Rabbit in Red

Volume I: Follow the Rabbit

By Joe Chianakas

Horror Block Exclusive Edition

Rabbit in Red

This edition: Horror Block Exclusive, 2016

Original edition, 2015

ISBN 978-1-63310-030-5

www.joechianakas.com

www.facebook.com/chianakas

Other Books by Joe Chianakas

***Rabbit in Red Volume II, Burn the Rabbit*, is available now.** Get it on Amazon or request it at your favorite bookstore.

Also pick up the author's collection of short horror, *Nightmares Under The Moonlight*.

The *Rabbit in Red* trilogy concludes in the fall of 2017 with the release of *Bury the Rabbit*!

Follow the author at www.joechianakas.com or www.fb.com/chianakas.

Praise for *Rabbit in Red*

"A love letter to the horror movie genre. If you are a fan of horror fiction, horror movies, or just want to read a good book, do yourself a favor and pick up *Rabbit in Red*!"—Bryan Fitzgerald of Fitz of Horror (www.fb.com/horrorfitz)

"If you're a horror fan, you NEED to read this book!" – Meg Bonney of Pure Fandom (www.fb.com/bepurefandom)

Dedication

For my mom, who still goes shopping with me to buy horror films. She's battling the worst horror, though. Keep her in your thoughts. There are many more scary movies to see, and I wish that the only horror she has to experience is on the big screen, not this big C.

And for my dad. ALS took him from this world. When he lost the use of his body, he still wanted to read. The last book I got for him was King's *Under the Dome*. Stories matter. So much. Don't believe me? Picture a man on his death bed smiling and begging for more of the story. It matters.

I love you both. Always.

Cover Illustration by Camron Johnson

www.camronjohnson.com

AUTHOR'S NOTE:

Camron's art is mind-blowing. We're using his work for *Rabbit in Red Volume Two*. He also did the art for *Nightmares Under The Moonlight*. He has a variety of talented, twisted, cool, incredible pieces on his website. If you're looking for art illustrations for any kind of work or just for your own personal collection, be sure to check him out. He's a talented and professional individual, who I hope to work with for all of my publications.

– Joe Chianakas

Part I

Follow the Rabbit

"There's something infectious about youth. We old people adore our pasts for many reasons, but the biggest reason is primal in nature. Youth's ravenous appetites for everything—sleep, food, sex, anger—are justified without shame or guilt. Those consequences only come with age."
—Jay Bell from the *Rabbit in Red Blog*.

Chapter One

Bill Wise hunted the rabbit in red, and his best friend Jaime followed.

Bill found his mother slumbering on the couch, like he did every morning. His primary contact with his mom took place in these moments, saying good-bye to a passed-out shell of a human. Bill groaned at the sight of the empty vodka bottle on the coffee table, but he bent over and kissed her as he always did, even if she never realized it or felt it only in a dream. He adjusted the blanket around her and tucked a pillow more firmly underneath her head. Drool drizzled out of her mouth, and one arm dangled to the floor. Bill took her arm and wrapped it around her chest.

"Bye, Mom."

She smacked her lips, mumbling the unintelligible nonsense of a dream.

Since he didn't have a car of his own, he waited for the school bus. He took out his phone and clicked on the bookmarked story *Rabbit in Red* that he and Jaime had discovered a few weeks ago. The contest would launch tonight, and they only needed to get through this one school day before their lives would change forever. He hoped.

Bill had the story memorized, but he read it over again. He didn't want to miss a single detail.

Eccentric Horror Producer to Host Fright Fest Contest

Hollywood's strangest horror producer, Jay Bell, is making himself public for the first time since opening Rabbit in Red Studios over a decade ago. Known for the creepy demands on his staff, directors and actors, Bell, or JB as he is more often called, first made news when taking a group of actors and film staff to an allegedly haunted location in the middle of Germany before filming his first feature film, Haunted Mind. *For his second movie,* The Devil in You, *JB flew the entire cast and crew to an old African village, where members supposedly had once been possessed by demons. JB made the cast and crew participate in these and a variety of other hands-on experiences to make his films as genuinely real and terrifying as possible. He even requires his workers to sign a non-disclosure agreement.*

The media have asked JB for numerous comments, but he's been strictly quiet, never appearing on screen himself.

Until now.

Now the Rabbit in Red producer has launched a website that introduces a special challenge for horror fans. The headline on JB's website reads: FOLLOW THE RABBIT IN RED TO A GREAT REWARD FOR THOSE WITH THE MOST KNOWLEDGE OF HORROR. *The specific details on the website tell all lovers of horror to register online and await notification from the rabbit.*

A test begins on Friday night, September 25th. Participants will need to download the Rabbit in Red app on their smartphones or tablets to play. The contest will continue all weekend and involves a series of riddles that must be decoded. And here's the incredible prize: Those with the highest scores will be invited to his infamous studio, which has been strictly closed to the public and the media, to participate in a variety of horror quests. To quote the website: "Those with the greatest knowledge will then be invited to a hands-on adventure. Imagine an amusement park of horror. You'll play with the rabbit all weekend, and the winners of those quests will receive a cash prize, and will be offered an internship in the horror industry."

JB and his Rabbit in Red studios are looking for young fans of horror to bring fresh ideas to the genre. He welcomes aspiring actors, writers, directors, and those interested in any aspect of the film industry to participate. Contestants must be free all Halloween weekend and are currently restricted to ages 17-21.

"We want fresh young minds," JB posted on his website. "But for you older fans of horror, don't worry. Think of this year as a beta test group. You'll get your turn, I promise."

If you're interested in taking the Rabbit in Red challenge, go to www.frightfest4d.com *for more information.*

The bus pulled up as Bill finished reading the article. His eyes remained glued to his smartphone as he took a seat, and the bus jerked forward on its path to the horror that was high school. He and Jaime had already downloaded the app, but first they had to get through one more boring day. They both were seniors, and Bill couldn't wait to get out and leave the standardized tests and standardized jocks behind.

Throughout the morning classes, his phone burned a hole in his pocket. He wanted to stay on the Rabbit in Red website and text Jaime, but he couldn't risk having his phone confiscated, not today of all days. The morning classes were the longest he had ever experienced, and when the bell finally rang for lunch, he ran to the cafeteria. He sat at a table by himself and took out his phone.

"Dude, what's with that lame shirt?" some sports guy asked just as Bill took a seat. Bill wasn't sure which sport. They all looked the same to him — their faces, tans, and sharp jaw-lines would bully him in his nightmares, but he tried to forget their names. They weren't worth remembering.

Bill was wearing one of his favorite t-shirts, a red and yellow shirt that read *Stephen King Rules,* something he first saw in the '80s horror comedy *The Monster Squad* that he had purchased on eBay for ten bucks.

"If you knew how to read," Bill said matter-of-factly, "you might find something more meaningful than what's in between two goal posts."

"You're a real loser," the sports guy told him. "You know that?"

"Your mother tells me the same thing about you," Bill replied. You could never go wrong insulting one's mother. Well, maybe it could go wrong if the guy you were insulting was twice your size. Bill was tall, but skinny, and this guy was as thick as a punching bag.

The nameless jock grabbed Bill's tray and dumped the food on his lap. Bill wanted to stand up and punch him. For one dark moment, he envisioned the jock in a horror film, getting that arrogant head cut off by Jason Voorhees' machete or being gutted by Freddy's claws.

But it wasn't a movie. Instead, Bill sat there embarrassed, thinking a thousand ways to get revenge but doing absolutely nothing. Now his lap was covered with the school's tater tot casserole. Yeah, he needed to get out of high school.

Bill walked with his head down to the bathroom to clean himself up. He was angry at the sports guy, angry at himself for not being stronger, and angry that the few precious minutes the high school allowed students for freedom would now be spent cleaning off his pants. How nice would it have been to sit with Jaime at lunch instead of always by himself? He didn't have many friends here, not anymore, but he did have one best friend: Jaime Stein. She lived far away though, out East, quite a distance from the small Illinois town that Bill longed to escape.

Bill had first met Jaime in an online group for kids who had lost a loved one. There were three types of things Bill looked for online: forums and groups about losing a family member, anything related to horror, and, well, a third thing all teenage boys like to look up. But not necessarily in that order. On a support group, Bill had found a girl from across the country looking for answers. As he picked the crumbled tater tots off his pants, he wondered what Jaime was doing and wished she were by his side.

*****

"How was Suzie-what's-her-face?" Bill asked Jaime. They were on FaceTime, and Bill smiled at the unflattering view of Jaime's face. He was sitting on his bed, staring at the *Halloween* poster in his bedroom, and counting down the minutes until the contest would begin. Jaime must have had the phone pinned between her chin and shoulder. He heard her swing open the front door and walk inside her house. When she repositioned the phone so he could see her face again, Bill looked away so she wouldn't think he was staring. *Dumb, I know.* He shook his head. He just loved looking into her brown eyes.

"Eh, you know, the same. I gotta get away from high school. Get away from her and everyone. Does every school have a Suzie-what's-her-face?"

Bill nodded. He didn't have to answer. If he had a dollar for every time they had a conversation about a mindless jock or a beauty queen that only valued appearance, he could pay to go to the best college in the world.

"Hi, honey. Hi, Bill."

"Hi, Mrs. Stein," Bill said. Jaime held the phone out so Bill could wave. "What movie are you watching?" He could see her on the couch with a box of tissues in one hand and a glass of wine in the other. She didn't even look up from the TV.

"Oh, I think you'd both like this one. This woman's boyfriend is in a terrible accident. He's been in a coma for years and then he—"

"Wakes up, which makes her cry, which then makes you cry," Jaime said and stuck her tongue out at Bill on the phone. "Isn't it always the same?"

"Bill!" Tara yelled from the kitchen, and Bill again got a 360-degree view of Jaime's house as she spun the phone toward her little sister.

"Hey, Tara," Bill said. "Whatcha doing?"

"Just making a peanut butter and banana sandwich," said Tara around a mouth full of peanut butter. "Want one?"

"Sure. Got a drone that will fly it over to me?"

Tara giggled, and Bill then got a view of the kitchen ceiling as Jaime went to make her own afternoon snack.

"You really should dust," he joked.

"Jaime, clean?" Tara laughed. "Ima watch TV."

Bill heard the cling of a butter knife banging against the countertop. "Do you want me to stab you?" Jaime said. Bill pictured Jaime pointing the innocuous blade at her little sister.

Tara giggled again.

"You think it's funny, but Dad left Mom like how many years ago? If my baby sister turns into one of those girls who thinks life is not complete without a guy, I'll make my own horror movie right here, and you'll be the star. No Lifetime Original Sap Crap for you."

"Hey, you watch those stupid horror movies all the time," Tara said. "What about the women always running up the stairs instead of out the front door? And they are *always* having sex. There's a lot of pretty stupid women in your movies. I think those are much worse than what Mom watches."

Jaime picked up the phone, and Bill finally had a better view than the ceiling. Jaime patted her sister's head with her other hand. "That's true, and you're a smart one. But that's why I like to write. I'm making my characters stronger and smarter."

"Like me?" Tara joked.

"No joke," Jaime said. "Like you."

"Cool. Okay, write me a story."

"What do you think, Bill?" Jaime asked. "Do we have time for a story?"

"I'm always up for one of your stories." He flopped back on his bed, his head now on a pillow, his feet dangling off the corner of the bed. "Besides, we've got like an hour to kill before this contest starts."

"Yay!" Tara cheered.

Seeing the two girls together made Bill wish he had a sibling. Someone he could be as close to as Jaime was with Tara. Would Jaime and Tara always be this close? Life had a way of changing things, and certainly not always for the better.

Jaime walked up to her bedroom, and she handed the phone over to Tara. Tara waved at Bill, and he smiled back. She faced the phone toward Jaime so he could see what she was doing. Jaime sat at her desk and opened her laptop. Tara plopped herself face down across the bed, kicking her heels back and forth as she waited for Jaime to tell her the story. Jaime typed for several minutes. Bill kept quiet and studied her face. He loved how focused she could become. He could hear her breathe out of her nose. Whenever she took a moment to think, she'd gently pull at her hair with her right hand. Then her eyes would widen and she'd resume typing. Bill loved watching her.

When she had finished writing, she read it out loud.

"Laurie sat in the last row of the church. She didn't want people to see her cry. As the ushers carried the coffin out of the church, Laurie sobbed into a tissue. Then she looked up. The wife — or the widow, to be more accurate — made eye contact. Laurie's eyes were wet. But the widow's eyes? Dry as the desert."

She paused for a moment, and Bill felt a lump in his throat. He didn't think the story was about his own mother, Sally, a widow for almost a decade. He knew Jaime had only been to one funeral in her lifetime. Her Uncle Tim had committed suicide. She had only briefly spoken about it to him, and she never went into details, but he had gotten the basic facts from their online grief support group. Jaime would tell him that story when she was ready, and he'd be there for her when she was.

Jaime coughed lightly and continued reading. "Laurie hadn't seen Tim — TOM, I mean — in years, but thinking of the end of life, that this is the final destination for all of us, brought rough tears to her eyes. She wondered how Tom's own wife managed not to cry."

"That's a sad story," Tara said. "Why didn't the wife cry?"

"I don't know. Why do you think she didn't cry?" Jaime closed the laptop and curled up next to her sister in bed. Tara angled the phone so Bill could see both of them.

"Because she was stronger than her friends?"

"Or maybe she was still too much in shock to cry?"

"What if she already cried so much she couldn't cry anymore?" Tara kicked her feet against her butt as she thought.

"Maybe. I don't know."

"You wrote it! Why don't you know?" Tara slammed her feet on the bed when Jaime shrugged.

"When I write, I like to think of a situation, that's all. It's not about answers. It's about thinking about the situation, coming up with your own answers."

"You're weird." Tara stuck out her tongue.

"But that's why you love me!" Jaime jumped on Tara's back and started tickling her ribs.

"Stop! Oh, God, please!" she cried.

"No way, never, and certainly not today!" As they playfully wrestled, the bed bounced and the phone fell on the floor.

"Hey, you guys!" Bill yelled from below. He heard Tara sigh in relief as Jaime jumped off the bed. "As much as I love seeing you torture your sister, it's almost time to begin."

Jaime nodded, and Bill saw that focused determination reappear on her face. *We're really gonna kick ass. The two of us on the same team. This is gonna be so awesome.*

"Okay. Yeah." Jaime looked over her shoulder. "Wish us luck, Tara."

"After you tried to kill me? Yeah, okay. Good luck." Tara planted her feet on the floor and looked at Bill on FaceTime before leaving. "You don't need it though. You're the smartest people I know."

Tara skipped out of the room, and Jaime looked Bill straight in the eyes. "So are you ready to follow the rabbit?"

"I'm terrified," Bill replied, his arms stiffening as his heart pumped with excitement. "Why do I feel like this?"

"Because it's the coolest thing we've ever done. And we want to win. We're going to win. I already have the app downloaded on my phone. You?"

"Same. I'll Skype you. Wait one sec and I'll be right back." Bill ended the call and opened the Rabbit in Red app. He stared at the timer as it counted down the final minutes until the contest would begin. He jumped off his bed and grabbed the tablet on his desk where he used Skype to call Jaime back.

Bill looked back down at his iPhone, where a white rabbit hopped through a splattering of blood. All he had to do was press the button *Follow the Rabbit* and the game would begin. With one hand, he held the phone, and with the other he adjusted the tablet where Jaime now appeared on Skype. Bill saw a faint sheen of sweat glisten on Jaime's forehead. They were hundreds of miles away from one another, but they wanted to begin this journey together.

"One minute to go."

"I want this so bad." Bill closed his eyes for a moment, took a deep breath, and looked at Jaime. "Oh-right. We're gonna win, right?"

"Right," she said. "This is for your dad."

"For your uncle," he told her.

"For *us*." She smiled at him, but it was the focus in her eyes that made him feel ready.

"For us. Oh-right. Let's count it down, and press the button together."

She nodded and they counted with the timer down from ten. "Three, two, one, now!"

The rabbit spun on their phone screens, then the image magnified, the rabbit growing, until they could only see its teeth. Its smile morphed into a snarl, and the rabbit cackled, spun around again, and disappeared. On their phone screens, a riddle awaited them.

Follow the Rabbit. Follow the Rabbit in Red to the masquerade. Tell me when the crystal legend upgraded from homemade.

The text disappeared and the rabbit returned along with a countdown. They had thirty seconds to answer the question.

"Jesus, that's not enough time to Google anything," Bill sighed. "What is it even asking?"

"Talk it out loud. That's the first step."

"Did you get the same riddle?"

"Yes, thank God." Jaime laughed nervously. "But I'm guessing that's a little beginner's luck. Okay, what do you think?"

"Got it!" he shouted seconds later. "I know what it's asking, and we know the answer."

Chapter Two

Bill repeated the riddle out loud. "Follow the Rabbit to the masquerade. Tell us when the crystal legend upgraded from homemade."

"The masquerade means it has something to do with a mask, right?" Jaime asked.

"Yeah," Bill said. "And the crystal legend?"

"Jason! *Friday the 13th*! Camp *Crystal* Lake. How cool. When he upgraded from homemade means . . ."

"When he ditched the sack he put over his face and put on the iconic hockey mask."

"Yeah!" Jaime cheered. "Okay, are you typing in the number three or the full title?"

"Full title. *Friday the 13th Part Three*. Go! Only ten seconds left!"

Jaime and Bill entered their responses to the first Rabbit in Red challenge on their phones, holding their breath.

CORRECT! The white rabbit danced again in a rain storm of blood and smiled at them. *Press CONTINUE when you are ready for the next challenge.*

Bill let out a deep breath. "One down!"

"We stay up all night," Jaime said. "We have to get the highest score."

"Absolutely."

"That was a cool first riddle. I'm always surprised that a lot of people our age don't even realize Jason wasn't the killer in part one."

"Not until the very end!" Bill smiled. "One of the best endings ever."

"You ready for the next one?" Jaime asked, taking a deep breath. "We may not get the same riddle, but at least we can keep track of what we've answered correctly."

"I'm ready," Bill said and pressed *CONTINUE* on his phone. The rabbit spun, danced, and grinned again, and the next riddle appeared.

Follow the Rabbit. Follow the Rabbit in Red to where mama tried. Tell me the movie in which those poor faces still died.

Bill read it aloud to Jaime. "Did you get the same one?"

"Yes! How is that possible?"

"Who cares!" Bill replied as the rabbit appeared with that awful timer, counting down from thirty seconds. He closed his eyes. Why couldn't his brain have a search tool like a computer? "Mama tried, mama tried. Where do I know that from?"

"*Mama*?" she wondered. "Could it be that movie with Jaime Lannister? God, I can never remember his real name."

"Yeah, the one with the girls who were raised in the wild. Let's try that." They entered *Mama* as the answer but the screen responded with a bold *INCORRECT* and the rabbit took a wound, shooting blood at the screen.

"Damn. That can't be good."

"Screw it, I'm gonna Google it," Jaime said, quickly typing on her tablet with only fifteen seconds to go. "It's a song! I got song lyrics. 'No one could steer me right but mama tried, mama tried. Mama tried to raise me better but her pleading I denied.'"

"Ten seconds, shit!" Bill shouted. "Those poor faces still died," he read aloud again from the clue.

"Faces. Mama tried," Jaime repeated. "I got it! The song is played a lot in the background in this movie. The faces is the hint!"

"Oh yeah! The movie was originally titled *The Faces* but got changed to —"

"*The Strangers!*" they both yelled. They typed as fast as they could with only seconds remaining.

"Nice!" Bill cheered. "Jesus, I'm gonna have a heart attack before this night is over."

"No kidding."Jaime laughed. "If you could feel my heart beating now, it could knock you out."

Holding his phone in one hand and looking at Jaime through Skype on his tablet, his heart beat as if he had been sprinting. For a moment, he wondered if it also had something to do with the girl across the country, the one person he knew who shared in his enthusiasm.

"I love that movie," he said. "That line at the end gives me chills every time."

"When Liv Tyler's character asks why?" Jaime said. "Yes, best answer in any horror flick."

"Because you were home," Bill whispered. "No other reason than that they were home." His body twitched for a moment, his saddest, darkest memory stinging him like a wasp that appeared out of nowhere. *Shake it off. No time for that now.*

Their screens flashed *CORRECT* and the bloody rabbit danced.

*****

Bill sat up in bed slowly, his thin shoulders and long arms trying to stretch away the fatigue of such little sleep. Standing up, he leaned on his bookcase and ran his hand over the covers of the *Goosebumps* series that defined his childhood. He scanned his DVD and Blu-Ray tower proudly displaying several of the movies that had come in handy during the all-nighter he and Jaime just pulled, and he soaked in the atmosphere of his bedroom full of posters, from Jack Nicholson's creepy face in *The Shining* to *Halloween's* butcher knife and ominous pumpkin.

He grabbed a t-shirt from a pile of clothes on his dresser, knocking over some of his Horror Block boxes. He subscribed to the most kick-ass monthly subscription ever, full of horror collectibles, and he kept every box. His mom never gave him trouble for his messy room. Too much of a mess herself, he thought, as he searched for a clean shirt among a pile of clothes he never put away. He had a simple rule: *on the floor, wear no more, on the dresser, smelling better.*

Now that he was awake, he checked his phone to see if he had a message from Jaime. Nothing yet. He was eager to text her back, but if she were lucky enough to sleep a bit longer, he didn't want to wake her. They had until Sunday at midnight to answer as many riddles as possible, and the fresher both of their minds were, the better their chances.

The riddle challenge so far had been such a rush. What would it be like to actually tackle the hands-on quests at Rabbit in Red studios? As he waited for Jaime to text him, Bill searched online for more information about JB, the eccentric Rabbit in Red producer. It had to be helpful to know as much as they could about him. According to JB's biography, he was forty-five when both of his parents died in a car accident. In his young adult life, he had lived by doing any job he could get his hands on at any movie studio: janitorial work, maintenance, mail, whatever. He had grown up in the Eastern United States, but travelled all over the country before making California his home. When he'd inherited a fortune from his parents' estate, he opened his own film studio: Rabbit in Red. Notoriously private, JB had given the entertainment media a whirlwind of news stories with the launch of his Rabbit in Red challenge by publishing blog posts and updates at frightfest4d.com.

Bill checked his phone again as he read about JB and sent Jaime a quick good morning text. He was getting excited to continue the riddles, and while waiting for her to reply, he re-read one of JB's blogs.

I've been a fan of the horror culture since I was a young boy. Films like The Exorcist *and* The Texas Chainsaw Massacre *terrified me as a child, but I found a strange excitement in losing myself in their stories. I quickly became frustrated with Hollywood horror though: it was always another sequel, always a remake of an original, always the same idea. Hollywood is a business after all, and they are more willing to put money into ideas that will guarantee a profit than to take a risk. I've eavesdropped on or participated in every conversation from New York to Hollywood that you can imagine, and most would rather make a 10th* Paranormal Activity *than try something new.*

But that's going to change, my friends. I'm proud to announce that I am opening the doors at Rabbit in Red to invite others to join me. Unlike Hollywood where only the elite make the decisions, you and I will work together. I know what it feels like to love something and to want to be a part of it. To begin this journey, I will create a contest to gather the most committed young horror fans in the world.

Bill's sleepiness slipped away, and the adrenaline rush returned. He wasn't a writer or an actor, but in a high school film class, he had studied digital editing. He'd felt a pure high after creating his first scary scene in a group project, and he'd known right then and there that if he could make a career out of editing movies, especially scary ones, then he'd never work a day in his life. Would they let him try some of that at Rabbit in Red Studios? To work side by side with JB, the master of horror, would be a dream come true.

Jaime still hadn't replied, so Bill selected *Boogeyman: The Killer Compilation* from his film collection to watch and ate a bowl of Peanut Butter Cap'n Crunch. Just as he got into a scene from *Hellraiser*, his tablet sang the theme song from *Halloween*, alerting him that Jaime was calling on FaceTime.

"Morning, my wise friend," she greeted.

"Hey. How you doing?"

"Good. How long did we sleep?"

"I think I got three or four hours. It's enough for now."

"Yeah, we can sleep when we're dead," she joked.

"Oh God, why are you wearing that awful shirt again?" Bill asked.

"*Season of the Witch*? This is one of my lucky shirts. We've got a long day ahead and can use all the luck we can get."

"Lucky for you. I can't stand that movie."

"You just hate it because your lover Michael Myers isn't in it."

"It's a damn *Halloween* movie, you know! How dare they use the title and not make it about Michael."

"Happy, happy Halloween, Silver Shamrock!" Jamie sang that movie's theme.

"How are we friends again?" Bill asked and they both laughed.

"I don't think I've ever seen you with your hair all a mess like that," she giggled. "So this is morning Bill. Hmmm. Maybe *I* should be asking why we're friends."

Bill laughed and rubbed his short, blond hair. "Maybe you should look in a mirror before insulting me," he joked back.

"What? This is what perfection looks like." She smiled and tossed back her thick, shoulder-length brown hair.

"You're as funny as you are smart. So when do you want to continue?"

"I'm gonna eat something quick. And then let's play. We should try to take breaks though. Rest. This is a marathon, not a sprint."

"Oh-right. Do you think it's weird that we're getting the same riddles? I thought it'd be random."

"JB is clearly smart," Jaime said, furrowing her brow. "I imagine he's thought of everything and that there's a reason for everything."

"I hope we get to meet him," Bill said. He paused, swallowed hard, and plunged ahead. "And that I get to meet you in person, too."

"It's going to happen," Jaime reassured him. "Just gotta stay positive. I was thinking how weird and cool it would be though. I mean we don't live anywhere near one another, and we'd both be flying somewhere new to us."

Bill looked out his bedroom window to where the trees touched in the middle of the streets. It might be pretty, but it was also pretty boring. It would make for a good scene in a horror film, though. Plenty of bushes to hide behind. Maybe Jaime could write the script, and Bill could edit the movie. Someday.

"Bill?"

"Huh?"

"Did you zone out?"

"Sorry. I was thinking of Ray Bradbury."

"That meme you share on Instagram like every day?"

Bill could almost hear Jaime's smile when she teased him. "Why do you hate on the things I love?"

"I'm just kidding."

"I know. It's just . . . you know, we've got something special." He rubbed his hand over his hair again. "Like he wrote, we're cups filling up every day, but how do we know when to let it out? I don't think I'll know until I get out of this damn town. At least you have the ocean."

"Ahh, it's like the sky," Jaime sighed. "When you take a minute to look up, it's always beautiful. But you get used to it and it's like the same old thing all the time."

He doubted it would ever get old if he were there with Jaime.

He didn't really know what they were — Jaime made him feel warm, like talking to her flushed his skin with blood. It was awkward sometimes and hard to explain, something that was more than friendship, but not exactly romantic. She was really cute with her long brown hair, the way it brushed over her shoulders, and her slender body projected confidence and strength. She'd never make it as a horror actress (she was way too flat-chested). As much as Bill admired big boobs in his movies, he found Jaime's physique to be real.

What would it be like to cuddle up next to her while watching a horror movie? Would she jump into his arms during scary moments? Would he feel goose bumps on her arms and legs? Would he be uncomfortable watching a sleazy sex scene next to her? He would be lying if he didn't admit that another reason he wanted to win JB's contest was to meet her in person.

"Okay," Jaime said. "I've eaten. You ready?"

"Always," Bill said. They pressed *CONTINUE* and watched the rabbit dance to another riddle.

Chapter Three

Through the webcam, Bill could see Jaime's bedroom. She had a bright white comforter, and the bed was neatly made. Next to her bed was her writing desk where she usually sat to talk with him. She would often Skype with him on her tablet or FaceTime with him on her phone and multitask with the laptop: a movie or story would almost always be open on one of her several technological devices. The desk had an upper shelf, where there were several books about screenplays, writing, and of course some horror stories. She had every Anne Rice vampire book as well as the popular teen read *Twilight*. But only the first book. Jaime said the characters, especially the girls, were too weak for her taste. He remembered her commentary: *We need books with strong female characters, not some girl always gushing over a guy. I am going to write stories where the girl saves the guy. Or a girl that doesn't need guys. Not some whiny brat who cries about her insecurities and boys.*

Bill liked that she was an avid reader, too. Most horror fans he met could talk hours about movies, but ask them a question about a book and suddenly their face looked stoned as if the word "reading" was some kind of bad drug.

Jaime moved from her desk to the bed and took the tablet with her. "Are you ready to finish kicking this rabbit's ass?"

"Oh-right!" Bill said, putting his fist into the webcam for an online fist bump.

"You are such a dork." She laughed, but she put her fist up, too. "You and your oh-rights! Now let's finish this game."

The rabbit danced and their next riddle appeared. *Follow the Rabbit. Follow the Rabbit in Red to meet the shape. This most famous babysitter made quite the narrow escape.*

"Easy one!" Jaime said.

"Yeah," Bill agreed. "The shape is the original name for Michael Myers."

"And *Halloween* was first titled *The Babysitter Murders*."

"And so the answer must be Laurie Strode! Let's type it in. Quick!"

CORRECT.

Wasting no time, they hit *CONTINUE.*

The next challenge read: *Follow the Rabbit. Follow the Rabbit in Red to where the snow shines bright. Then get warm with a hot bath here, or die, you just might.*

"Oh, perfect for us," Bill laughed.

"Reminds me of our first argument," Jaime giggled back. "Let's enter the title and see if we have a match." They both entered *The Shining* but received that dreadfully bold *INCORRECT.*

"Damn, we went too fast. There's more to it than just the title, right?" Bill asked. "Okay, think. The snow shines bright. That has to be a *Shining* reference."

"What about the hot bath?"

"Where you might just die? Exactly, it's more than the title. Dammit!"

They stared at the riddle on their phones as the terrible timer pressured them.

"I got it!" Jaime said. "It must be the room number. There was one room in particular that was haunted. What was that number?" She pulled on her brown hair and nearly chewed on it with frustration. "Two thirty-seven! Let's try that." Jaime typed impetuously before Bill could interrupt, and Jaime's screen flashed *INCORRECT.*

"No!" Bill yelled. "Damn. Well, that serves you right for liking the movie better than the book. Kubrick changed it to two thirty-seven in the movie, remember?"

"No time for your fun facts! What's the room number, dammit?"

"Two seventeen." Bill chuckled and they both entered the number. "And all I was going to say was that the Stanley Hotel, where they filmed the scenes for the Overlook, didn't want to use the real number, in case guests would no longer want to stay there. You can visit the Stanley Hotel now and, get this, the rates start at two hundred seventeen dollars. I thought that was cool."

"Yeah, yeah. We got a contest to win. Save your vacation plans for later." She grinned.

They hit *CONTINUE* and read the next challenge.

Follow the Rabbit. Follow the Rabbit in Red to the back seat. Every now and then I get a little bit lonely. Tell me the movie and don't miss a beat.

"What the hell?" Bill asked.

"Oh, man. Okay, let's start with back seat. What's it mean to you?"

"A killer in the back seat?"

"Seems logical. That's what I was thinking. Who gets lonely though?"

"Norman Bates?"

"Definitely," Jaime said. "I guess you have to be lonely if you also pretend to be your dead mother. What about the back seat though?"

"When Marion takes the money and runs, where does she put it? Could she have put it in the back seat of the car?"

"I don't remember." Jaime bit her lip. "I think it's rolled up in newspaper, and I know it's forty thousand dollars. But isn't it in her briefcase?"

"I don't remember where she keeps it either. Damn. Well, it's a good guess. Let's try it."

They entered *Psycho* as their answer, and the screen flashed *INCORRECT*.

"Damn!" they each cursed.

"Okay, from the top and quick," Jaime instructed. "Back seat. Every now and then I get a little bit lonely. Why does that last line sound so familiar?"

"You're right," Bill said. "Turn around!"

Jaime looked over her shoulder. "What?"

"No. The song. There is a song called 'Turn Around.' Or 'Bright Eyes.'" He sang a little. "'Turn around, bright eyes, every now and then I fall apart...'"

"Oh yeah! It's the opening scene of *Urban Legend*. Oh that's perfect. JB is freakin' brilliant."

They entered the text *Urban Legend* and the screen again flashed *CORRECT*.

"That's a great scene, too. The killer in the backseat, the woman driving off, and the song that comes on the radio says 'turn around.' That's where the line 'every now and then I get a little bit lonely' comes from!"

Their next challenge read: *Follow the Rabbit. Follow the Rabbit in Red to the semi. What holiday treat would our pranksters most enjoy?*

"Let's start with movies with semi-trucks," Jaime said.

"There's one at the end of *Texas Chainsaw Massacre*."

"And *Pet Sematary*," Jaime added. "Gage gets killed by a semi, right?"

"Yep. And there's *Maximum Overdrive*, another King movie. You know, the cheesy one with Emilio Estevez where the trucks come to life?"

"That was ridiculous," she snickered. "Okay, quick, what has pranksters? And a holiday?"

"I don't think any of the ones we just said had anything to do with those."

"No, me neither." Their smiles melted, and Bill rubbed his chin hard enough to nearly remove skin. Only silence accompanied the timer as it now counted down from ten.

"Damn, c'mon." Bill squeezed the bridge of his nose. He couldn't think. "Semi. Holiday treat. Pranksters."

"Name some holiday treats," Jaime suggested.

"Peeps," Bill said.

"Candy canes!" Jaime said louder. "Candy cane! That's the answer."

"Candy cane? What's that from?"

"Enter the damn text!"

With only a couple of seconds remaining, they entered *candy cane* and the screen flashed *CORRECT*.

"Wow, what was that from?" Bill asked.

"C'mon. A semi-truck," she said. "A couple of pranksters talking on an old CB with truck drivers. Paul Walker!"

"Oh, shit. Yes. *Joyride*. They give the nickname Candy Cane to the truck driver. The one who went mad and then started chasing them down."

"And by the way," Jaime said, "Peeps? No one likes Peeps. Gross."

"I like Peeps," he defended.

"You would." She chuckled and rolled her eyes. "Cheapest holiday treat ever. And they go stale the moment you open them."

"Why do you have to knock what I like?"

"If you're going to suggest Easter candy, you should at least suggest Cadbury eggs."

"True. I would consider killing for a Cadbury egg. If there's not a movie about that, there should be."

The two worked hard, and they worked well as a team. They filled in the gaps in one another's knowledge of horror trivia. It was helpful to bounce ideas off of one another, even in the short amount of time they had to answer each question. The weekend flew by, and with less than one minute to go before the end of the contest, they tried to complete one final riddle.

Follow the Rabbit. Follow the Rabbit in Red to the turkey. Don't reject the Rabbit. Welcome it. And sing this with the quirky.

But before they could answer, midnight arrived, and the game shut down. The rabbit hopped around the screen and a new message read: *Calculating results. Scores will be posted live on frightfest4d.com at 5:00 p.m. PST on Monday September 21.*

"That's tomorrow." Bill glanced up at Jaime incredulously. "We really have to wait until tomorrow to find out?"

"Now what do we do?" Jaime asked. "I feel completely drained. Excited, but drained."

"Yeah, I guess we sleep. I don't know how I'm gonna get through school tomorrow."

"Me neither. But tomorrow . . . God . . . everything could change."

They talked for a few moments longer until exhaustion completely consumed them. After saying goodnight, Bill shrank into his blankets and closed his eyes.

All he wanted was to dream of the Rabbit in Red. To dream of possibilities. But he wasn't that lucky.

Chapter Four

Bill heard a crash outside of his bedroom. It sounded like a car had slammed into the living room. His hands pulled at the blankets and he lay rigid. The family dog, a small cocker spaniel named Sparky, slept in his bed, but he had woken up with the noise, too. Bill grabbed the old dog, trying to quiet his growl. Looking around the room, his eyes adjusting to the dark, he tried to listen but could only hear the thumping of his terrified heart. Sparky's upper lip rose and his mouth curved, almost like a smile.

A moment passed and then he heard another sound he would never forget.

His mother screamed.

Bill didn't know what to do, and he couldn't hold back the tears stinging his eyelids. He wanted to run to his parents, but fear paralyzed every muscle in his body. He slid onto the floor as if another force was moving him. He hugged Sparky and grabbed a blanket. It wasn't exactly a controlled movement or intentional. He fell, blankets and dog still clasped against his chest, and he slithered underneath his bed.

"What do you want?" he heard his mother cry from down the hall.

Bill opened his mouth but nothing came out. His cheeks were wet and he tasted the tears as they rolled onto his tongue.

"On your knees," a voice demanded. Bill did not recognize the voice.

Then he heard his father.

"Leave her alone! What do you want?"

"Quiet," the intruder barked. "You, on the floor, now. Where is your son?"

"He . . . he is —" his mom started to answer, the words interrupted by a sob.

"He's spending the night at a friend's house," his father interjected.

"You better be telling me the truth," the man snapped. Bill thought he sounded relieved. "Now, on your knees. Hands behind your back."

Bill took several deep breaths. Sparky looked up at his young master and licked the tears from his face. At fifteen years old, Sparky had been the family dog long before Bill was born. But when a baby entered the Wise household, the dog took to him like he was one of his own pups. As soon as the baby moved from a crib to an actual bed, Sparky had been Bill's longtime sleep companion, always cuddling up to keep him warm, always licking away the pain when Bill had a nightmare.

"Sparky," Bill whispered. "We have to help them." He knew the dog didn't understand the words, but Bill sensed Sparky understood the fear. Sparky hadn't chased a squirrel or barked at a noise in the house for a couple of years now, but Bill hoped he had one good fight left in him.

The boy and the dog crawled together, out from under the bed, to the doorway of the bedroom. His parents' bedroom was down the hall, only steps away. At the edge of the doorway, Bill saw the legs of the intruder, heavy legs in dark jeans. In front of the intruder, he saw his parents, both down on their knees.

"Stay still," the intruder commanded. He had what looked like silver wiring and the intruder wrapped it around his parents' wrists, tying their arms tightly behind their backs. The man then took out a large sack that looked like a pillowcase. "I want your cell phones, jewelry, valuables and any cash you have. Tell me where everything is and no one needs to get hurt."

Bill's mom cried, and his dad spoke in a tense, shaky voice. "You'll find our phones charging, one on each side of the bed. My wife has her jewelry in a box in the drawer under the mirror over there." He nodded at the vanity table. "In our closet, I have a safe. It has some cash. Take it. Just don't hurt her."

Bill watched as the intruder first grabbed the phones, then walked to the other side of the bedroom to where his mom kept her jewelry. With the intruder out of sight, Bill had a direct visual of his parents. His mom had her chin against her chest, sobbing. His dad's gaze followed the intruder briefly, and then he snapped his head and looked straight into Bill's bedroom.

"Dad," Bill mouthed quietly, holding on to Sparky, crawling enough to poke his head out of his bedroom door.

30

His dad shook his head furiously, eyes wide, and mouthed "HIDE" over and over. Bill felt the tears rise into his throat and choke him. He wanted to help his parents, but he was also terrified. The fear was a palpable weight in his gut that made movement nearly impossible.

"HIDE," his dad mouthed again.

Sparky's eyes widened with primal instincts, and what the pup saw triggered his loyal and protective spirit. Finding the energy of his youth, Sparky darted out of Bill's hold and charged into the other room.

"Sparky!" Bill slammed his hand over his mouth as he cried out, catching his mistake too late, and the dog did not listen anyway. Hearing the noise, the intruder moved quickly across the room.

Bill saw the man's whole body. But there was no face to see. It was covered in a black mask.

"You lied," the intruder said to Bill's father, and he backhanded him across the face.

"No!" Bill yelled, standing on his feet. At that moment, Sparky leapt at the intruder, but the man kicked the little old dog hard with a boot in the face. Sparky squealed and flew into the hallway wall.

"Stop it!" Bill cried louder and ran to his loyal pup. He knelt down and wrapped his arm around Sparky, his only companion in this home besides his parents. He hugged him and bawled while Sparky moaned.

"Take the damn stuff and get out of this house," his dad shouted, getting to his feet.

"Get back down on your knees," the intruder demanded. He swung his arm behind his back, reached into his waist, and pulled out a gun. He pointed the gun first at Bill's father. Even though the intruder was wearing a mask, Bill could have sworn he saw a smile, and the intruder moved the gun away from Bill's dad and pointed it at his mom.

"Now," the intruder said.

"Get that gun away from my wife!" Bill's dad yelled and charged at the intruder. The man in the black mask quickly pointed the gun once again at Bill's dad, and this time he fired.

Bill and his mother screamed at the same time. The boom was deafening. Bill thought his heart had exploded as he watched a chunk of his father's head splatter the wall. The bullet hit him above the eye, skin and blood shooting out everywhere. Bill hugged Sparky tighter and put his head on the dog and sobbed. Bill's mother fainted and fell sideways on the floor.

The intruder grabbed the phones and the jewelry quickly like a child eagerly taking candy on Halloween. He lunged over Bill's mom and darted past the sobbing child who was covering Sparky like a blanket.

As the intruder rushed out, Bill sat up and cried, "Why? Why? Why?"

The intruder in the black mask turned to Bill.

"Sometimes there is no why, boy." And then he turned and went away.

* * * *

Bill shot straight up in bed, waking up in a cold sweat from the nightmare memory, wanting to cry, wanting to scream. He settled for slamming his fist into his pillow. Over and over again.

* * * *

Bill pretended to be sick Monday morning. It wasn't very hard. He stayed in bed and binge-watched shows on Netflix until he knew Jaime would be home from school. He tried not to think about the nightmare, but it was impossible to forget. He had relived that night many times.

When he got bored with Netflix, he started *The Last of Us* on a PlayStation 4 he had bought just before school started after saving enough money from mowing lawns in the neighborhood. He watched the game's introduction, shocked at the emotion in just the opening sequence. He rubbed his wet eyes at the end of the introduction, anxious to kill some damn zombies.

When he felt satisfied at getting some revenge, he paused the game, paced around his room, and then pulled up more of JB's blog on his tablet.

The young understand horror much more than adults. As we get older, we lose our imagination and the terrors we felt as a child are replaced with boring but necessary adult worries. Adults complain about their jobs and their bills. They have nightmares about being late to work or forgetting their pants. The monsters in the closet have all moved out, and life becomes a boring routine. For a child, those monsters are real, and they live in the basement, under the bed, and in the closet. They sleep and breathe and eat inches away from where the child sleeps. And they watch the child. The child can feel them, and they wake up screaming for mom or dad, and when mom or dad come in the room, the monster disappears. Adulthood is kryptonite for monsters, but a child's imagination is their magnet.

As we look at the best horror stories ever created, the main characters are often children or teenagers. Teenagers are the perfect characters in a horror story. They may be on the bridge to adulthood, but they still have a child's imagination, and they still can hear the monsters in their room play. But they have an adult's eye too, and they can fight back. It's almost as if they have two sets of eyes: the child's eyes let them see the monster and the adult's eyes show them how to fight the monster.

Unfortunately, our horror audiences want sex and gore, not real fear. Gore without fear is like sex without love; you'll squirm, but it's better when your heart's in it. The first primary element of a horror story is fear. Fear as seen through those child's eyes: the monster living all around us. Sometimes those monsters are literal: something from another world, something that can reach our own world and harm us. Sometimes those monsters are humans, and humans can be the scariest of all monsters. Especially adults, corrupted by the world around them. Politics, relationships, drama, work, money: there are so many elements that poison adults, but the largest consequence is that they no longer see the monsters. They may not even see themselves as monsters. There is a kidnapping of the imagination. Think of imagination like how you felt about your local fair. When you're a child, the fair is a place of magic. When you're an adult, it's a place that sucks the wallet dry.

As we work here at Rabbit in Red Studios to produce the next great generations of horror stories, to reinvent the genre, we must think of these things. We need the imagination of our youth and their great ability to fear and see all of life's monsters. But most importantly we need the ones with great courage to fight back.

A great teacher once told me "reading is the inhale and writing is the exhale," and so it is with my contest. Every great writer knows that to write well one must first be a great reader. Horror movies and books are much of the needed inhale to win this contest, but it's not only about books and movies. What we inhale should be all of life, all of the subtleties around us. We are surrounded by all of the great makings of a horror story in our day-to-day lives. You only have to open up your eyes and observe. Those are the people I want to work with in my studio: young, fresh eyes full of observations who have inhaled so many books, movies, and elements of life that they will explode if they don't exhale.

And to exhale is to create. I always thought traditional education was focused too much on knowledge and not enough on application. A real education inhales all of that knowledge in order to create. In my contest, you will be evaluated not only on what you know but what you can do.

Bill sighed when he looked at his phone. Jaime still had a couple hours of school left. To kill some more time, he put on his running shoes and stretched out for a jog. After all of the scary movies he had seen, he always wanted to make sure he could outrun any killer. The number one rule to survive the zombie apocalypse, as *Zombieland* brilliantly stated, was cardio. He grabbed his iPod and selected a playlist. He had a variety of great songs from the classic, spine-tingling violin notes of *Psycho* to the electronic beats of John Carpenter's *Lost Themes*, and to his preferred music when he needed to really get moving: some crazy, energetic pop-punk by his favorite band, Terribly Happy.

After hitting play, he stepped outside his house and jogged toward the nearest cemetery. It was full of hills and trails, nearly the size of a small town. Some of the tombstones dated back to the early 1800s. He tried to lose himself, to make himself feel small among the thousands of buried dead whose names he never knew. But he looked over his shoulder, too. Maybe he had seen a few too many horror flicks, but he could never be certain that someone wasn't following him.

When he returned home, he paced his bedroom again until Jaime called.

"Now I'm getting butterflies," Bill answered. "How are you feeling?"

"I'm fine. Just spent the day thinking about everything."

Through the FaceTime call, Bill saw her toss her school bag on her bed. She kicked off her shoes and sat on the bed, curling up next to her bag. *Lucky bag,* Bill caught himself thinking.

"JB hinted at this contest in his newsletters for months," Jaime continued. "But the actual contest wasn't announced until just a couple of weeks ago. That's not much time to prepare. It's perfect for brushing up on what we already know, but you aren't going to learn the entire horror genre in less than a month." With her back on the bed, Jaime held the phone directly above her face. Bill shook other thoughts from his head.

"That was intentional on JB's part," Jaime continued. "He wants the people who have spent their youth obsessed with horror. He wants people who are resourceful. He wants people like himself. We got this."

"I hope you're right." Bill ran a hand through his messy blonde hair and clenched his fists until his knuckles turned white. He wanted to know the results. His head felt fuzzy with impatience, and he caught himself thinking about other things, too. Things about Jaime. Things he wanted to shake from his mind. For now.

"Who else do you know that's read every Stephen King book by the time he's seventeen?" Jaime walked over to her desk, opened her laptop, and went to frightfest4d.com.

Bill sighed. "I haven't read them all by a long shot. More than half, but not all."

"Oh yeah, you skipped Bachmann?"

"Yeah. I thought it'd be cool to read all of the ones he wrote and intended to write as Bachmann after I finished the others to see what he does differently, you know?"

"That's cool. Did you run today or something? You look kinda gross." She chuckled, tossing her leaf-brown hair out of her eyes.

"Yeah. Through the cemetery. Tried to clear my mind to keep it sharp."

"One day I'll visit and you'll have to show me this cemetery you're always talking about."

"It's the coolest. It's so big. It makes me want to be remembered. To do something big with my life so I don't end up a name on a tombstone that no one knows."

"Not everyone can be famous like JB. Besides, I think fame would kinda suck." Jaime straightened a picture she kept on her desk, one with her, a really tiny Tara, and their Uncle Tim. "I want to be remembered by friends and family who really knew me. Just because someone recognizes your name on film credits or something doesn't mean they really know you."

Bill nodded, and they both paced their bedrooms until the clocked ticked down. Finally, at 5:00 p.m. PST on the dot, the results of the Rabbit in Red challenge were posted.

Rabbit in Red's Fright Fest web page swirled with *Matrix* style numbers to reveal only one number, the number nineteen. A message appeared on screen: *We have selected nineteen participants to join us in Hollywood to participate in the Rabbit in Red Fright Fest 4D Adventure. Thank you to the thousands of people who tried. Based on a variety of calculations including total number of riddles tried, total solved, and total missed, nineteen of you have been determined to be good enough for the next round. And those nineteen are . . .*

The screen changed again, this time counting down from nineteen. Next to each number, it listed a person's first name and last initial, the state they were from, and their ranking. They didn't recognize any names but as the list started to reveal the final five selected contestants, both Jaime and Bill held their breath, their eyes widening, absorbing every name, waiting and hoping desperately to see their own on the screen.

Number five: Daniel L from California
Number four: Wes P from Georgia

Number three: Rose D from Louisiana
Number two: Jaime S from Massachusetts
Number one: Bill W from Illinois
Congratulations. An e-mail is being sent to you now. Please confirm your identity and travel arrangements.

"Bill! You are number one! Oh my God, congratulations!"

"Congratulations yourself! Number two! We got the two highest rankings in the world! I can't even believe it. Oh my God!" They were silent for a moment, smiling wider than their faces. Bill added, "You know, we'd probably be tied for number one, if you hadn't —"

"Shush now, don't remind me!"

"This is fantastic!" Bill jumped up and touched the ceiling in delight, and an alert on his tablet notified him of a new e-mail.

"I got one, too," Jaime said. "Let's open it together!"

They both received the same e-mail and the subject line read *Rabbit in Red Fright Fest: Open Immediately.* With eager anticipation, they did exactly that and began to read it aloud.

But the e-mail was not from JB. It contained no identifying information at all.

You are in grave danger. Do not go to the Rabbit in Red Fright Fest. It's not what you think. I repeat: DO NOT GO!

Chapter Five

"What is this?" Jaime asked, her brown eyes squinting in disbelief at the computer screen.

"I have no idea. A joke?" Bill stood up and leaned against the wall, trying to comprehend it.

"This is weird."

Another alert notified them of a new e-mail. This one was titled: *Congratulations, Rabbit in Red Hunters* and the sender was listed as Jay Bell.

The e-mail read as follows: *Dear friends, congratulations! You have the great honor of participating in our Rabbit in Red Fright Fest 4D Adventure! I know you must be anxious about what you will be doing, but I promise that you will have the time of your lives! The next part of our contest will put your horror knowledge to a bigger test. We have created special sleeping accommodations for you right here at the studio. We will need you to fly in by Friday evening October 30. The next part of our contest will begin at midnight sharp. Throughout October 31, there will be a variety of fun contests. Imagine if* Willy Wonka and the Chocolate Factory *produced horror stories instead of candy—that's the experience you will have.*

Attached to this e-mail is a waiver all of you need to sign, and if you are under 18 you will need a parent/guardian signature as well. You have nothing to worry about. It's something my lawyers say I must do. You'll also need to click "confirm" here so I know you are coming, and then fill in the travel arrangements. Transportation to your nearest airport, an airplane ticket to Los Angeles, and transportation to our studios is all being taken care of. You need not worry about any cost or money for this weekend adventure. You will return home Sunday night November 1st in time for school on Monday, which I am sure you are excited to know.

Pay attention to the website for updates and announcements. In the meantime, continue to immerse yourself in our favorite genre, as your knowledge will need to be sharper than ever for the next

part of the contest. Once again, congratulations and good luck. –
JB

"Okay, now I don't know how to feel," Jaime commented after reading it. "I want to be excited. There doesn't seem to be anything odd with this, right?"

"Right." Bill leaned against his bookcase and laughed quietly when he saw a book titled *Misery* right in front of him. It was one of the King books he hadn't read, but the title was the answer to how he felt. "You know, that first e-mail could have been anything." He walked away from the bookcase and nervously fidgeted with an empty Horror Block box. "A jealous computer nerd who hacked the system. A jealous competitor of JB's. I mean, if you are going to send a message like that, grow a pair and say who you are."

"Agreed. Why anonymous? I don't like that."

"It will be you and me and seventeen others," Bill said. "We're not living in a horror movie. We have cell phones and intelligence."

"And balls." Jaime laughed. "Well, one of us anyway. Do you think you will have any problems getting your mom to sign the waiver?"

"Nope. She's a zombie. My living room is like a slow episode of *The Walking Dead*. She'll sign it and not even realize I'm gone. What about you?"

On FaceTime, Bill saw Jaime walk to her bedroom door. She poked her head out and looked downstairs. "My mom will argue with me, but I'll win in the end. I have a way of winning arguments."

Bill rolled his eyes. "I never would have guessed."

"I say we get these waivers signed and returned and confirm our travel arrangements. If there's really something creepy about all of this, if we are really in *grave danger*, I'm sure we'll hear more. The event's more than a month away. If nothing more happens, I'm sure we have nothing to worry about."

*****

The next month flew by. Like waiting for a big vacation, the first couple of weeks seemed to pass slowly, but at the end of each night Bill looked back and was surprised by how quickly time disappeared. During the days leading up to Halloween weekend, news of JB's Rabbit in Red Fright Fest went national and several televised news networks were trying to find and interview the contest winners. Jaime and Bill both agreed to not contact the media. It was an unnecessary distraction and they thought it would be better (not to mention safer) if they avoided the spotlight. Not everyone felt the same.

Appearing on several news networks for interviews was a contest winner named Daniel Lloyd who came out immediately to the media. He was eighteen years old and lived in San Diego, California. Bill and Jaime caught a couple of his interviews, and neither were a fan of Dan.

"Tell us why you entered the contest," one interviewer asked Daniel.

"I'm going to make a living directing and starring in horror movies," Daniel said confidently, flashing his white teeth. "I've already received a film scholarship to one of the best universities in California. Go, Trojans! Naturally I've studied virtually everything there is to know about horror and I wanted a chance to be a part of this contest. Winning it and doing whatever internship that follows will be a nice addition to my resume."

Jaime called Bill to contribute her commentary. "He sounds like a D-bag. Gag. You know how much I hate hashtags? Well, he's earned one. HashtagDbag."

The interviewer continued talking to Daniel. "So you are confident you will win. Why is that?"

"I always win." Daniel looked directly into the camera and smirked. "The only reason I'm not ranked as number one after the riddle challenge was because of typos. I was typing too fast. But that was a test of the brain. I think this next part is going to be brain and body, and as you can see, I've trained for that as well."

With bright blonde hair, much brighter than Bill's, Daniel stood with an arrogant grin and flexed his right arm. With his left hand he lifted up a USC Trojans t-shirt to reveal a firm six-pack. He was ripped, a stereotypical So-Cal kind of body, with a stereotypical idiotic mind to go with it.

"You can know a lot and still be stupid," Jaime told Bill.

The media kept searching for the other winners, asking anyone with information to please contact them immediately. Jaime and Bill managed to keep under the radar. No one at Bill or Jaime's schools outed them to the media because Jaime and Bill hadn't told anyone outside of the family.

Daniel might have been the only one to contact the media directly so far, but several other contestants had been outed by friends or family. Rose Dawn was one such unlucky winner, and was now hounded by the media after friends reported her. Rose made the mistake of posting a status update on Facebook about the contest. The day of the riddle challenge she posted, *Wish me luck! Following the Rabbit in Red tonight!* When the website listed Rose D. from Louisiana as the third place winner, her friends sent screen captures of her Facebook posts to the media, and the news wasted no time showing up at her front door.

When asked why she entered the contest, Rose looked shy on camera. "I enjoy being behind the camera. Not on it." A seventeen year old New Orleans resident, Rose's name matched her face: soft red hair, a petite body. Her eyes were hard and dark, as if guarding a secret, but her face was cute in a little-sister kind of way. She might not stand out in a crowd, except for her hair and the little black purse she held tightly against her side, but she possessed a deeper beauty, something harder to see for most people. She spoke quietly into the camera but never looked directly at it.

When asked why she entered the contest, Rose looked shy on camera. "I enjoy being behind the camera. Not on it."

"So you want to be a filmmaker too?" a reporter asked.

"Yes."

"And why is that?"

"Because I like it."

"And you want to make horror films?" the reporter pressed. "Why horror?"

"Horror needs art, and I like art. I think JB would agree," Rose answered simply and matter-of-factly.

Jaime, who was quicker to form an opinion than Bill, admired her. "She's smart but doesn't flaunt it. And you can tell she really wants to be an artist. The way she looks away from the camera. It's like she's thinking of something else, but she doesn't let them know it. I like her."

"What's that written on her purse? Do you see that? Something in purple."

"Looks like a quote but the only word I can read is silence," she told him. "It's pretty."

The fourth place winner was also outed to the media. Wes Pike from Savannah, Georgia, loved to write and shared his passion for writing horror stories with his high school creative writing teacher. During the days leading up to the contest, Wes told his teacher all about it, and on the Monday following the riddles, Wes went early to school to excitedly let his teacher know he had won. Thinking it would be good PR for the high school, his teacher talked with the principal and they surprised Wes with an interview from local media that afternoon, or at least that's how the reporter introduced the story that Bill and Jaime were watching.

"Congratulations, Wes," a reporter began. "Tell us about the contest and why you are doing this."

Wes held a small red ball that he squeezed in his hand as he answered the questions. In the background, his teacher smiled and nodded with enthusiastic encouragement.

"Well, I don't know what we will do next," Wes stammered, "but I've always been a big reader. I read horror books and like to write horror. The contest sounded fun. It sounds like something worth writing about."

"Indeed it is," the reporter agreed. "So what's your favorite horror story?"

"Hmmm," Wes thought. "Probably Stephen King's *It*."

"Why is that?"

"It's the only book I've read that made me terrified of something in real life. I hate clowns now. I always thought it was cool though that a story had that kind of power. I absolutely hate clowns."

"Kind of like how people reacted to Twisty the Clown on

American Horror Story: Freakshow?"

"Yeah," Wes answered. "Like that. And Twisty is terrifying all right, but I don't think anything will ever top Pennywise."

Wes was a bigger boy and wore an even bigger sweatshirt while being interviewed on camera. He was dark-skinned and had a boyish face that made him look like he should be in middle school and not about to graduate into college.

"I think you'll like him," Jaime told Bill. "You both love *It*."

"Yeah. I like that he's kinda like Rose, too. He seems honest. Straightforward. Not looking for fame."

"You can tell a lot by how someone appears on camera."

The news stations continued to discuss the next part of the contest, bringing on so-called horror experts: actors, writers, teachers, and anyone who would give them face time. In one interview, an English professor discussed her thoughts on the contest.

"Four-D obviously means four dimensional," she said animatedly. They were probably lucky the professor was too old to enter the contest; she was clearly excited about it. "The first part of JB's contest was to find those who knew the most about horror. I suspect that this second part of the contest will put them in four-dimensional style challenges, perhaps a combination of computer simulations and physical simulations. I'm guessing it will be something like being a part of a movie."

The media also contacted JB of course, but JB was silent and no new information had appeared on his website. Frightfest4d.com had displayed the same message since the day of the trivia contest: *We eagerly await our nineteen contestants who will be arriving on October 30. Our next round of the contest begins at midnight sharp. Return to our website then and you will get to view some of the fun from the comfort of your home.*

The media dug up every contestant they could, searching hashtags related to Rabbit in Red, JB, and Fright Fest. As the weeks passed, the only two contestants that hadn't been interviewed were Jaime and Bill.

"It's to our advantage," Jaime said, "to learn as much as we can about them and to make sure no one knows about us, I think."

"I'm sending you a YouTube link of another girl's interview," Bill said. "What do you think?"

An annoying ad played first, and then a reporter came on the computer screen. "We're live with Annie Walker from Estes Park, Colorado," the reporter stated. "Annie, tell us about yourself and why you're entering the Rabbit in Red Fright Fest."

Annie was pale and voluptuous, with hair as dark as the night slashed with sporadic splashes of gray that contrasted with her youthful face. "I'm so excited!" she told the reporter. "I've always wanted to be an actress. I love horror movies, and horror seems like a great way to build a career. I mean, look at Jamie Lee Curtis! She got her start as a scream queen on *Halloween* like decades before I was born and now she's back this year with that new show *Scream Queens*! I think it goes to show that a powerful voice and a great horror story can live quite a long time."

"Can we hear you scream?" the reporter asked with a laugh.

"Absolutely!" Annie smiled, opened her mouth, and let out a roar that made the reporter jump and grasp her ears.

"Well, channel nineteen viewers, now I'm deaf!" the reporter joked.

"I like her," Bill said after Jaime finished watching.

"She seems okay. Naive, I think. Innocent."

"She's got a hell of a pair of knockers. No wonder she can shout so loud."

"Why must boys be pervs?" Jaime rolled her eyes.

"Just an observation." Bill grinned back. "But damn. How does she stand up straight?"

"Bill!"

"Sorry." He laughed. "Here, I have one more for you to watch. This is the last one." He sent a new YouTube link, and a boy named Dexter Lange from Seattle, Washington, appeared on camera.

"How are you preparing for Rabbit in Red, Dexter?" the interviewer asked.

Dexter had dark eyes, a build similar to Daniel's, but a focus that revealed a deeper maturity. Whereas Daniel appeared cocky and arrogant, Dexter's eyes revealed pure confidence, in a way that was almost frightening.

"I'm going to be an actor and director," Dexter informed the interviewer. Not "I want to be an actor," or "I hope to become a director," like others had said, Bill noticed. There was clearly no doubt in Dexter's mind about his future career. "This is an opportunity for me to do something outside of a traditional college. I'm studying everything. Not just pop culture hits, but all the classics in literature and film from Poe to Hitchcock."

"There's something off about him," Jaime said. "What is it?"

"I dunno, but listen to what he says next."

The interviewer on the screen continued. "Who is your favorite horror villain?"

"Easy. Patrick Bateman from *American Psycho*."

"He's pretty nasty, isn't he? Why is he your favorite?"

"He destroys anyone who makes him feel inadequate," Dexter replied and then looked away from the camera, formulating a thought. "It's the fantasy that dark horror like that can provide. In real life, you can't axe someone for making you feel small. But in that movie, you live the vicarious fantasy of brutally killing anyone who makes you feel inferior."

"Well, okay," the reporter said, flushed. "Dexter, we wish you good luck."

"Wow," Jaime responded. "Yeah, okay. Keep an eye out on him. He's got some issues."

"Just don't make him feel bad." Bill laughed awkwardly.

Jaime and Bill watched all the news excerpts they could, wanting to learn all about the competition. And they studied. They searched for internet lists on the best horror books and horror movies of all time, trying to read and watch as many as they could in the small amount of time they had. They reported back to one another on their studies, summarizing what they read and saw. They avoided the media, and they both agreed on one other idea.

"When we get to Hollywood, we should introduce ourselves right away to Wes and Rose," Jaime stated. "Annie seems nice too. I also think we should stay away from Daniel HashtagDbag. I don't trust him. And we should stay away from Dexter. He's a little . . . uh, scary, don't you think? I think if there's any kind of team events, it would be good to have other connections like Wes and Rose and maybe Annie. But I definitely don't want Daniel or Dexter looking over my shoulder."

"Oh-right. So what do you think about this four-dimensional stuff?"

"I think the professor they interviewed is right." Jaime shrugged. "I mean, 4-D is real life plus simulation, right? Who knows what specifically, but it sounds fun."

Although they studied and paid attention to every detail in every horror story they could absorb before Halloween weekend, they completely ignored the first e-mail they had received warning them about this contest. No other contestant said anything about it on the news. No media outlet reported any danger or suspicion. And the anonymous sender never contacted Jaime or Bill again. But Bill, at least, had been lying when he told Jaime that the warning e-mail didn't worry him. Although he ignored it as much as possible, it was like an itch in the furthest spot on his back. It nagged at him, but he couldn't reach it, so he did his best not to think about it.

Chapter Six

Under the covers the night before the flight, Bill struggled to sleep. He looked at his phone, and *1:00 a.m.* glowed back.

"Ugh," he sighed. "Why can't we be like cell phones? Just plug me in and charge my battery."

He started the Netflix app on his phone instead of trying to fall asleep and browsed the horror section. So many movies, so little time. He clicked on a random horror flick he had yet to see, *The House of the Devil.* Maybe he could fall asleep watching it.

Something made him jump a few minutes later, but it wasn't the movie. There was a crash somewhere below in the house. Bill crept out of bed and peered downstairs from his bedroom doorway. He kept still and listened closely. There it was again, another bang, the sound of dishes hitting the floor.

He tried to tell himself what he thought most people would have thought: *Oh, it's nothing. Go back to bed.* But what if this was the one time he shrugged off a noise and someone was actually in the house? He thought of how many random noises had woken him up in the last decade. One of these days, the noise would be more than the floor creaking or the wind blowing, wouldn't it? They never did catch the intruder who killed Dad.

What if he came back for Mom? What if he's just been waiting ten years and picked tonight to return?

Bill shook his head and sighed. "You're so stupid, Bill. You know what the noise is."

"Mom?" He spoke softly, and his voice cracked as he worried what he would do if someone else actually replied.

"Billy?" his mom called from the kitchen. "Sorry, honey. Did I wake you?"

"No, I couldn't sleep."

He walked downstairs toward the kitchen. He should have known better. A large bottle of vodka sat on the counter, nearly empty. His mom had knocked over some glasses on the countertop, and she was making herself another drink.

"Can't sleep either?" he asked, looking at the glass full of vodka and ice and nothing else.

"Can I ever?" she returned.

"Yeah, I know."

Bill had grown up watching his mom drink every night. After his father was murdered, they stayed with their grandparents for nearly a year. His mom sought therapy and tried several prescription drugs over the years since the home invasion, but vodka was always her drug of choice, especially when the sun went down.

They eventually moved out of their grandparents' house, and for a year or so, Bill thought everything had stabilized and might turn back to normal. Sally Wise was an elementary school teacher who took an extended leave of absence after her husband's death. She never did muster the will to return to work and eventually quit. Months later, Bill saw her browsing help wanted ads while sitting at his grandparents' kitchen table.

"Mom, are you gonna get a job again?" he remembered asking her.

"I need to do something, honey. I don't know what to do, but I need to do something."

"I don't want you to go back to work," he told her.

"I know, baby, but we have to have a home of our own again."

She was hired as a receptionist at just a little more than minimum wage, but they found a small house to rent, and moved out of her parents' home a little over a year after the murder.

That was when the drinking started. On her own, with no one to watch over her but her child, she took to the bottle. Every single night.

"I think it's good you get away for the weekend," she told Bill now, snapping him from his memories.

"Yeah, but I'm nervous."

"What's this about again?" she asked, taking a large swallow.

"I told you. It's a horror contest."

"I'll never understand why you like that shit. Haven't we had enough horror in our lives?" she asked. Her eyes were swollen. Bill remembered how beautiful his mom's eyes used to be — brilliant blue enhanced by light blond hair.

You got that blonde from your mom, his dad used to say. *I just hope you got her brains, too.*

"When will you be back?" his mom asked.

"Sunday night." When he looked at his mom, it was like looking at a ghost.

Sally Wise never moved beyond answering phones. She never tried to teach again. She'd get up at 7:00 every morning, take a quick shower, and head to work. On Sunday, they would go to the grocery store together. She'd let him pick out a new cereal every Sunday, but that was all Bill ever had for breakfast. He didn't mind though. He loved cereal, and he loved getting a new flavor every week.

She'd come home from work by 4:00 each day, and sometimes she'd make something for dinner. But if she was cooking, it was usually hot dogs, a frozen pizza, or something microwavable. She'd greet Bill when he got home from school, and then like clockwork she'd make a drink. Vodka on the rocks. She'd drink until she had enough to sleep. Bill worried of course, but he didn't actually mind. Sally was more likely to talk to him about his day when she had a few drinks first, and as limited as the conversations were, he enjoyed talking to her.

Years passed and nothing changed, and so Bill made friends with his movies and his books. They helped him fall asleep, they kept him company, and they were always there for him. After they moved, he left most of his childhood friends behind, and he never made much effort to find new ones. He missed the days of having a bunch of kids over to watch a movie or play a game, but with the way his mother was glued to the bottle, who would want to bring new friends over anyway?

"I wish you'd find a different hobby," Sally told him.

"I wish you wouldn't drink so much," Bill said.

Bill knew she'd get angry if he said something about her drinking. This wasn't the first time he had made such a statement. And sure enough, she glared at him, her once beautiful eyes hollow and hurting.

"Look, Bill," she started. "I've told you before. It's different for me. You have had your whole childhood to grow and adapt. You have a whole life in front of you. You can move on. What do I have? I have nothing. Nothing to look forward to. No life to live anymore. It's not fair for you to say such things to me. All I have is nothing."

Bill felt himself getting mad. Tears of anger were forming. They'd had this fight before too, and Bill hated it.

"Nothing?" he snapped. "You have me. You have always had me. But you choose that damn drink instead."

Sally started to cry. "Oh, Billy, don't say such things to me."

"Why don't you love me?" he asked. The tears fell from his eyes as the words came out. He stared at his mother, and she gasped but no words followed. Bill's heart raced as if he had just finished running. He didn't know if he asked the question because he really believed it to be true, or if he asked the question to hurt her. Probably a little bit of both.

Tears rolled off her cheeks, but instead of answering, she poured another drink. She swallowed it all at once and then turned and looked at her son.

"You know I love you," Sally whispered. "But every time I look . . . at you . . . I see . . . your father. Do you know how hard that is? Every day I see you and every day I see him and I will never get over this."

Bill let himself cry, choking on the awkward, painful sobs. Why did parents have the power to hurt kids so much? Even crappy parents? And no one could make it hurt as much as his mother, Bill thought. It wasn't the first time this had happened either.

She didn't comfort him. She poured another drink and looked out the window.

Bill stood up, walked toward her, and hugged her. At first she didn't hug back, but then she set her glass down and wrapped her arms around his head.

"I'm sorry, Mom."

"Me too, baby. Me, too."

He kissed her cheek and turned around and walked back upstairs to his bedroom. Getting under the covers, he took out his phone and pressed play on the movie he had started watching. He let the horror of the film wash over him and pull him away from reality. Maybe it would help him sleep.

Chapter Seven

The next morning, Bill went to say goodbye to his mom. She was still asleep, so he didn't wake her. He quickly cleaned up the kitchen, threw away the empty vodka bottle, made a bowl of cereal, and waited for the ride JB arranged to pick him up and take him to the airport.

His eyes widened as the brightest black he'd ever seen glowed outside his home: an ostentatious limo pulled up out front.

"Good morning, Mr. Wise," the limo driver greeted, tipping his hat and opening the back door for Bill.

"Wow," Bill managed to say.

"Your host for the weekend has instructed me to take you to the airport." The driver smiled. "Mr. Bell said you should be treated like royalty."

The limo drove him into Chicago, and from there he flew to LAX. Another driver waited outside the terminal at LAX with a sign shaped like a hockey mask. Across the Jason-themed mask, Bill saw his name: *Mr. William Wise.*

"That's me," he told the driver.

"Welcome, young sir. I've been given specific instructions to escort you to Rabbit in Red."

Bill followed the driver to another limousine. He stretched his legs out in the back and laughed, soaking in the luxury.

The driver pulled up to the front of a warehouse, and Bill took a deep breath and jumped out of the limo. It was time to focus on the here and now. This was what he had been waiting for.

Outside the limousine, Bill put his hand on the warm sidewalk. The driver handed Bill his duffel bag and bowed slightly.

"So this is Hollywood," Bill said aloud, taking his bag and studying the obnoxiously large warehouse of a building, several stories tall, stretching almost as far as his eyes could see. His small neighborhood back in Illinois could fit in this building. Outside the main entrance was a big plastic banner that read *Welcome to Rabbit in Red's Fright Fest 4D!* in bloody red italics. Bill thanked the driver and walked toward the banner. He looked around the outside of the building, and it seemed to stretch further than he could even see. He expected to see some palm trees, but there wasn't even grass, merely endless pavement surrounding the building.

He crept toward the doors even though he wanted to run. Trying to soak in every sight and sound, he listened for noise, work, or people, but heard nothing. It was evening on Friday, October 30, the sun was hanging on to the day by a thread of orange and purple, and all Bill heard was a quiet breeze.

That all changed when he opened the doors.

"Welcome, Bill Wise."

Bill spun around. An animatronic clown, its purple mouth wide open, leered down at him. Its enormous head bobbed right next to Bill's face, and Bill jumped back a step before he recognized it as the fat clown from *Killer Klowns from Outer Space*.

"Your friends," continued the clown in the same terrifying voice Bill remembered from the movie, "and our host of the evening are waiting for you in the studio commons. Straight ahead but watch your step. You're in for a night of surprises. Ha hep. Ha hep. Ha hep."

The clown laughed, then settled back into its resting position and went still.

That was a cool greeting! Bill waited, but nothing else happened, so he guessed he was supposed to move on. He looked around. Several large halls extended to the left and the right.

The hallway on his left resembled that of a hospital. Looking closer, he saw a nurses' station, white *Happy Halloween* letters on an orange banner, and a black witch hanging on a wall. It didn't take him long to realize this was an allusion to the hospital in *Halloween II*.

To his right, the hall changed into a giant hotel hallway: it had white wallpaper with small purple flowers and beige paint on the trim. JB had decorated this hallway to resemble one of the hotel halls in *The Shining*.

He heard chatter from up ahead, so he moved forward. The center hallway looked like a street with realistic sidewalks and tar-covered roads.

As he walked further, houses and trees appeared on the

roadside, and a soft rain began to fall. In the hallway? He wiped his wet forehead and laughed. *What is this place?*

A paper boat floated into a gutter at the end of the road. Bill nearly skipped down the road he recognized from Stephen King's *It*, where little Georgie was eaten by the killer clown in the gutter. Bill peered into the gutter and held his breath in case Pennywise decided to jump out. But he only heard a whisper.

"We all float down here."

Wes, the guy who was afraid of clowns, must have loved this. Or hated it. Bill laughed to himself and marched forward.

This hall ended in a set of double doors. Bill pushed through them and into a cavernous room. It resembled a high school gymnasium, and Bill looked straight up to the ceiling. Yep, there it was. A bucket of blood suspended over a stage in the back of the gym. His eyes followed voices, from the ceiling to a series of tables, all decorated for prom.

Four rooms so far, and three of them from Stephen King stories. *It's a good thing I'm a King fan,* Bill thought, but now he wished he had finished all of King's books. Why did that guy have to be so damn prolific?

Bill's excitement shifted from the scenery to the people. He immediately recognized Daniel from the media interviews. The athletic blond boy already seemed to have a gang of kids listening to his every word. Daniel stood like Captain Morgan, one leg on a chair and one on the floor dictating some kind of egotistical bullshit to kids too ignorant to know better.

Next to that table, he saw Rose and Wes, who were talking excitedly and already seemed to be friends. They didn't talk with the big gestures, tall posture, and loud vocals like Daniel. Rose and Wes talked with their heads angled down, leaning toward each other, but Bill could see their lips moving. There were several other tables where people sat in pairs or threes and were shaking hands and getting to know each other.

Bill examined the individuals at every table, but the one person he was looking for was missing. For the first time that day, he frowned. Had he simply beat Jaime here? Where was she?

Then his glance landed on the corner of the room, past the

tables near the stage, and he saw her. Jaime saw him, too. Their eyes locked, and Jaime stepped out from the shadows. Running her hand through her shoulder-length hair and straightening her shirt (it was the *Halloween III: the Season of the Witch* shirt), she stepped toward him from across the gym. He wondered if her heart was racing as fast as his.

Bill couldn't help but smile. He thought of those cliché, cheesy moments in movies where two people dramatically run across a field and embrace. But it *was* kind of like that. He walked toward her, too, and each step was quicker than the last. *Jesus, what do I even say?* His breath quickened, and for a moment, he thought he would choke and be unable to speak.

Thank God she spoke first, as he had no idea what to do. It was like seeing Freddy Krueger for the first time on screen. Well, not frightening, of course, but a powerful moment. One he'd never forget.

"You're here," Jaime whispered when they were finally face to face.

"You're here, too." The walk across the gym had left him breathless, but not because he was out of shape. His voice cracked as he spoke. *Why do you have to be such a dork? Say something real!*

"I arrived right before you." She gestured to one of the other tables. "I thought about going to sit with Rose and Wes, but I thought I'd stand back and people watch for a bit."

"It's so great to see you in person," he said. They stared awkwardly at one another for a long moment. Bill slung his duffel bag over his shoulder and nervously put his hands in his pockets. *Stupid, stupid, stupid,* he thought again. He dropped his duffel bag and slowly opened his arms.

She stepped forward and hugged him, skipping the handshake and formalities. Jaime smelled of vanilla and flowers, and Bill breathed deep, feeling his senses blur as butterflies tingled his stomach.

"It's nice to meet you in person," she said, easing out of the hug. She ran a hand through his golden hair and smiled.

"You, too. I don't even know . . . I mean, does this even feel real? Wow." He liked the way her hand felt in his hair. It made the little hairs on the back of his neck stand up. He wanted to touch her again, but he could only stare, his muscles paralyzed.

After a few moments, he broke eye contact and looked at the floor. He tried to compose himself. "Have you met JB?" he asked.

"Not yet. You're actually the last to arrive. I imagine he'll greet us soon now."

"Should we sit?"

"Yeah, let's go introduce ourselves to Wes and Rose."

"Oh-right."

She smiled at the familiar phrase. He grabbed his bag, and they took a seat at Wes and Rose's table. Daniel glared at them from across the room. Bill felt Daniel sizing him up but refused to make eye contact. He focused his attention on Wes and Rose instead. Out of everyone in this room, it was only he and Jaime, the two people with the highest scores from the riddle contest, that no one had seen on TV. He felt a dozen pairs of eyes suddenly fall upon them.

"Hi, guys," he said, trying to focus on the two people they thought were the most honest from the TV interviews. "My name is Bill Wise. And this is Jaime Stein. Mind if we sit with you?"

"No," Wes answered. "I'm Wes Pike. Nice to meet ya." Wes put out his hand, and Bill and Jaime shook it.

"I'm Rose Dawn."

"Hi Rose," Jaime greeted, shaking hands with her, too. "You have such beautiful hair. Rose Red, I bet they call you?"

She covered her mouth as she gently laughed. "Yes, but I prefer just Rose."

"You got it. So what do you think about all of this so far?"

"It's so big," Rose answered. "I never imagined it would be this big."

"That's a beautiful purse," Jaime told her. "What's it say?"

"Oh, it's a favorite quote of mine," Rose answered. "'Speak only if it improves upon the silence.' Gandhi said that."

"I love that. The purple stitching is very beautiful."

"Thanks." Rose looked down and ran a finger across the lettering.

"You can tell JB is loaded," Wes commented. "I've only seen the hallways out front and this room, but look at his attention to detail. The same blue stars up on stage exactly like in *Carrie*. And the *It* hallway. How amazing is that!"

"I know!" Bill nodded enthusiastically. "I can't wait to see more."

"So we're actually the top four," Jaime said. "Has Daniel talked to you? Or anyone else?"

"Daniel," said Wes, "came over here and said, 'You must know who I am.'" Wes stood up and put one leg on the chair and a hand on his hip, mimicking Daniel's posture and condescending look perfectly. "'And I saw you on TV too, but so you know, I plan on winning this on my own.'" Wes titled his chin up, and the three giggled at his impersonation. "'If you need help,'" he continued in a voice uncannily like Daniel's, "'which by the looks of you I'm sure you will, I'm guessing you're screwed.'" Wes sat back in his chair. "And then he laughed and walked away."

"It looks like he already has a gang of admirers," Jaime said, nodding at the group gathered at Daniel's table. "Ugh, his interviews on TV made me sick. And he's the only one out of anyone in this room who continually sought out the media. That says a lot right there."

Wes rolled his eyes. "Yeah, he seems like a jerk. And he's always drawing attention to his body. Look at those shorts. Might as well wear nothing but underwear. It's gross."

The four of them laughed, even Rose who had more of a soft giggle. She still covered her mouth when she laughed, almost as if embarrassed to do so.

"He's the Richard Simmons of horror," Jaime added. "HashtagHorrorFashion."

"More like HashtagWhoreFashion," Bill joked.

"Is he gay?" asked Wes. "I mean, why would you wear shorts like that?"

"Nothing wrong with being gay," Rose chimed in.

"Not at all, girl," said Jaime. "But don't be a jerk, and generally don't wear shorts in any situation where people can see your junk. Does he actually think people want to see the shape of his stuff?"

"HashtagGross," Bill groaned. "Small as it is, I suppose it's the best he has to offer. When you don't have much on the inside, you show off as much as you have on the outside."

"He's so nasty," Wes said. "Ugh, I hate him already."

"Don't say hate," Rose snapped. "Hate is a powerful word."

Wes grinned at Rose, and Jaime turned and also smiled at Bill.

"Look, there's Dexter, the *American Psycho* fan," Bill whispered to Jaime. Dexter laughed at something Daniel had said and put his hand up to receive the bro fist bump.

"I'm not surprised they're friends," Jaime said. "Just keep an eye on them. Do you see Annie?"

"Over there." Bill pointed to a table on the opposite side of them. Annie Walker sat with a few other girls who all were laughing and getting to know one another. "Should we say hi?"

It looked like all nineteen of the contestants had found a table and friends, and just as Jaime started to stand up to say hello to Annie, the lights dimmed. She sat back down, and like the energy before the headliner at a big concert, an electric wave of adrenaline shot through the room.

Bells started playing in surround sound around the room, so loud that everyone jumped and covered their ears. It was the bells from *The Exorcist*, perhaps even more haunting in this setting than in the actual film. The lights slowly came back on and now there was a spotlight on the stage.

The bells quieted, replaced by the theme from *Jaws*. A *duh-nuh, duh-nuh, duh-nuh* sound echoed throughout the commons, gradually increasing in both volume and speed. When the *duh-nuhs* reached their height, the bucket over the top of the stage tipped and spilled blood across the floor. Then the stage shifted, and the wall with the senior prom sign and all the stars from *Carrie* slid across stage revealing a new wall with two giant elevator doors.

The elevator doors opened, and more blood washed out of it, across the stage, and onto the floor of the commons. It was a tidal wave of red, and it roared through the room, splashing everyone and covering the floor.

A hole opened up in the floor of the commons, and the blood drained into that hole, leaving shimmering red puddles scattered across the floor. Then the hole widened in the floor until it was the size of their tables. No one screamed—instead everyone cheered and laughed. Bill sniffed the blood on his arms and, hesitating for moment, licked it. It was syrup.

The spotlight turned to the table-sized hole in the middle of the commons. A claw made out of knives was rising out of the hole. Moving upward on some kind of platform, the hand became an arm, the arm became a full body dressed in a red and green striped sweater and a brown hat. It was Freddy Krueger, or a guy with a lot of great makeup and costumes at least.

The terrifying nursery rhyme from *Nightmare on Elm Street* now played through the room. Childlike voices sang, *"One, two, Freddy's coming for you. Three, four, better lock your door."* Everyone in the commons started singing along. "Five, six, grab your crucifix. Seven, eight, gonna stay up late. Nine, ten, never sleep again!" Freddy laughed, a perfect cackle almost as good as the great Robert Englund.

The music quieted, and the lights focused on Freddy.

"My name is Jay Bell. And I welcome you to Rabbit in Red's Fright Fest 4-D!"

Everyone applauded, cheered, and whistled. For nineteen of the greatest young horror fans in the world, this was no nightmare. It was a dream come true.

"You are now beginning an incredible journey through the world of horror," Jay shouted over a microphone. "There will be games, surprises, challenges, and so much more!"

They jumped to their feet, clapping and hollering back.

"What will you experience, you must be wondering? Well, you will experience the legends of horror!" He slashed at one side of the room, and that wall changed to a giant video screen. Michael Myers approached on video, chasing Laurie Strode in *Halloween: H20* in the great scene where they meet for the first time in 20 years through a small window on a door. Michael stared at everyone in the commons, in full 3D form. They could hear his breathing. The *Halloween* theme music played, and the nineteen contestants roared.

"You have demonstrated great knowledge, and you will be

rewarded with the night of your lives!" JB's Freddy claw slashed at the opposite wall, changing it into another giant video screen. This time a scene straight out of *Evil Dead* was playing, where the tools and objects in the cabin became possessed and start flying. In full 3D effects, all the weapons flew at the audience. They all ducked, but again they cheered.

"But you will also be tested. Although I can promise all nineteen of you a weekend that you will never forget, this is a challenge. And I am looking for the best of the best!"

JB waited for the contestants to quiet down before he continued. "This is a place of celebration. I had a saying when I was growing up. Don't hang with those who shame. Not everyone celebrates our passions, but it's important to remember that there are others like you. Find the friends who do celebrate your dreams, and you will live a very rewarding and happy life."

When the group settled down after another long applause, JB continued. "And now, let me introduce our helpers."

Four people came out onto the stage, each dressed as a different horror character. There was Sam, the creepy childlike character from *Trick 'r Treat*, wearing a green mask with stitching over the mouth and holes for the eyes with an orange dress suit. Another assistant was dressed as Pumpkinhead from the '80s horror film of the same name. Pumpkinhead had a green alien-like body, pointy wings, long claws, and a devil's tail. The third assistant appeared as Captain Spaulding from *House of 1000 Corpses*, wearing a small patriotic red, white, and blue hat with clown makeup on the face, a full beard, and grossly yellow-stained teeth. The final assistant presented herself as Samara, the girl from *The Ring*, with long, wet, dark hair that covered much of her face. She was hunched over but looked out at the contestants with dark, determined eyes.

As Freddy, JB stood in the center and the four others surrounded him. It was a haunting and exciting display of horror.

"These are my assistants for the weekend," JB continued. "They will show you to your resting quarters. I say *resting* quarters as there will be little time for sleep!" JB, imitating Freddy's voice again, roared with laughter. "Take a few moments to put away your things and get ready for the most intense weekend of your lives. And I suppose you should take a moment to clean off the blood that splashed you, but don't worry. I promise you there will be more blood tonight! Oh, YES," he shouted. "MUCH. MORE. BLOOD!"

Chapter Eight

"Gentlemen to your left. Ladies to your right," the assistant dressed as Pumpkinhead announced. "We shall show you to your quarters."

Bill pushed his chair back and discovered he had been holding hands with Jaime without even realizing it. He must have grabbed her hand during JB's introduction. He looked down, surprised at his own actions, and caught Jaime smiling at him. He slowly released his grip on her hand and smiled back.

"See you soon," she whispered. She put an arm around Rose's shoulder and walked to the right of the stage.

Bill and Wes stayed together, keeping their distance from Daniel and his little rat pack. They were escorted behind the stage on the left and entered a new part of the building. The setting changed into cement floors, brick walls, and steel doors, with a wet glossy glow and a musty smell.

"What's this from?" Bill asked Wes. "*Session 9? One Flew Over the Cuckoo's Nest,* maybe? Or what about *American Horror Story: Asylum*?"

"You must choose a roommate and a room," Pumpkinhead announced. "Two people per room."

Daniel and the others sprinted forward. Bill nodded at Wes, and Wes smiled back.

"Look at that quote over there." Wes pointed at a memorial past the rooms, which as far as Bill could tell was supposed to be the outside of the psych ward. "It says, *Remember us for we too have lived, loved, and laughed.* That's from *Shutter Island*."

"Creepy! But you're right," Bill agreed. "I'd say it's more psychological than pure horror, but it does have one hell of a good setting. This room cool with you?" Bill pointed at the first room on the left.

"Close to the main stage, far away from Daniel." Wes snickered. "Works for me."

Bill opened the door and walked over to the furthest bed.

"I think we can expect ghosts in our rooms," Wes said. From the way he spoke, Bill guessed this setting made Wes a little nervous. "I wonder if the girls have as luxurious accommodations as us."

"I hope so. Wouldn't be as fun or fair if they didn't."

"We will meet in one hour," Pumpkinhead shouted from outside. "Please take the time to get to know one another, freshen up, and then meet us back at the commons precisely at 11:00 p.m. Games begin at midnight."

"I'm too pumped," Bill said, pacing the room. He tossed the small duffel bag on the bed.

"Yeah. I think I'll wash up a bit."

There was at least a sink in the room, and Wes washed his face. Bill sat down on the bed, and then Wes walked over to the bed closest to the door. Bill watched him unpack and saw that Wes had only brought sweatshirts. Bill opened his mouth to tell Wes that it was a little hot for sweatshirts in California, but Wes walked to the corner of the room and changed before Bill could say it. Even with Wes's back completely to Bill, he saw Wes's fat rolls. Maybe his choice of clothing wasn't that surprising.

Bill went to the sink and washed the syrup off his face and arms. He changed his shirt too, putting on a *Rocky Horror Picture Show* t-shirt, black with the giant red lips on the front. They each sat on their beds on separate sides of the room and faced one another.

"This is all surreal," Bill started.

"Yeah. This place could be a theme park."

"Maybe that's the idea."

"What do you think the game will be about tonight?" Wes asked.

"Something four-dimensional, right? We've already seen 3-D effects in the commons. I'm guessing we will have some kind of game where we will have to interact with those effects. That's what I think of when I think of 4-D."

"Are you and Jaime a couple?"

Bill blinked and looked away. "No. We met online a while back, so we knew each other before the contest. Tonight's the first time we've ever seen each other in person."

"Oh, that's cool."

"What about you? You have a girlfriend?"

"No." Wes put his head down. "Never had one." He took out a small red ball and squeezed it. Bill remembered that Wes squeezed the same ball during his TV interviews.

"I've never had one either," Bill said.

Wes looked up. "Really?"

"Yeah."

"Wow."

"Why wow?"

"Well. I mean, you look . . . good. I know I'm fat. Don't say anything. It's true. But you. You're thin . . . kinda athletic looking."

Bill laughed. "Well, thanks man. I don't know. I mean I want to of course but I just never really had a chance, I guess."

"Until now, right?"

Bill gave a fake laugh and turned around. "Maybe. Hey, what's that in your hands?"

Wes looked at the small red ball and back up at Bill. "Oh. This? Nothing. It's stupid."

"Remember what JB said? Don't hang with those who shame? I don't do that."

"It's a stress ball, but I pretend it's a clown's nose."

"Oh. That's cool," Bill said. "Whatever floats your boat."

Wes laughed, catching the *It* reference. "I'm terrified of clowns. Ironic, I know, considering how much I love that story. And I get kinda anxious in general. So I got this stress ball to squeeze when I'm nervous, and I pretend it's a clown's nose. Don't laugh, but I got the idea from *Batman*. Keep what scares you close, so you learn to control it, and not the other way around."

"I get that. Good for you. So what about you and Rose? You two seemed to hit it off."

"Yeah. She's so pretty, isn't she? I wasn't expecting that kind of distraction when I got here. I mean, she looked hot on camera, right? But when I saw her in person I swear I blanked on King's first name. That's not good. But I don't think anyone like her would like someone like me anyway."

"You can't think like that."

"It's true." Wes nodded and squeezed the stress ball.

Bill sighed and tried to think of the right words to say. "I think people are attracted to confidence, not just appearance. Have more confidence in yourself and everything will work out. And I tell you what. I got your back. For the whole weekend. Okay?"

"Okay. Cool." Wes had a good smile, honest and genuine. Sure, he had some extra baggage, but that was something, especially at his age, that could still be changed. Bill spaced out for a minute, trying to think when the last time was he had a face-to-face conversation with a friend. The only conversations he had were with Jaime through a webcam or his mom after she had several drinks.

There was a knock on their door, snapping Bill out of his thoughts. Daniel and a group of other guys entered their room. Wes leaned back as Daniel's tan body—and tightly clad junk—stopped way too close to him.

"Hey losers," Daniel greeted.

"Richard Simmons called," Wes said. "He'd like his shorts back." Bill snorted from across the room.

"That's funny, fat boy," Daniel retorted. "Have you heard of this twenty-first century invention called exercise?"

"If you're looking for a date," Bill jumped in, "you're in the wrong room." Dexter was standing behind Daniel and laughed at Bill's comment.

"Shut up, Dexter," Daniel said, and Bill saw Dexter give a sharp look back at Daniel. Dexter had a hard face and a muscular body, but didn't flaunt it like Daniel. Bill wondered what made any of these guys want to hang around Daniel, but he also wondered what thoughts were bouncing around Dexter's head. Horror could bring out the crazies.

"We just came to say hello," Daniel said. "You don't have to be rude." He looked around the room and saw Wes's backpack. Without asking, he picked it up, turned it upside down, and shook out the bag's contents. "Damn, kid. Got enough snacks?" he laughed as half a dozen candy bars fell out, mixed in with a couple of sweatshirts, pants, and underwear. "Oh, nice boxers! Looks like a dress my grandmother wears." He grinned as he picked them up and pulled them wide, stretching the boxers to twice the width of his own body.

"Leave his underwear alone, man," Dexter said from behind. "That's nasty. I'm out of here." He shook his head, then turned around and left the room.

"Whatever." Daniel turned his attention back to Wes and Bill. "I'll leave you guys to play with yourselves."

"Play with themselves!" Another boy laughed from behind Daniel. "That's funny."

Daniel gave him an odd look. "You're a fool, too, Leroy."

Bill peered around Daniel and tried to study this kid named Leroy. He was short and skinny with a determination on his face that wasn't as much about winning as it was about fitting in with the guys. He was awkward, the kind of follower who laughed too easily at bad jokes. Too bad he chose Daniel to be the one with whom he wanted to belong.

"Can't wait to see you lose," Wes said back to Daniel.

"I can't wait to see that bed break. Don't think it's meant for whales." And with that, Daniel and the rest of the guys left the room.

"He really is a hashtagDbag," Wes groaned.

"Don't pay him any attention," Bill said. "Guys like that are trying to compensate for something, you know? And we've already seen what that is." Wes laughed. "Forget them," Bill continued. "Let's check on the girls. See what their rooms look like."

They proceeded with caution — were they even allowed in the girls' wing? No assistants were visible in the hall of their psychiatric ward quarters, and they heard laughter from the other rooms, so they assumed all of the other guys were occupied. They walked quickly out of their quarters, back to the commons and crossed the main stage to the other hall, where the girls were escorted.

As they suspected, their living quarters had its own unique setting, too. It was the Bates Motel from *Psycho*. The hallway was painted to look like the hotel, and in the distance, there was a projection of the large family house that overlooked the rooms.

"Well, their rooms might look better than ours," Bill said, "but I sure wouldn't want to take a shower in any of them."

"I wonder what room Rose and Jaime are in."

"Jaime? You here?" Bill called, raising his voice but not too much in case they weren't supposed to be here.

Jaime popped out of the second room on the left. "Hey! What are you doing?"

"Looking for you," Bill answered. "We wanted to see what your rooms look like."

"Come check it out. I am totally not showering here."

The inside of their room looked exactly like the motel room from the film: simple, a standard bed, a small desk, and of course a bathroom with a shower.

"JB has a twisted sense of humor, that's for sure," Jaime said. "Go freshen up? Yeah, that's funny. I'll stick with the sink for now."

"A sink is all we have in our rooms," Bill told her. "We're in a psych ward."

She laughed. "How appropriate!"

"Hey now," Bill said. He grinned at her. "Don't be a wise ass."

"Don't steal my lines." She pushed him jokingly.

"I still can't get a signal," Rose said from behind them.

"Have you guys checked your phones since you've been here?" Jaime asked. "We've been trying to call home and let them know everything is cool. But we have no service. Must be all the big steel walls in this warehouse."

Bill had forgotten all about his phone. He had forgotten about anything that wasn't in the here and now.

"What about you, Wes?" he asked.

Wes looked at his phone and shook his head. "Nothing."

Bill and Jaime made eye contact. Was she also thinking of the warning e-mail they had received when the winners of the riddle contest were announced? He thought so, but he didn't want to say anything about it in front of the others.

"I'm sure it's fine." Jaime broke eye contact and spoke to Rose. "We'll ask JB about it after the game tonight."

"That's a much better shirt, by the way," Bill told Jaime. She had changed out of her *Season of the Witch* shirt and now wore a black t-shirt with a static white TV and an outline of a little girl sitting in front of it. "Now *Poltergeist* is a good flick."

"Carol-Anne!" Rose spoke in a high pitched voice, making them all jump.

"Rose, you are full of surprises." Jaime laughed.

They overheard a few other girls giggling in the hallway. "Let's say hi," Jaime said, stepping out of the room.

"Hey, we saw you on TV," one girl said to Rose. "I'm Annie. I'm staying in the room across from you."

"Cool," Rose said. "I didn't want to be on TV, you know. A friend of mine ratted me out to the local news."

"I could tell. It's cool," Annie said. *Now here's someone who could star in a horror movie,* Bill thought, as he stared at her huge chest. Jaime caught him gawking and slapped him on the shoulder. Embarrassed, Bill tried to smile and looked away.

"I'm Kim," another girl introduced herself. "And this is my roommate Trish. We're next door to you."

"Cool. I'm Jaime. You met Rose. This is Bill and Wes." They all shook hands.

"So what do you think so far?" Annie asked.

"This place is incredible," Jaime said. "The attention to details put in everything, I mean wow. It's like living in a horror movie."

"Yeah, like a dozen horror movies!" Trish said. "I can't wait to see what these games are."

The bells from *The Exorcist* rang once again. "Is it time already?" Bill looked at his phone, which still had the time even if it had no service. "Wow, we only have ten minutes. I guess we should get back to our rooms in case the assistants check in on us. Nice to meet all of you."

He hesitated. He thought about hugging Jaime, but everyone was watching. And would it be weird if he were to hug her again?

"Good luck," Annie said.

"Yeah, you, too," Bill said back.

"See you in a bit," Jaime told them and waved. The boys ran out of the Bates Motel quarters, through the commons, and back to their *Shutter Island* section.

"Do you want one?" Wes asked Bill, grabbing a Snickers that

Daniel had shaken out of his backpack earlier. Bill thought for a moment that he should tell Wes to stop eating candy bars if he was so worried about his appearance, but instead he said, "Sure, thanks" and enjoyed a quick snack. As Bill bit into his candy bar, Daniel poked his head into their room again.

"Boo," Daniel said, apparently trying to spook them with that always smug grin on his face. Dexter and Leroy were behind him again and a few other guys that Bill didn't know yet, but that smug grin of Daniel's must have been contagious since they all possessed it. "Pretty sweet rooms, eh? We found a secret. Want to know?"

"What?" Wes asked.

"Like a real mental hospital, the doors for these rooms lock from the outside." Daniel slammed their room door shut, locked it, and ran off laughing with his rat pack.

"Hey!" Bill shouted after him. He jumped off the bed and tried the door but it was no good. They were locked in. "Hey! Unlock this door! Let us out!"

But no one answered, and no one came. *The Exorcist* bells rang again. They were supposed to all meet in the commons, and Bill and Wes were now locked in their room with no way out.

Five minutes passed and Wes took over for Bill banging on the door and shouting to anyone who might hear them. "Surely Rose or Jaime will wonder where we are," Wes said in between slams. "C'mon! Anyone! We can't get out."

"What a jerk," Bill snarled. "In these rooms, no one can hear you scream."

Another five minutes passed, and now both Bill and Wes were banging on the door together. Wes had broken into a sweat, and Bill already had a bruise forming on his arm. Finally, they saw someone outside the door: Samara the assistant, the girl from *The Ring*.

She unlocked the door. "You're late. JB won't like that. Hurry."

"It's not our fault," Wes began, but Bill grabbed him and ran toward the commons. There wasn't any time to waste.

They saw Jaime and Rose at the same table from earlier that evening, and Jaime mouthed, "What happened?" Bill glared over at Daniel and his table, which had grown in number, now a mix of guys and girls. Daniel smiled back.

JB was on stage, out of costume, dressed only as himself. "Bill and Wes, is it? Tardiness could have cost you the entire game, boys. Thank you for deciding to join us."

"But we —" Wes tried to explain but was interrupted by JB.

"Shhhsh," JB said sternly. "Have a seat."

Now that JB was out of costume, they saw what he really looked like. He could have played Frankenstein's monster. He was as tall as Bill, but not skinny. He had a strong athletic build, like Dexter and Daniel put together, a football player's build. It was JB's forehead that made him think of Frankenstein's monster. It was as wide as it was high, covered by thin black hair sporadically patched with gray.

"Now, as I was saying," JB said, "there are two main reasons for our first round. One is to find out how well you know these stories. The second is to pay tribute. Art inspires art. The best of it inspires us to create, don't you think? And at the end of this weekend, that's what I hope to have inspired in all of you. I hope to deepen and strengthen your passions to create. You've all followed the rabbit in red here. The next step is to play." He paused and grinned at all nineteen contestants.

"Are you ready to PLAY THE RABBIT IN RED?" he shouted.

All nineteen roared in excitement.

"Our first round of games will begin at midnight sharp," he told them. "You will work individually to solve a very special challenge, not only testing your horror knowledge but also your ability to problem-solve and think on your feet. You will be escorted to a special chamber in the studios that has been designed with a game portal for each of you. It looks like this."

JB pointed to the screen behind him. The screen displayed a small room with a bench about chest high that contained some kind of helmet and pair of gloves. It looked like the Oculus Rift, a real virtual reality experience Bill had read about. The room possessed a giant curved screen that engulfed the walls 360 degrees.

"These are the game rooms," JB continued. "When you enter, you are to put on the helmet and the pair of gloves. This is very unique technology. Images will play on the curved screen and through special lenses on the helmet. The layering of images enhances the special effects. You'll see 3D effects out of the corners of your eyes, in your peripheral vision, and even behind you. The gloves act as motion sensors, much like an enhanced Wii remote. The gloves will allow you to interact with your environment: you can pick things up, throw items, punch, claw, clap, and anything else you could normally do with your hands. And now look at the floor."

On the screen behind JB, the floor of the game chamber was revealed. It was also curved with a conveyer belt of sorts. "The floor will move with you. If you move forward, it acts like a treadmill. But you can move side to side, backwards, jump, crawl, duck, run and the curved shape of the floor will go in any direction you choose. Thus begins the 4D element of the game. You are a part of it, not sitting in front of a computer, but physically a character in our game.

"That's not all." JB gestured toward the screen again. "The room is equipped with full digital surround sound, and the speakers in your helmet will give you the best audio quality you have ever heard. You will feel the air and hear every little detail in the games. And one last thing: the room itself can move. If something were to hit you, for example, the room will shake and bump and knock you on the floor. You will feel everything. That is 4D!"

The group applauded, although not as vigorously as before. There was nervousness and hesitation in the air, a mysterious uncertainty. It was like getting excited about an approaching thunderstorm, but seeing ominously dark clouds and feeling a strange quiet in the air that could abruptly change at any moment.

"The best way to learn is to jump in," JB said. "I know this is new to you. But this is the next level of our contest. You will find that your horror knowledge will be most useful, but you will have to apply that knowledge in this 4D environment in a series of challenges. And because I'm nice, I'm going to preview those challenges for you. Here is your first!"

JB turned and faced the screen to watch with everyone else as a demo about the first challenge began to play.

"Your first challenge," the video explained, "is to survive a series of horror fights. In your first fight, you will choose to be either Freddy or Jason and re-enact the showdown between our two legends in *Freddy vs. Jason*. Points are awarded based on how closely you fight as whichever character you choose. You must re-enact this fight in the film, punch for punch."

The screen showed a quick scene from the movie, when Jason dragged Freddy through a burning cabin.

"After that fight, you will jump immediately into our favorite cabin in the woods from *Evil Dead II*, where you will battle demons as well as your own hand."

The video feed changed to show the comedic and horrific hand of Ash attacking its own body.

"Finally, you will leap into the original *Fright Night* for the final battle between Charley and Vincent on one team and Jerry Dandridge, the vampire next door. This may be the hardest of all as you will have to move between two characters. They are both in your control in this final scene. And once again, in each of these challenges, you will receive points for re-enacting the specifics within the movie. Good luck."

A clip of *Fright Night* played, Jerry facing Mr. Vincent with his cross, Charley in the background, and Jerry laughing, "You have to have faith for that to work, Mr. Vincent. Remember?"

JB faced his audience of nineteen. "Are you ready?"

Everyone stood and cheered, and Bill looked around at each of them. Did they know these movies better than him? Were they confident or just excited? His eyes narrowed and he stared at JB. He was ready to play.

"Assistants! Escort our players to their game chambers. Get ready to PLAY THE RABBIT IN RED!"

Part II, Round I

Play the Rabbit in

Red

"Groovy!"

—Ash from *The Evil Dead*

"I should warn you, princess. The first time tends to get a little messy."

—Freddy from *Freddy vs. Jason*

"Welcome to Fright Night. For real."

—Jerry from *Fright Night*

"Time to nut up or shut up."

—Tallahassee from *Zombieland*

Chapter Nine

The assistant dressed as Captain Spaulding guided Bill into his private game chamber. Bill stepped onto the movable floor, jumped around a bit, moved side to side, and even did a quick sprint to get a feel. Exactly as JB described, the floor was curved, and standing on it, Bill felt like he was balancing on the ball of a computer mouse, something that could move in any direction. He put on the game helmet and wireless gloves and had a flashback to a book he read a couple of years ago that took place about twenty years in the future with virtual reality technology but was ironically all about the 1980s.

But this was not the future. This was the here and now. He closely examined the gloves, and although they were black, there was a silhouette of a rabbit on the left glove and an axe on the right one. With the gloves, he could directly interact with the 4D environment he saw through the virtual enhancement provided by the helmet. The helmet was like an oversized pair of 3D glasses except these covered his peripheral vision and his ears to enrich sound. On the giant curved screen that engulfed the game chamber room, the Rabbit in Red logo appeared, a white rabbit in a red box with a splattering of blood.

The logo whirled and vanished, and then standing in front of him were two life-sized, characters. It was Jason Voorhees and Freddy Krueger, and a voice in his helmet instructed, "Select your character."

Among horror fans, there was debate as to who won the epic fight between two of horror history's biggest undead serial killers. In the end, Jason Voorhees walked away with Freddy's head, but Freddy winked back at the audience. Of course, it would appear that both remained well and alive for any future sequels.

Bill selected the Camp Crystal Lake slasher master. If he was to re-enact what actually happened in the film, he figured Jason would be the easiest to copy. These horror legends had two epic fights. In the first, Jason was tranquilized and entered Freddy's dream world, where the Camp Crystal Lake killer was useless. Bill would mostly have to remain still and let Freddy repeatedly toss him around, and he didn't think it would be too hard to simply let Freddy kick his ass. In the second showdown of the movie, Freddy was captured and taken out of the dream world, where he lost his power. In this scene, Bill as Jason could unleash a real beating on Krueger.

Bill cracked his knuckles, squeezed his fists within the computerized gloves, and pointed at Jason. The room vibrated, the floor beneath him hummed like a motor warming up, and that *cha cha cha* classic Jason music chirped in his ears. Freddy remained on screen, and Bill knew he had now become Jason. Freddy turned forward, faced Bill, and smiled. He opened his hand with the knifed glove and laughed. In the curved shape of this room, a spell of dizziness overtook Bill for a moment. He had to close his eyes and take a deep breath.

But then he smiled. "I'm Jason freakin' Voorhees, bitch!" he yelled at Freddy.

The screen pulsed bright white, nearly blinding Bill for a moment, and then the setting changed. As he had expected, the game began in Freddy's dream world. There wasn't much Jason could do, and when Freddy attacked, he used mental powers that threw Jason around the room with staggering force. Trying to adjust to the 4D environment, Bill felt every blow. The movable floor shifted beneath him, sound effects blasted through the helmet, and the room spun fast like a planetarium star show.

Stay calm, Bill told himself. *It will be my turn in a moment.*

The combination of sound effects, floor vibrations, and rapid screen changes made Bill slightly sick. Everything he saw and heard was from Jason's point of view. And that point of view was pretty pathetic at the moment. He was being violently whiplashed around Freddy's dream world.

"It's almost over," he said aloud. "Don't lose focus." Once this scene ended, Bill only had a moment before the film fast-forwarded. Now it was Jason's turn.

Freddy stood in front of him now in a scene near the end where Krueger had been removed from the comfort of his nightmare world. He was on top of a woman in a cabin, his claws spread open. Freddy looked at the girl and said, "Die, bitch." Suddenly, the room filled with heat. Bill looked behind him and there was fire, huge flames up to the ceiling. He couldn't tell if this was real or virtual, but the room's temperature increased rapidly and sweat poured down his forehead within the helmet.

Focusing back on Freddy, Bill realized he had a machete in his hand, Jason's weapon of choice. Bill/Jason was in the same room as Freddy. Freddy looked up, annoyed that he was interrupted.

Bill knew what to do next. He stepped in toward Freddy and slashed the machete at Krueger's head. Krueger ducked and cut at Bill's neck. Bill swore he could feel those finger knives slashing on his very own neck.

"Ahhhh!" Bill grabbed his neck, checking for blood. Was he really hurt? He couldn't tell, but he couldn't let it stop him. He turned and swung his machete at Freddy's core. Freddy danced backwards. Bill swung again, feeling the heat of the room intensify, and his machete struck the floor in front of him. Krueger laughed in his face and kicked his right foot toward Bill's groin. Bill saw the foot coming and knew he had to do exactly what Jason did in the movie if he was going to win this game. He grabbed Freddy's foot and Krueger's laugh morphed into a surprised scream. Using all of his energy, Bill swung his arms upward, launching Krueger into the cabin wall behind him. From the corner of his eye, Bill saw the girl Freddy was going to kill escape with a boy, two of the lead characters in the film. He ignored them and chased down his rival, grabbing Krueger by the back, picking him up with unbelievable ease and slamming him through a huge window at the back of the cabin. From there, he ran Freddy through a series of windows that lined this wall of the cabin.

Krueger continued his screaming, but Bill remained silent. Jason never talked. He was sure breathing hard, though, and Bill's face was sweating. He wished he could wipe the sweat, but the computerized helmet fully covered his face. The fighting alone would have been enough for anyone to break a sweat but the extra heat in the room, courtesy no doubt of JB's 4D enhancements to the game chamber, made it feel like Bill was actually on fire. But he had to finish Freddy. He had to win.

Dragging Krueger through the last of the windows, he ripped the body right through the wall to the cabin's door. Bill picked him up and tossed him once again with incredible strength out of the cabin.

He had never experienced anything like this. He was living out a fantasy of being a part of a horror franchise he loved, of getting to really feel it without the dangers of the "reality" of the situation. He fought the fight until the end, walking away with Krueger's head until Freddy winked, and the screen went black.

The room immediately cooled, and Bill exhaled deeply. He could use a break, but there was no time. The images on the screen went into rewind this time, moving counter-clockwise, as if going back in time. Ash from *The Evil Dead* series stood in front of him on screen.

Bill laughed. These were movies he first watched with his childhood friends years ago. These were not movies to watch alone, and not because they were all that frightening. They were absolutely hilarious, and some of Bill's favorite childhood memories contained those moments of gut-busting, uncontrollable laughter by a bunch of boys up too late, high on sugar and candy and the imagination of childhood. *The Evil Dead*, in fact, was the last movie he had enjoyed with the boys in his neighborhood before that terrible night when his father was murdered. He had laughed so hard, and it had been an incredibly long time before he found that kind of laughter again. Although he still enjoyed watching *The Evil Dead* movies, they never were quite as a good as in his memories when surrounded by childhood friends.

Ash charged right at Bill, and Bill yelped as Ash appeared to tackle him, causing the entire room to vibrate. But he didn't get tackled. Just like Jason, Bill had to become Ash.

The computerized glove in front of him took on a life of its own as the screen focused on the cabin in the woods from *Evil Dead II*. This was the most iconic scene in all the films and still the funniest in all of horror comedies. Ash's hand became possessed, and precisely like the movie, JB's game chamber's 4D effects empowered the computerized glove to act out the attacks of Ash's hand.

Bill felt his right hand raise on its own. The glove tightened around his hand and forearm. He tried to move his hand, tried to stop it, but he was no longer in control.

"What the — How?"

The palm of his hand turned and faced him. His fingers wiggled at him, but it wasn't Bill wiggling them. It freaked him out, watching his body do things that he wasn't able to control. Then his fingers spread wide in front of him, his hand thrust right at his own face, his own fingers pressing against his cheeks and forehead. It pulled Bill around the game chamber.

He ended up in the kitchen. His hand grabbed a plate and smashed it on Bill's head. It grabbed the back of his head and pushed him into the sink — not just once, but three times. It moved from the back of Bill's head to the front, yanking him against the wall, then down near the floor, back and forth with powerful momentum. Bill screamed and tried to fight the hand but there was nothing he could do. The hand shoved him on the floor, and Bill rolled, the floor rolling with him. He tried to stand up and fell again. The hand found more plates and bashed Bill on the skull with one after another.

Bill lay on the floor. He wanted to fight, but he had to remember where he really was and what he was supposed to be doing.

Focus, he told himself. He was distracted by the technology within this glove and the amazingly real special effects. *Remember what happens. Think!*

He lay still and let the hand drag his body across the floor. How was this even happening? Bill couldn't tell if somehow the computerized glove actually had the power to move him, or if perhaps it was the floor that was actually moving him. Whatever it was, it felt real, and it made Bill dizzy.

The hand moved toward a meat cleaver. His heart rate doubled as he tried to focus on the images on screen. He knew what he needed to do, and he would have to time this next part exactly right. He watched as his independent hand snatched the cleaver, which it would have used it to kill him if Bill didn't act right away.

This was the moment! He seized a knife that was on the kitchen floor and stabbed the hand — his own hand! — pinning it to the floor. He hesitated a moment, looking at this image in front of him. It was the strangest thing Bill could have imagined. There he was, on the floor of JB's game chamber, but all around him he only saw the infamous cabin in the woods from *The Evil Dead*. And he had stabbed his own hand, but thankfully he felt no more than a sharp pinch. The knife was virtual, but the glove was real, and whatever technology JB programmed in it, the glove reacted in perfect real time to everything happening on screen.

He knew what he had to do next, and he was both excited and terrified at the idea. This was the epic moment with Ash in *The Evil Dead*. He had to cut off the possessed hand. That was the only way to get rid of the evil, to not become fully possessed. With his right hand pinned to the floor gushing out blood, Bill reached for the chainsaw that Ash had used earlier in the movie, which of course happened to be right next to him. Remembering this iconic scene from those younger memories when he and his friends cheered, Bill picked up the chainsaw with his left hand, bit on the cord and yanked it back with as much force as he could to start the gas-powered hacking device and brought it down on his right arm. The screeching noises, the loud mechanics of the saw, the crunching of bone, and the splattering of blood coalesced in a cacophony of noises, an orchestra of pain.

Bill cut off the hand. The gloves provided another strong pinching sensation, but he had done it. He stood up and cheered, still in the cabin in the woods, and laughed as everything came to life, the deer head dancing on the wall, the lamp shaking behind him. Bill roared and laughed like Ash in the film, in part because he was having so much fun and in part remembering that he needed to act like Ash to win this game, and so he yelled, feeling maniacal and powerful.

The screen went black again, and Bill hoped he had a moment to relax. He had no idea how much time had passed. Everything seemed to happen so quickly. He wondered how everyone else was doing and if these games were being recorded. It would be great to watch Jaime kick ass, too, and he laughed out loud picturing Wes and Rose fighting. Shy, little Rose as Jason Voorhees or big Wes fighting his own arm would be a great sight to see. He also hoped that Daniel was getting his ass kicked.

But there wasn't much time to think about these things. The screen moved clockwise. There was one battle left in this round, and it would be harder, Bill thought, because it was lesser known by his generation. For sure, that was intentional on JB's part.

He was now in Jerry Dandrigde's house from *Fright Night*, the 1985 original, not the 2011 remake. This time Bill had two characters from which to choose. Peter Vincent was the charlatan vampire killer who had his own TV show in the movie. Charley contacted Vincent for help, and Vincent certainly got a lot more than he expected. He swiped on Peter Vincent's character, taking on his first person point of view with Charley standing next to him. He guessed this final scene would be harder, not only for the film being more rare and difficult to remember, but that he would have to swipe back and forth between each character. Bill tried to recall the fight scenes at the end of the movie. He would need to act as both of these characters, and if he was going to do well, he needed to remember what each of them did.

The scene started with Vincent staring at Jerry's vampire companion. Charley and Vincent/Bill were at the top of the stairs, staring down at this vampire. JB programmed this scene without giving him any time to think at all. He had to shoot the vampire now. Bill looked down and in his computerized glove he now held a gun. Bill shot the vampire as quickly as he could. The vampire fell down the stairs but refused to die. Bill shot and shot again, screaming, until the vampire picked him up in both hands.

He had to jump characters if he was going to be able to defeat them. Just as the vampire was about to toss him, Bill swiped over to Charley. Now, as Charley, Bill held a stake in his hands and knew exactly what he needed to do with it. Without hesitation, he thrust it into the heart of the vampire. Jerry, the main vampire, briefly left the scene, but Bill heard the scream and prepared himself for Jerry's return. Jerry's companion was the easy one. This would be the real battle, but Bill knew where to look. He turned to face a beautiful, large stained glass window at the top of the stairs, and just as he remembered from the movie, Jerry flew through the window, shattering it, hissing at Charley and Vincent.

Bill had to swipe again and become Vincent. As Peter Vincent, he held an arm up, holding Charley back as he took out a cross and thrust it at Jerry, the vampire antagonist. Jerry put his arms up and winced for a moment but then began to smile. Bill focused on Vincent now, the charlatan vampire-killer who didn't believe in vampires. It was Vincent's turn to change, to find the faith he had lost.

"You've got to have faith for that to work," Jerry snorted, unaffected by the cross. He moved in on Bill, but Bill remained strong with the cross. Faith here was about having confidence, and Bill wasn't going to let Jerry pass. As the bells chimed 6:00 a.m. warning the vampire that it was close to sunrise, Jerry yelled, morphed into bat form, and attacked Bill.

Time to swipe characters again. Bill switched over to Charley and jumped at the vampire bat, but the bat turned and bit him on the arm. Sunlight began to shine through the window and the bat screamed, flying for cover into the basement. Bill froze for a moment, trying to remember if he was swiping characters correctly. He replayed the very end of the movie in his head, searching his memories for who did what.

Bill changed back to Vincent for the final part of the fight. He hoped his memory was correct. He ran downstairs and chased after Jerry, ready to end this once and for all. In the basement, the vampire had already retreated to his coffin to protect himself from the sun. Bill threw open the lid to the coffin and without wasting another second of time to think, he staked Jerry in the chest. The vampire sat straight up and screamed, the noise deafening within Bill's helmet.

Working together with Charley, they tore down a layer of the basement wall that protected the area from the sunlight. Bill reached high with both arms and tore at the walls quickly and violently. He turned to see the sun hit Jerry, and the vampire burst into flames. Everything in the game chamber became brighter and hotter once again, but Bill smiled as he watched Jerry melt. This part of the game was finally over.

He took a deep breath, exhausted but exhilarated. The screen went back to the Rabbit in Red logo and flashed a message: *Congratulations. You have successfully completed all challenges in round one. You may exit the chamber and return to the commons for refreshments. The next round will be announced shortly.*

Bill took off the 4D equipment. He was drenched in sweat. All he wanted now was to see how his friends performed. He laughed out loud, once again picturing Rose as Jason Voorhees, throwing Freddy outside the cabin. He chuckled, although maybe he shouldn't have, at the panic he could perfectly picture on Wes's face when he had to remember which character he needed to be during *Fright Night*. He grinned even wider as he approached the commons, betting without a doubt that Jaime had just as much fun as he did.

He couldn't wait to hear how they did, and he couldn't wait to play more. There was still a whole weekend of adventure yet to experience.

Chapter Ten

The assistant dressed as Sam from *Trick 'r Treat* escorted Bill back to the commons after the game. Bill looked around for his friends but only saw Daniel and a few other contestants. For a moment he wondered how so many people were finished already; he thought he was pretty spot on during all of the games. A buffet had been set up near the stage, and Bill wasted no time grabbing a plate full of food.

Devouring one slider on the spot, he headed back to the table where he first met Rose and Wes. He was on his second helping at the buffet when Rose returned.

"Hey! How'd you do?" he asked.

"Good, I think," Rose said. "That was so much fun! I love the *Evil Dead* movies! The last one was a bit trickier. I think I hesitated too long when switching back and forth between the characters in *Fright Night*. Oh, food!" She grabbed a strawberry off of Bill's plate. "Sorry!" She giggled. "I'm so hungry."

"Help yourself." He smiled. "There's plenty more."

Wes returned next, and Rose yanked a chicken leg off of Bill's plate.

"Wes! Hey man, how'd you do?" Bill asked.

"I don't know." He frowned. "I chose Freddy. He's always been my favorite. I kicked ass in the first fight scene, but I messed up in the second. I tried to fight back when I wasn't supposed to. And when Jason was dragging me through the windows, I think I hurt my back. I fell and was literally rolling around on that damn floor. And at the very end, I saw Jason walking around with my head. Unreal but so cool."

"Ouch," Rose mumbled with a mouth full of Bill's watermelon.

"Get your own!" Bill laughed at Rose. She grabbed a plate from the buffet and quickly filled it up.

"Yeah." Wes shook his head. "I'm worried that scene messed me up. How about you two?"

Before they could answer, Jaime appeared, one of the last to return. Bill quickly counted how many were there now that Jaime had returned. Eighteen in total. Missing one.

"That was the coolest thing I have ever done in my life!" Jaime said. They took a seat at a table near the buffet. "Ooh, that looks good," she said, taking a chicken leg off of Rose's plate.

Literally snapping her teeth at Jaime, Rose said, "Get your own, girl!" They both laughed. Jaime stood up and filled a plate with so much food she could barely lift it. She rejoined the table, and, in between mouthfuls, she described her experiences.

"That was so badass beating Freddy." A bite of a hamburger. "I felt invincible." A bite of a chicken thigh. "And Ash! I cut off my own freakin' hand!" A mouthful of cheese. "I think I took too long with the last game, but other than that, I feel pretty great!"

"I wish I had a picture right now." Bill laughed. "Oh, wait." He took out his cell phone and snapped a photo of Jaime. She gleefully smiled with a chicken wing between her lips. "Now all four." The four of them huddled together and Bill extended his long arm, snapping a selfie of the group.

"To kicking ass!" Bill said, raising his third glass of water.

"To a *groovy* weekend!" Jaime added. "That was incredible."

They ate and laughed, and Bill looked around the room, counting one more time to see if everyone had returned. Still eighteen. JB walked up on stage and the giant screen turned on behind him.

"Well done, ladies and gentleman. Well done. I do hope you enjoyed yourselves playing the game as much as you seem to be enjoying this food." He chuckled. "Now it is time for you to view your results. The game is far from over, and you have several more challenges to complete. After our first round, let's take a look at your performances. These are based on how closely your actions re-enacted the actual actions in the films, everything from your timing to physical movements."

The screen lit up and in JB's dramatic style the theme music from *Friday the 13th* played, the *cha cha cha* that Bill always interpreted as *jay jay jay jay, son son son son.*

"In first place," JB broadcasted, "Daniel! Congratulations! You matched the movies with a ninety-eight percent score! Well done!"

Daniel beamed, an extra-large mouth full of teeth grinning and pissing off Bill's table. "How?" Jaime asked. "How did hashtagDbag do it?"

"Shh," Wes said, anxious to see the rest of the results.

"In second place, we have . . . Bill with a ninety-six percent score! Not bad!"

"Yeah, Bill!" Jaime screamed and hugged him on the spot. If he was mad about Daniel, that emotion was quickly eliminated by the support and cheers of his best friend.

"In third place, Rose! Our little red-headed darling had a dazzling ninety percent!"

"Rose!" Wes cried. "Wow! Congrats!"

"In fourth place, we have Jaime with eighty-four percent matching!" JB continued.

"Oh-right!" Bill cheered and high-fived Jaime. When their hands touched, he briefly wondered if he should have hugged her instead.

JB went through all of the scores, and Bill paid particular attention to Dexter, who only earned thirteenth place, and all got very nervous for their friend Wes, who had not been yet congratulated when JB entered the double digits. Seventeenth place went to Leroy, one of the kids that hung out with Daniel and laughed at his stupid jokes.

"In eighteenth place, we have Wes, with a sixty-five percent score."

"Okay, man, sixty-five isn't bad!" Bill said. "It was a lot to do."

"Whatever." Wes's head drooped. "I sucked. Dammit. Everyone from Daniel's group beat me. I had a hard time keeping up and blew it fighting Jason."

Rose put an arm around his shoulders. "It's okay," she said. "It's not over yet. Head up, okay? You'll get them on the next one."

Wes forced a half smile at Rose, and Jaime and Bill gave encouraging and empathetic looks. "Okay."

"That's all of the results we have for the night," JB continued. "I know we began with nineteen of you, but we lost one person during the games. It would appear that our 4D Fright Fest was too much for her. She ran out of the game chamber during the first simulation. She has not returned and has yet to be found. If you happen to see Annie, please let me or one of my assistants know right away. You've already helped yourselves to food, so now I suggest you help yourself to some sleep. Our games continue in the morning. My assistants will get you when it's time. Good night all and good luck. Get your rest. This first round was only the beginning."

And with that, Jay Bell walked off stage and left the room.

"What the hell?" Jaime snapped. "That's not okay. Someone is missing, and they're not doing anything about it?"

"Why would she leave?" asked Rose. She wiped the corners of her small lips with one hand and ran the other through now slightly messy red hair.

"Maybe she got hurt," Wes suggested. "If she was as uncoordinated as me, she could have fallen and hurt herself. There was a moment in that first match when I almost thought of giving up."

"I guess," Bill said. "Or she could be flat out scared. If she ran out and they haven't found her, she could be hiding somewhere."

"That's right," Jaime agreed. "We should try to find her. She was staying in the room across from ours. You remember what she looked like?"

"Yeah," Rose said. "She was a bigger girl. Dark hair. She seemed pretty energetic. Sat over there." Rose pointed at the table in the corner of the room, opposite that of Daniel and his group.

"She had the big knockers," Bill added—it was a way to identify her, right?—but Jaime snapped him a dirty look. "Sorry."

"Let's go check her room," Jaime suggested, leading the way, her brown hair flopping over her shoulders as she walked.

The foursome went into the girls' section, the Bates Motel-themed quarters. Jaime knocked on the door of the room that Annie claimed. When no one answered, she opened the door and walked in.

"Hello? Anyone here? Annie?" This room was identical to the one Rose and Jaime were sharing. It was made up to resemble a motel room from *Psycho*, a double bed, a small table in between, and of course a bathroom with a shower.

"No one's here," Wes said.

"Look. That's different." Rose pointed at a desk near the side of the room next to the door, where a window would have been had this been an actual motel room. On the small desk sat an old-fashioned typewriter. "That's not in our room."

They examined the typewriter. "It's missing a letter," Bill said. "Look." Moving in closer, they saw that it was missing the letter *n*. "Do you think this means anything?"

"I don't know. I doubt it," Jaime said. "These rooms are supposed to be like old motel rooms from the '50s, right? It makes sense that JB would decorate them with old stuff like typewriters. It's probably missing a letter because it's an old prop."

"Did she have a roommate?" Wes wondered.

"I saw only her enter this room," Rose said. "But that was only for a moment. Someone else could have been staying with her."

"We should ask around," Jaime said. "See if anyone else has seen anything."

"Okay," Bill said. "But not Daniel."

"Everyone," Jaime said emphatically. "If we really want to know what happened, we ask everyone. Even hashtagDbag." She sighed.

"How the hell did he get first place?" Bill still wanted to know.

"Hey, at least you got second," Wes responded. "Not last."

They proceeded to exit the room, but Wes bumped the desk and a drawer popped open. "Wait up, guys. What's this?" He pulled it open and found a bundle of paper. "It says *Fast Cars*. Does that mean anything to any of you?"

"Doesn't ring a bell," Jaime replied, taking the manuscript from Wes. "Look. It says *Fast Cars* on the first page but the rest of this is simply a big heap of paper. It's probably nothing."

"I don't recognize it," Rose said. "You, Bill?"

"Hmm, I don't think so. But my brain is fried. It's definitely odd though."

"This place is full of randomness," Jaime said. "If only our phones had service and we could Google. Let's not make puzzles out of nothing until we have nothing left to work with. But let's find this girl. Can you imagine being lost in a place like this? She's got to be hiding somewhere, and if that's the case, I can only imagine that she's scared and alone. C'mon."

As they walked out of the room, Bill hesitated at the door for a moment. *Fast Cars*? No, he didn't know anything about that, but a strange sensation crept upon him. It didn't feel right. That wasn't the kind of feeling he wanted to have.

His brain may have been tired, but for a moment the memory of the cautioning e-mail entered his mind. This first round of games had been incredible, and this place was by far the coolest he had ever seen. It was the Hogwarts of horror. But was there something evil hiding here? As he thought about Annie, he couldn't help but feel that something was off, that this place wasn't just fun and games.

He desperately wanted that idea to be false and tried to push it from his mind. *Just find Annie, and we'll know everything is okay,* he thought. *Find Annie, and we'll get a little sleep. Find Annie, and we can play another game in the morning. It's all fun, games, and friends. There's nothing to worry about. It's like the noises you hear late at night. You go to investigate and it's nothing. Nothing at all, right?*

Chapter Eleven

They decided to split up and search in pairs. Jaime suggested that she and Rose pair up and Bill and Wes stick together, that way it wouldn't be too suspicious and they could thoroughly search their own gender's quarters without getting questioned. Bill agreed it was a good choice, but he was a little disappointed to not be able to explore the studio with Jaime.

The girls started in their own sleeping quarters to search the rooms and ask the other girls if they had seen anything, while Bill and Wes agreed to tackle the boys' section.

When Bill and Wes returned to the commons, it was already empty. Apparently everyone was taking JB's advice and had gone back to their rooms to get some sleep before the next round of games. The two boys went back to their psychiatric ward sleeping quarters and started knocking on doors. Wanting to get the one person they dreaded out of the way, they started at Daniel's room.

"What do you want?" Daniel snickered. He had his shirt off and rubbed his well-defined chest. "Advice on how to be first place? Sorry. Can't teach talent."

"No, but you can teach how to be an ass," Bill countered and folded his long arms across his chest in response to Daniel's exhibitionism. He really wanted to ask for details on Daniel's games, but he kept to the task at hand. "We're looking for Annie. Have you seen her?"

"Why are you looking for her? If she's too scared to play the games, let her go home."

"We're worried that she could be lost somewhere in these studios," Bill replied. "We've only seen a small portion of them so far. She could be anywhere. What if it were you who was lost? Wouldn't you want someone looking for you?"

"I would worry about yourself, second place," Daniel sneered. "And you, fat boy. I'd worry about last place for sure. Unless there are candy bars at the end of the next game, I don't see how you're gonna catch up."

Daniel chuckled. Bill clenched his fists, fighting the urge to smack him. Daniel stood there basically letting it all hang out in a short pair of boxers. Although he was very muscular, he was also unnaturally tan. Bill had a mental image of Daniel posting selfies on Facebook with a GTL hashtag. How someone like that made it to this contest and did that well was as big of a mystery to him as the missing person.

"Thanks for your help," Bill muttered, wanting to say so much more. "You better get some sleep. Your eyes look all puffy and baggy." Daniel's head snapped toward a mirror, and Bill let out a sarcastic laugh and left the room. "C'mon," he told Wes. "Don't let that asshole get you down. Not worth it."

"You know what pisses me off?" asked Wes. "There are a dozen guys like that in every high school. I've dealt with him before. Well, not him exactly, but you know what I mean. In junior high especially. I'd go home and escape in movies, books, video games. Anything to get my mind off jerks like that. And then the same jerks end up here. I don't get it."

"Me neither. Not at all." Bill sighed. "Let's keep looking."

They knocked on all the doors asking if anyone had seen Annie or knew anything about her. Most of the time, the guys who answered were half asleep and mumbled "I have no idea what you're talking about" responses. A few others, the ones that Bill recognized had hung out with Daniel, were rude.

"Who cares? Get out and let us sleep," Dexter said, slamming the door in their faces. *They say the apple doesn't land far from the tree about how children resemble their parents,* Bill thought. *Well, the hairs aren't far from the asshole when it comes to friends.*

No one seemed to know anything, and the rooms looked all the same, nothing suspicious to be found. They were all bleak and depressing. He'd have preferred the Bates Motel to this setting.

"What now?" Wes asked. "We should get some sleep too, right?"

"Yeah, but I hate to go back to the girls in the morning with no answers. Let's explore a little more."

Their first thought was to revisit the areas they already knew about: the main entrance halls with the street from *It*, the hotel-themed hall from *The Shining*, and the hospital floor from

Halloween II. They exited the boys' quarters and walked through the commons.

They glanced back at where the buffet was earlier. "Those games made me really hungry," Bill said. "Let's see if there's anything left."

The food had been removed, but the plates and silverware were still there. There was an electric knife where the cheese cubes once sat but no food was left except a few crumbs.

"Doesn't look like it," Wes said.

They left the commons and walked down the hallway that was the street from *It*. They passed the gutter and saw again the shadow of a paper boat that slipped inside.

"Want a balloon?" a voice whispered. They ignored it, knowing it was part of the setting, but smiled at one another.

"That was probably the first big book I read as a kid," Wes said. "I tried to start it when I was in fifth grade. Couldn't finish it. In part because it was so big but also because it gave me nightmares. But I saw the made-for-TV movie that same year. It was so good, I had to go finish the book."

"Same here. I actually saw the movie first, too. The book was even more shocking."

"Yeah, do you remember the sex scene with all the kids? I couldn't believe that was in the book."

"Yeah, that was the weirdest thing." Bill shook his head. "I hear they're remaking the movie. I wonder if they'll incorporate that scene somehow."

"I doubt it," Wes said. "And no one will be a better Pennywise than Tim Curry."

"Not for those of us who loved the original. But hopefully it will inspire a whole new generation of horror fans."

"Why do you think Daniel is such an ass?" Wes asked.

"Some people hate what they don't understand," Bill said. "Maybe Daniel doesn't understand why we didn't try to hang out with him. So he hates."

"I was so happy to get away from that prison they call high school even for a day or two," Wes said. He looked at the floor and pulled at his baggy sweatshirt. "But somehow the jerks still find me."

"So, like, what did these other jerks do to you?"

Wes took out his clown nose stress ball and squeezed it tight. "Uh, the usual, you know. Hey, what's that?" he asked.

The hall was dark, but they had each taken out their cell phones and were using them as flashlights, looking for anything out of the ordinary, not an easy task in JB's studios as everything was unusual. They didn't see anything suspicious in the *It* hall, and when they got to the end, they chose to go left to explore the hall from *The Shining*.

"Look," Wes continued. "I don't remember that when I first got here. And it doesn't seem safe either."

An axe was leaning outside one of the hotel room doors. They went closer to examine it. It was no prop. It was a real axe, heavy and sharp.

"Jack uses an axe to hunt down his wife and son, right?" Wes asked.

"In Kubrick's movie, yes. In the book, it's a baseball bat."

"So do you think this means anything?"

"I don't know," Bill said, "but I'm not exactly comfortable knowing there's a weapon laying around for anyone to grab. Let's take it back."

"Hey!" Wes started. "Did you take a close look at your gloves in the game rooms?"

"Oh yeah!"

"On one was a rabbit. On the other was an axe. Is that a coincidence?"

"I doubt anything here is a coincidence," Bill said. "Let's definitely take it back then. It has to mean something."

They picked up the axe and not seeing anything else in this part of the hall, they turned around and explored the hospital setting from *Halloween II*.

"What's your favorite *Halloween*?" Bill asked.

"The first one," Wes said. "It's not about cheap scares, you know? It was done with the intention to be genuinely frightening. What about you?"

"The first is also my favorite," Bill conceded. "But honestly

H20 comes close. There's something about seeing Laurie Strode become a bad ass and chase Michael with an axe that I love. And all of the allusions."

"Oh yeah!" Wes laughed. "Like Laurie's secretary in the movie is played by her real life mom who also was the actress that played Marion who was stabbed in the shower scene in *Psycho*. She even makes a pun about motherly instincts."

"Right," Bill said. "And the car her mom drives is the one she drove in *Psycho*, too. And the book Laurie is reading to her students is like the one that she discussed as a high school student herself in the first movie. I love that stuff. That's why we're here though, right?"

So far they hadn't seen anything out of the norm in this hallway, but when they were about to turn back, they heard voices coming from one of the hospital rooms. Bill put a finger up to his lips, and the two walked very quietly near the room.

"You put the axe where?" JB's commanding voice asked.

"Right outside a door, down the other hall," a woman's voice answered. They recognized it as the assistant who played Samara from *The Ring*.

"I didn't want to make it too easy, Donnie," JB responded.

"I thought you wanted them to find it," she said.

"Yes, Donnie, but we have very smart kids here. There's a lot more work we have to do and I don't want them figuring it out too quickly."

"Okay, I'll go get it now."

"No, leave it. It's fine. Maybe it will throw them off. And what about you, Chester? Did you modify the settings for the next games?"

"Yes, boss." A man's voice this time. It sounded like the assistant who dressed as Captain Spaulding. "I've programmed the twist as you requested."

"Good. I want their scores to reflect originality. We've seen them re-enact scenes. It's time for something deeper. And darker."

"Are you sure about the last part of this module, sir? You don't think it's too . . . haunting?"

JB laughed. "Chester, you should know me well enough to

know that I don't think there is such a thing as too haunting. We need to bridge the gap between fantasy and reality. It will prepare them for the final test."

"Sir?" Donnie asked. "What about the girl?"

"You let me worry about the girl. I'll handle her." He chuckled again. "Let's start working on breakfast. Our contestants are going to need all the energy they can get in the morning."

Hearing them shuffle inside the room, Bill yanked Wes toward the exit and then ran out of that hall, down the *It* hallway, into their sleeping quarters, and finally back into their room, where he slammed the door shut.

"Don't you think you should have put that axe back?" Wes panted.

"No way. It means something. But what? We can keep it under my bed for now."

"What does it mean?"

"I don't know," Bill said. "We know it's something JB wanted us to find. Maybe not so easily or even tonight, but he expected someone to find it. And maybe to throw us off? That's weird."

"Let me see it."

Wes examined the axe, and Bill didn't know what he expected to find. It looked normal as far as he could tell. A wooden handle, a steel blade.

"Wait, what's this?" Wes pointed to a small engraving on the handle.

"It's a rabbit," Bill said. "Look closely. It's the Rabbit in Red logo, the same one that appeared just before the first game. It definitely belongs to JB. Other than that, we know it was in *The Shining* hallway and that Jack in the movie uses it."

They both stared in silence at it for several minutes, passing it back and forth. Wes yawned, and Bill nodded. "I'm getting tired, too. Let's sleep on it and tell the girls at breakfast. Sleeping on an idea always helps, right?"

"What about everything else JB said? We have to tell that, too."

"Yeah," Bill agreed. "We have some clue as to the next round of games. Still, it's pretty vague. The next set will test our originality and be deeper and darker. So I guess it's not a reenactment? Something different? And what could be 'too haunting' do you think?"

"I don't know." Wes shook his head. "God, I'm not going to get any sleep tonight."

Bill looked at his phone. There were only a few hours left in the night before they were supposed to meet for breakfast and the beginning of the second round of games. Out of curiosity, he tried to text his mom to see if it would send. The message failed. Still no signal in these halls.

"Hey, Bill," Wes said. "I almost forgot. Happy Halloween."

Bill chuckled. "Happy Halloween, Wes. I almost forgot, too. We've only been here a few hours, but it feels like forever."

"Yeah. Let's get some rest. I have a dozen questions but if we don't sleep, we're not gonna do as well tomorrow. I have to get better."

"You will, man. We have some inside info now. You'll do great tomorrow."

"Thanks."

"Goodnight."

"Night, Bill."

Bill tried to force himself to sleep, but the axe under his bed kept entering his mind. What did it mean? Sure, it must be from *The Shining* but how did that connect to anything else? He pictured Samara explaining to JB that someone had already taken the axe. Would JB be surprised? Maybe there were video cameras — JB would know that he and Wes took the axe, and probably that they were eavesdropping, too. And what in the hell was going to be "too haunting" tomorrow?

And what about Annie? JB said he would "handle her." What did that mean? This was already pretty crazy shit, he thought.

How much more intense can it get?

Part II, Round II

Save the Rabbit in

Red

"It's Halloween. Everyone's entitled to one good scare."

—Sherriff Leigh Brackett from *Halloween* and Norma Watson from *Halloween: H20.*

"We all go a little mad sometimes."

—Norman Bates from *Psycho.*

"I am eternal, child. I am the eater of worlds, and of children. And you are next!"

—Pennywise from *It.*

"If I wanted to listen to an asshole, I'd fart."

—Captain Spaulding from *House of 1000 Corpses.*

Chapter Twelve

He was seven years old again, and it was Christmas Eve night. He sat between his parents, and they asked him a question they already knew the answer to.

"Okay, Billy," Arnie started. "It's tradition. You get to pick a Christmas movie to watch before bed. What will it be?'

"Gremlins!" Bill shouted.

"That is not a Christmas movie." Sally smiled, shaking her head.

"Yes, it is!" Bill insisted. "It takes place during Christmas. And Gizmo is a Christmas present! It's the best Christmas movie ever!"

"Okay, Gremlins *it is," Arnie said, giving in. "But then it's time for bed. You gotta give Santa time to drop off the presents."*

"OKAY!" Bill clapped his hands.

He sat snuggled in between them and watched it intently. "Sparky!" he called and the family dog, with a little help, got up on the couch too and rested on Bill's lap. Bill could recite every line of dialogue, and he laughed whenever his mom would moan in disgust. Sally found the birth of the mogwais particularly disturbing and looked away when one of the gremlins was going to explode in a microwave. Sparky would bark whenever someone screamed on TV, and this made Bill giggle even more.

At the end of the movie, Bill asked, "Again?"

"No way, José," Sally groaned. "That is so not a Christmas movie. You are lucky we love you. Now time for bed. I can't believe I'm going to have nightmares on Christmas Eve night." She kissed him on the forehead and Bill hugged her back. "You want Dad to tuck you in tonight?"

"Yes, please!" Bill smiled, and his dad scooped him up in his large arms like he weighed nothing more than a small pet.

"Okay, buddy. No getting up in the middle of the night. We'll open presents in the morning. But can you give us until seven?"

"Six, please!" Billy cried.

"Oh-right. You come wake us up. But not a minute before six, okay?"

"Oh-right!" Bill said.

The memory faded, and now he was in another one. He returned to that terrible night, as he had so many times before. He tried to hold on to Sparky so he wouldn't bark at the intruder. He tried to hide as his dad said. If only he had hidden, if only he had been quiet, then maybe the intruder would have taken what he wanted and left his family in peace.

Then his dream fast-forwarded ten years and he was meeting Jaime for the first time, just today. He was hugging her, smelling her perfume, but when he pulled away, it was no longer Jaime. It was his mother.

"It's your fault!" she cried. "You killed him. And it's your fault I drink. You, oh, you remind me of Arnie every day. That's why I drink. Why couldn't you have done as you were told and just hide? They never caught the killer, but they never needed to. You're the killer!"

Bill woke up. He looked around, but everything was dark. Wes was snoring softly, but other than that, the room and these quarters were completely silent. He couldn't go back to sleep after that, and there was only one thing he really wanted now: to talk to a friend. His best friend.

He crept out of the room, walked across the commons, and into the girls' quarters. Knocking lightly on the second door on left, he whispered, "Jaime?"

He heard the creak of the box springs move. He said it again, a bit louder. "Jaime?"

"Bill? Is that you?" she answered groggily. "What are you doing?"

"I couldn't sleep."

"Hold on." A moment later she appeared in the doorway. "Are you okay?"

"Yeah. I just wanted to see if you might be awake. Wes is snoring."

"So is Rose." She giggled. "Let's go to the commons."

The halls were dark and quiet, and their footsteps made a soft echo down the hall. They walked toward the commons and found the table where they sat earlier that day.

"Sorry if I woke you," Bill said.

"No, don't be. I was barely sleeping. Between Rose's snoring and my mind going a thousand miles an hour, it was hard to sleep."

"Same here."

"How bad were the dreams?" she asked.

"It started off so good." He tried to smile. "I relived a good memory. And then it changed. I hate that. Why can't we have only good dreams?"

"If people had only good dreams, the horror genre wouldn't be nearly as successful."

He nodded with a half-smile. "That's true. I don't mind nightmares as long as they're about Freddy or Michael Myers. Anything that's not real."

"You still have your Michael Myers dream?" she asked him. *Halloween* was one of the first horror films Bill had seen, and that ghostly pale mask of Michael's still sporadically haunted him.

"It's been a while, but yeah. But with those kinds of nightmares, you know, I wake up and know it's not real. Sometimes I think they're even kinda cool, you know? The power of horror, right? But with the other kind, I wake up, and I can't shake the truth or memory away."

"I get it. I still dream of my uncle. I'd prefer getting bitten by vampires in my dreams any day instead of thinking about that shit."

She rested an elbow on the table, held up her head with a hand, and yawned. She was so pretty. The brown in her eyes was not only gentle, but also empathetic, even though she was clearly exhausted.

"And like you said," Jaime continued, "it's not fair. I want to remember all the good times, but dreams have a way of focusing on the bad. Worst of all, I have dreams of other friends and family killing themselves. It's terrible."

"Really?"

"Yeah. It's like once you know someone — really know someone close — who has committed suicide, you can't stop thinking about it. We missed it completely, you know? We didn't see it coming. We kept living our lives, and here he was struggling and we didn't even know it."

"How did he . . . how did he do it?" Bill asked. Was it even okay to ask something like that?

"He hanged himself." She took a deep breath, and Bill watched her clench her fists. "I've thought about this a lot, you know? Hanging. Jesus. It means he took the time to create a noose out of rope. It means it wasn't just a screw-my-life kinda day. The ceiling wasn't that high." Her voice changed, slipping into a robot-like voice. Bill knew Jaime was holding back her emotion. "His neck did not snap. He suffocated, slowly. Nothing instant. He let himself slip away."

Jaime's voice quavered. Bill could tell she didn't want to lose herself. She was always so strong.

"And why?" She looked down at her hands and sighed hard. "We don't know. We may never know. He had a wife and daughter, and if they know more, they aren't telling me. Supposedly there was no note. He was haunted, I think. You know what I mean? By like demons he never told anyone about. He kept them bottled up, and one day, I guess, he couldn't take them anymore."

"I'm so sorry." He didn't know what else to say. His first thought was that he wished her uncle were alive so he could punch him in the nose. How could anyone hurt their family like that? He looked down at his own hands and fidgeted. He felt like hugging her. Maybe a bad joke about *Halloween III*?

"It's not your fault." They sat there in silence for a moment, and Bill scooted his chair close to Jaime. She straightened in her seat. "You know, I've had that dream about you."

"What about me?" Bill asked, blinking hard.

"That you killed yourself."

"Oh, Jaime, no, I would never."

"I know." She shrugged, not meeting his eyes. "But you see that's the problem. I *think* I know. But do we ever really know? What if you start drinking like your mother? What if you change?"

"I'll never drink," he stated. That was one thing he could promise.

"My uncle used to say that when we're young, we make

promises about all that we dream of doing and all that we vow never to do." She frowned. "But the truth is, few of us accomplish what we dream, and most of us do what we vowed we never would. Do you think that's true?"

Bill lowered his head and shook it softly. "I don't know, J. But I promise you. I'm okay." He reached out and held her hand. "Seriously." There was another long stretch of silence, which was fine with both of them. Jaime scooted her chair closer and rested her head on his shoulder.

"What about you?" Bill interrupted the silence. "Are you okay?"

"Oh, yeah. I mean, I think you and I and everyone will always hurt at times. We'll never escape all the bad stuff. But I would never hurt myself, if that's what you mean."

"Why does anyone hurt themselves?"

Jaime sighed. "There are just some things we'll never understand. I think that's what my uncle would tell me. We can empathize. We can criticize. But we will never really know what goes through someone's mind — or what pain they have in their heart. All pain is unique." She squeezed his hand and moved closer to him, resting her head on his shoulders.

"Death sucks," Bill said.

"Yep. And look at us suckers. We surround ourselves with it voluntarily."

"We must really be messed up." Bill frowned.

"That's okay," Jaime told him. "Know who you are and know what you love. And as JB said, don't hang with those who shame."

Bill thought of his mother, wondering if she were still awake. If she was up, she was probably on her umpteenth drink. He wished he knew how to make it better. But he didn't.

He looked down at Jaime, her head on his shoulder, her hand in his. He didn't want to get up. Lowering his head so it rested on hers, he closed his eyes. *Maybe if everyone had someone they could talk to in the middle of the night and maybe if everyone had someone to hold them and tell them it would be okay, we would all actually be okay.*

Maybe he should tell Jaime what he and Wes found. Plus, he

was curious if Jaime and Rose had found anything. But then he heard a light snore coming from just below his ear, and he smiled. He closed his eyes and let himself drift off to sleep.

And then the bells rang, a deafening loudness, thunder after the calm.

Chapter Thirteen

The bells from *The Exorcist* sounded, a deafening and haunting alarm clock in surround sound throughout Rabbit in Red.

"Oh, shit." Jaime yawned. "What time is it?"

"I don't know. But I'm guessing that's our wake up call. We have a lot of catching up to do. I was about to tell you last night but then you fell asleep."

"I'm sorry." She stretched and then her lips curled into a smile. "But it was a nice night. I'll go get Rose and you get Wes, and we'll meet back here as soon as we're ready."

"Oh-right." Bill smiled. He wanted to hug her again. It felt so good to have a best friend, but it was time to get back to work. They had a mystery to solve, after all.

Bill ran back to his room and saw that Wes was still asleep. "Hey, wake up!" Bill tossed a pillow at Wes.

"Five more minutes, Mom," Wes grumbled.

"I'm not your mom." Bill laughed. While Wes slowly sat up, Bill glanced under his bed and was relieved that the axe was still in its place. "C'mon. Get dressed. Let's go."

It took Wes a few minutes to get up and a few more to get dressed. Bill quickly changed his clothes into something fresh, splashed some water on his face, and ran a comb through his hair. Then they left the room and briskly walked to the commons. The assistants were bringing out breakfast, another buffet style meal. Bill and Wes's eyes grew big with the sight and smells of all the food.

Looking closer, they saw this morning's food was prepared as only JB would have it. Pancakes in the shape of Jason's mask, special Freddy claw donuts, a fruit salad with dozens of toothpicks that resembled Pinhead from *Hellraiser*, biscuits shaped like the mask of Michael Myers, pumpkin-shaped omelets, and more. Bill and Wes helped themselves to several Jason pancakes and looked around for Rose and Jaime.

The girls were sitting at the table already eating. Rose was pouring strawberry syrup over her pancakes. "Bloody fun!" she praised, which gave a tired Jaime a case of morning giggles.

"Hey." Bill smiled back, wondering if Jaime told Rose anything about their night. Rose was happily devouring food, so he guessed she didn't know or couldn't care less. As much as he wanted to play with his food, it was time to discuss what they found.

"You won't believe what we saw last night!" Bill started and told Jaime and Rose about finding the axe and what they heard JB discuss with the assistants. "So we have to figure out what this axe means, what it means to be original in today's game, and what this extra terror is all about."

"Wow," Rose and Jaime said together.

"So what about you two?" Bill asked. "Did you find anything?"

"We talked to the girls," Jaime said between bites. "No one roomed with Annie. It looks like she was solo, and given our odd number of nineteen when we started, it makes sense that someone would room by themselves. So no one saw anything. Most of them didn't even remember her. But it was a dead end. No one knew anything. No one saw anything. We were going to check out some of the other areas of the studio like you did, but a couple of assistants were outside our hall doing their own checking, Sam and Pumpkinhead, I think. We guessed they were looking for Annie too, but they didn't say anything."

"At least you didn't have to talk to Daniel," Wes said.

"Yeah," Rose agreed. "The girls were all pretty nice about it except for the ones that had been hanging with Daniel. They didn't really want to talk with us."

"You think he's been trashing us?" Bill asked. "Maybe he targeted us right away because we beat him on the initial challenge with the riddles."

"That makes sense, given his competitive ego," Jaime said. "Bad mouth us to others to get them on his side."

"Do you think he had help last night?" Bill asked. He didn't see how that could be possible, but still. "I still can't see him doing that well in the first games on his own."

"Anything is possible," Jaime answered. "But now, thanks to you two, we have some inside information. Maybe that will help us today."

"So what do you think about the axe?" Wes asked.

"It makes sense that it has something to do with *The Shining*," Rose said. "It's the big axe Jack used when he chased his wife and son in the movie. It was right outside the hotel-themed hall."

"I agree, but it seems too obvious." Jaime shook her head. "Like, it can't be that easy right?"

"Exactly. And even so, what does the axe from *The Shining* have to do with anything?" Bill asked.

"I have absolutely no idea," Jaime said, and both Rose and Wes shrugged. *Well,* Bill thought, *I feel better knowing I didn't miss something too obvious at least.*

"Now, what about being original?" he continued. "And what about the extra terror?"

"I think we'll have to wait to see how JB introduces today's games. Then let's hope we can piece it together."

Feeling better, Bill got a Freddy claw donut and took some time to look around the room. Including himself, he counted eighteen total and tried to avoid eye contact with Daniel and anyone else at his table, but he could feel Daniel watching him, smirking. *I wonder if he knows something, or if he simply is that much of a jerk.*

"Did you guys see these?" Rose held up small note cards that had been placed on the table. "They're labeled conversation starters. JB must have put them here to get everyone talking and comfortable."

"Cool," Wes said. "What's the first one?"

"They're about favorite horror genres and films. The first one says: *What are your favorite science-fiction horror films?* Oh, that's easy. You have to go with *Alien!*"

"That's always a classic," Wes agreed. "I have to admit I'm partial to all the *Resident Evil* movies."

"*Invasion of the Body Snatchers*," Jaime said.

"John Carpenter's *The Thing*," Bill answered. "All good choices. What's another card?"

Rose read, "Best monster movies?"

"If you don't say *Cabin in the Woods*, then something's wrong with all of ya," Jaime said. "It has the best collection of every horror monster from like every movie. Absolutely brilliant!"

"I would say *It*, but I remember there was a clown in that monster collection too," Wes said. "Yeah, great movie! And Aquaman at the end. That was the best. I could do this all day! We should get together. You know, when this is all over."

Rose laughed. "Ooh, we could go camping in the woods and make our own little *Blair Witch Project* or something!"

"That would be so fun," Jaime said. "So, Rose you are from Louisiana? And Wes you're from Georgia? I live near Boston, and Bill is in Illinois. We could all meet somewhere in the middle."

"Until then we have Skype," Bill added. "Jaime and I even watch movies together. She'll play a movie on her laptop and keep me on Skype on her tablet, too. It's pretty cool."

Jaime smiled at him, and Bill would have sworn that this time she blushed a little.

"I'm glad I met you guys," Wes said. "You know what else? It's just nice to find people our age who have actually had a fairly uncensored childhood. Not that I have a lot of friends," he shrugged, "but where I grew up, the kids weren't allowed to watch R-rated movies. I'm glad my parents didn't care. I can't imagine my childhood without the fun of horror."

"For real. I mean, if you think about your favorites, not just in horror but in anything," Jaime added, "it's what we see when we're young that will have the greatest effect on our imaginations. That's what my uncle used to say. Of course, I think he was referring to *Harry Potter* and not *Friday the Thirteenth*."

"What's funny," Rose said, "is that my parents used to make me cover my eyes during sex scenes but they didn't care if I saw someone get their throat slit. Is that weird?"

"No, my mom had a simple rule," Jaime continued. "As long as I could understand the difference between reality and fantasy and as long as they didn't scare me so bad I couldn't go to sleep or to school the next day, she didn't care. She let me decide what was appropriate for me."

"What about your dad?" Rose asked her.

"He left my mom when Tara, my sister, was born. Tara's about three years younger than me."

"Wow, so your sister never met her dad?"

"Nope. I barely remember him. I don't think I really remember him at all, but you know, you hear stories when you're a kid and they kinda become reality."

"What happened?" Wes asked.

"My mom doesn't like to talk about it. Just says the bastard broke her heart, and she hopes he gets run over by a train. I got really close to my Uncle Tim. He was my dad's brother. He was like my dad growing up."

"What did he have to say about your dad?" Bill asked.

"He always said some people look inside and put themselves first. Others look outside and put others first. He said dad wasn't bad, but he was one who always looked inside first. And as to what really happened between him and my mom, Uncle Tim said that it was up to my mother to tell me that story. Not him." Jaime sighed.

"That's a hell of a story. Crazy. I'm so sorry, Jaime." Wes paused for a moment and then addressed Bill. "What about your parents?"

"They were pretty cool, too," he said and Jaime looked at him warmly. "They used to be pretty cool. It's another hell of a story. I'll tell you later. Look."

Bill pointed up at the stage where JB had entered with his four assistants. They talked briefly in a quiet circle on stage and then JB addressed everyone. "Good morning, Rabbit in Red hunters! What a day we have in store for you today! And happy Halloween!"

The conversations at all the tables quieted and attention was focused on JB. There were no cheers or applause this time. Instead, there was the unspoken dread about what had happened to one of their own. Where was Annie? It was difficult to get excited about the next round of games.

"Before we begin today's festivities, we do have a serious matter to discuss." JB's expression became solemn. "As you know, we are missing one contestant, Annie. I assure you that my assistants and I are doing everything we can to find her. We have searched the premises and are trying to make contact with her parents. We have left messages, but they have not called us back yet. We have not found her on studio grounds yet either. We suspect she is hiding somewhere, too scared perhaps from the first round of games. We know she hasn't left the building, as we do have security and monitoring systems in place that alert us if anyone comes or goes. While I know you are concerned and that this is serious, I have full confidence that we will find her before long. Don't let her actions ruin your fun."

JB was silent for a brief moment. Bill and Jaime made eye contact, and he wanted to ask if she trusted JB. As if she were reading his mind, she shrugged ever so slightly. Bill's attention returned to JB.

The volume in their host's voice intensified, and he even smiled. "If you thought last night was wild, wait until you see what is in store for you today! We have a new theme in today's games. Are you ready to SAVE the Rabbit in Red?"

The sounds of everyone shifting in their chairs, straightening up, and inching closer to JB resonated through the room. Those simple sounds suggested that the majority of the contestants had confidence in their host. Bill remembered what Daniel had said--if Annie couldn't handle the pressure then she can get out of the game. One less person to compete with. Bill wondered if it was their weakness for trusting him so quickly or JB's strength in earning back their confidence with only a few words. Regardless, everyone was now focused on the present moment. The dread of the missing girl dissipated with the anticipation of the next set of games.

Bill exchanged a silent look with Jaime, and he knew they were thinking the same thing. *Do what it takes to move forward and win but let's not forget about Annie. Keep your eyes open.*

"This morning," JB continued, "is the second round of games. You will return after breakfast to the game chambers. Last night, you were awarded points for successfully re-enacting horror fights. In this second round, you will be awarded points for successfully saving horror victims. Now is your chance to play the hero! In *deus ex machina* style, we are adding you to the movie scenes as an additional character. You will be able to interact with the victims and their killers in the same 4D style as you did last night, but your job is to be the hero. You get to change the outcome. Here are your challenges."

The screen dropped behind JB on stage, and once again, the contestants were given a preview of their upcoming tests.

The first clip revealed a brief montage of the opening scene from *Scream*, where Drew Barrymore's character, much to the surprise of audiences at the time, was killed off in the first ten minutes.

"Can you save Casey, Drew Barrymore's character?" JB laughed. "The clock is ticking, but be careful. Once you are added to the scene, the killer or killers will be after you, too."

Wes jumped at the sight of the second clip, one with which they were already familiar. There was the little boy, Georgie, in his yellow rain coat chasing a floating paper boat down a rainy street. The boat fell in a gutter, where a sharp-toothed clown named Pennywise grabbed Georgie and tore him to shreds.

"This famous opening scene from *It* has haunted audiences and readers for decades. Can you save Georgie? You won't have much time, and we certainly aren't going to make it easy for you." JB chuckled and made direct eye contact with Wes, who shuddered in his seat.

The final scene that played on the screen was one everyone knew. It was the perhaps the first slash that inspired all of the slasher movies to come. They saw Marion Crane in the shower at the Bates Motel. They saw the knife stab her again and again and again.

"Finally, will you be able to save Marion? How will you do so? I'll give you one more thing to think about: You're not going to be so lucky as to pop up right behind any of the killers in these scenes. It's not going to be that easy." JB snickered again. "But I sure do look forward to seeing you try."

The screen went black, and the assistants gathered around JB. "Oh, another thing. If you succeed in all three of these scenes, you will be awarded a bonus scene. I'm not going to tell you anything about this bonus scene, except to say that it will be unique for each one of you. Remember that your goal is to *save* the victims. Now, you have fifteen minutes to freshen up and get ready. Then my assistants will escort you back to the game chambers. Good luck and get ready to SAVE THE RABBIT IN RED!"

"Okay," Jaime said. "I think I got it. You overheard JB talking last night that he wanted originality, right? Now, we have to save each of these victims. I don't think he's looking for the easy way out. He's not wanting us to tackle and fight the killer this time. He's looking to see what we can do with our surroundings."

"Yeah," Bill said. "So we have to be extra observant. Look around for things in the scenes that could help us. Take risks, and be different than the other contestants." He sat back and crossed his arms. "I don't think these scenes are about fighting either. These scenes are about how adaptable we are. We got this!"

"Bill?" Jaime asked. "The bonus fourth scene?"

"Yeah, that makes me nervous."

"What do you mean?" Wes asked.

"JB said we'd experience even more terror last night, right? It makes sense that the fourth scene will be something much worse."

"Just remember that we know it's going to be bad," Jaime advised. "So whatever comes at us, tell yourselves that you can handle it."

"What do you think it will be?" Wes asked, his voice shaking slightly.

"I have no idea," Bill confessed. But he had a feeling it would be something that none of them would ever be able to forget.

Chapter Fourteen

Bill tried to recall all of the details from the scenes that he could. In *Scream*, Drew Barrymore's character was making popcorn when she got a prank call. She had to answer trivia questions about horror villains and she got one wrong, which resulted in her boyfriend, who was tied up in a chair on the back porch, getting murdered. The question she got wrong was "Who was the killer in *Friday the 13th*?" Under pressure, she answered Jason, but the killer in the original movie was Jason's mom. Jason Voorhees, with the exception of the first movie's epilogue, didn't appear until the second film.

Wes and Bill were escorted to the game chamber by Captain Spaulding — Chester, Bill remembered — and they silently wished each other good luck with a nod. Bill put on the computerized gloves and the virtual helmet, stretched out his arms and cracked his neck. He squeezed his fists a couple of times, looked at the dark shadows of the rabbit and the axe on the gloves, bounced around on the movable floor, and took a deep breath as the black screen around him came to life once again.

He thought at first if he could get the correct answer to the *Friday the 13th* question to Drew that he could save her, but if this game was programmed to resemble reality in any way, certainly she would freak out if a complete stranger walked into her house. Bill also knew that in *Scream* there were two killers, and certainly both were working together in this first kill even if the audience wasn't aware of it at the time.

The screen came to life and featured the Rabbit in Red logo, which quickly transformed into the setting of *Scream*. Bill found himself outside the front of the house. He ran to the window, and he saw Drew making popcorn.

The house phone would ring any second, setting her fate in motion. Bill looked around and saw some cables, and he ran toward them. Phone lines! Drew's character received the call on a landline to the home phone. He pulled at the wires, ripping them from the house. If he disconnected the phone, then her killers would not be able to call. For the killers in *Scream*, murder was about toying with the victim. If they couldn't toy with her, maybe they wouldn't kill her. He ripped the cords as quickly as possible, and then ran to the house's garage. He looked for a cutting tool, and grabbed a pair of garden shears. He went back to the phone wires and cut them in half to be safe, and then quietly snuck around to the back of the house.

One of the killers would be with the boyfriend in the backyard eventually. Bill remembered that Casey — Drew's character — turned on the back light and didn't see anything at first. The second time she turned on the light, however, her boyfriend was tied up in a chair. Bill had to find the boyfriend.

Near the front of the house, Bill saw one of the killers dressed as Ghostface. He had his cell phone out, and Bill could see Drew through the windows. She was walking around the kitchen, and she was not on the phone at all, Bill was grateful to see. Ghostface was attempting to make a call, but it wasn't going through. Bill saw the man's arms wave in frustration. Was he trying to get someone's attention? Surely, the first killer was going to discuss with the second a new plan, as Drew was not answering her phone. It also made sense that one killer would be out front and one out back, that way they could trap Drew no matter how she tried to escape. He saw the Ghostface out front make another call. He had to be trying to reach his partner in crime.

Where would the killers keep her boyfriend? They must have moved him quickly into the backyard for Drew to see. Bill looked around. Behind the garage! *Jesus, I was probably feet away from the second dude.*

Bill crept to the back and saw both Ghostface and Drew's boyfriend exactly where he had predicted. The boyfriend was already tied up, just a dozen feet away from the spotlight in the backyard where Drew was meant to eventually see him.

The killer's phone rang. Yes! The other Ghostface was calling him. The plan was working! This Ghostface answered the phone, grunted, took a sharp look at the boyfriend tied in the chair, and then ran to the front of the house. Bill hid in the shadows on the side of the garage and held his breath. He released a heavy sigh, and then ran to Drew's boyfriend. With the garden shears he took from the garage, he cut the boyfriend loose.

"Listen carefully. I'm here to help," he murmured in the young man's ear. "You are in serious danger. I'm going to cut you free. You need to get your girlfriend and run toward the street. Her parents will be returning soon. Get her now and leave through the back door and go around the right side of the house. The guy who tied you up went up the left side and he's talking to a partner who is helping him. You have to avoid them at all costs. Trust me. Go now."

Bill watched him run and grab his girlfriend who jumped at the surprise. Her expression turned to panic as he quickly explained what happened, but he followed Bill's instructions and not a moment too soon. When Drew and the boyfriend left the house, the first killer returned. Bill hid behind a tree and watched as the madman dressed in the Ghostface costume ran into the house searching for Drew and her boyfriend. Bill followed the two up the right side of the house and breathed a sigh of relief as they were already at the main road and they weren't stopping. Up ahead were car lights, and Bill knew these would be Drew's parents. He had saved both Drew's character's life and her boyfriend's, as well as saved mom and dad from the grief of losing a daughter. He smiled, and the screen went dark around him.

"Congratulations!" a voice announced. "You were successful!"

The screen didn't move but Bill heard a whirling sensation through his virtual helmet. He was being transported to the next scene. When an image did appear, Bill found himself in a sewer. It was wet and crawling with rats, and he shuddered as they appeared all around his feet. He was in the setting of *It* all right, but he was not on the street where he expected to be. Georgie would be somewhere up above, floating his boat, and Pennywise, a clown that represented all children's fears, was somewhere down here with him. He needed to get out of here and see where he was, and so he ran forward, hoping he wouldn't run into the clown, but knowing he had no time to spare. He ran until he found a ladder that led up to a sewer cap, and he pushed the cap open and crawled out. Ahead of him was Georgie, running along down the road. Bill must have crossed paths with him underneath the street only moments ago.

"Georgie!" he shouted, but George was too far ahead and didn't hear him. "Shit!" Bill yelled again and looked around. He saw Silver on its kickstand in a yard behind him. That was the bike Georgie's big brother, the character Bill, used in the story. The bike shouldn't have been there, but no doubt JB programmed the bike to be in someone's yard to make it look like it belonged there.

Bill ran to the bike, and as he picked it up, a small hatch opened in the floor in front of the floor on which he currently stood. Out of the hatch, a stationary bike like the ones in fitness centers moved toward him. He got on the bike in the chamber, thus getting on the bike in the simulation, and feeling like the Bill in the story, he pedaled as fast as he could and shouted, "Hi-yo, Silver! Away!"

He didn't have a second to spare. Anyone playing this simulation who didn't get out of the sewer quick enough and who didn't recognize and use the bike right away would never have a chance of saving Georgie. Bill neared Georgie and saw that the boat was approaching the gutter where it would fall to be captured by Pennywise. Bill sped right on past the little boy and went full speed at the paper boat. It was inches away from falling in the gutter when Bill leaned over and scooped it up. He couldn't resist glancing in the gutter. There he saw the clown in full white makeup, a big red nose, and pointy teeth as sharp as knives. Pennywise the clown growled at him, and Bill was not going to take any time to confront that beast. His heart racing faster than he could pedal, Bill quickly cycled around back toward Georgie.

"My boat!" Georgie cried.

"Here, little man. I picked it up for you because it was going to fall in the gutter. I'm a friend of your brother's."

"Really?"

"Yep, now what do you say you hop on with me and I'll give you a ride back home."

"I'm not supposed to talk to strangers."

Remembering the dialogue from the story, Bill knew Georgie said the same thing to Pennywise.

"Well, I'm Bill Wise, a friend of your brother. Now we're not strangers. Hop on the back and I'll give you a ride."

"Okay," Georgie said all too easily, and Bill pedaled away from the gutter and the clown that would end Georgie's life. Georgie held on tight, and Bill felt disappointed only because he wished he had more time to play in this simulation as the screen turned to black again. He wished he had more time to ride Silver and talk with Georgie. He would have loved also to meet Georgie's brother, but it was not in the game. The stationary bike in the chamber moved back into the hatch from which it came, and Bill stood up, awaiting his third challenge.

"Congratulations. You were successful!" a voice announced again.

As a new image formed on the giant screen, he found himself standing on the front steps of the Bates house, one of the creepiest homes in all of film. He appreciated that the TV show *Bates Motel* recreated the house, but seeing it on the black and white screen in the original *Psycho* was still one of the most haunting images in all of cinema.

He knew where he was, but *when* was even more important. Was Marion already in the shower? Where was she? And where was Norman Bates? He ran down to the hotel, crawling past the office windows in case Norman was in there, and peeked inside the room he knew she was renting. He saw her begin to undress, which meant she was moments away from entering the shower. Bill shouldn't have been surprised. JB wasn't giving them any spare time to think. Bill knew Bates would be watching her through a peephole in the back of his office.

He looked around. "Think!" Should he knock on the door and run away like a game of ding dong ditch? JB wanted them to be original, and the only thing Bill could think of was to take a risk.

He entered the office of Norman Bates and rang a little bell on the desk. Sure enough, Bates came from the back of the office, moments away from spying on Marion in the shower and then going to her room to stab her over and over again.

"Can I help you?" Bates asked.

"Yes, I need a room," Bill said. "Can you show me the inside of the room first? I'd like to see it before I pay for it."

"As you wish," Bates sighed, obviously annoyed.

Bates took the lead and walked out the office door, and Bill looked around, desperate for some kind of distraction. Even if Bill managed to distract Norman while Marion was in the shower, she would not be safe forever. He had to get her out of the motel and back on the road. He followed Bates past cabin one, where Marion was staying, to cabin six. On the inside, it exactly resembled the girls' sleeping quarters at the studio.

"Will this be sufficient for your needs?" Bates asked.

"It will do."

"Let's get you checked in then." Bates turned back to the office.

On the way out, Bill grabbed a memo pad and a pen from the desk in the room. When they returned to the office, Bill sat down and wrote a quick note as Bates gathered the check-in paperwork.

The authorities know you have taken the money and are on their way here, he wrote. *You need to leave now or you will be caught. Leave now. Don't think. Just act. From, a helping friend.*

"Would you excuse me for a moment? I seemed to have misplaced my wallet. Shoot, I may have left it back in town. I was at a little restaurant there earlier. Would you mind if I came back in a few minutes?"

Bates looked to the back of the office, anxious perhaps to get back to his peep show. "I'll be here for a little longer. Just knock first."

Bill left the office and walked slowly away, looking over his shoulder. He waited until Bates moved from the desk to the back of the office, and then Bill ran to Marion's room. He slipped the note under her door and knocked hard and fast. He then ran near the other end of the hotel and watched. Marion cracked open the door, and Bill could see that she was wet, covering her body and her hair with two different towels. He had saved her from getting watched by Norman Bates and hopefully saved her from being stabbed as well. She picked up the note, read it, and slammed the door. Bill knew that in the movie, Marion ends up staying at the Bates Motel because she embezzled money from her employer and hit the road running. He hoped he could scare her out of the motel and back on the road. A couple of minutes later, she was dressed rather poorly but had her suitcase and car keys. Without so much as saying good-bye to the deceivingly friendly face that checked her in, she got in her car and drove off.

The screen went black and once again a voice announced, "Congratulations. You were successful!"

Now, Bill held his breath and tried to think about what could happen next. It was time for the fourth challenge. He knew this was designed to be a surprise and to be the most terrifying of all.

The image on the screen slowly pixilated to form a scene from Bill's memory, one with which he was vividly familiar. Surprise turned to intense curiosity. "What? How?" he muttered. He was an eight-year-old boy lying in bed, cuddling with his best friend Sparky. It wasn't a perfect match, but it eerily resembled the appearance of his childhood bedroom. A wave of nausea punched Bill in the gut, and he moaned at hearing the noise of someone breaking into his house. His mother's scream came next. Sparky's head popped up at the sound, and Bill, trying to remind himself he was still in a game chamber, mumbled, "What the hell?"

But the simulation was so real. His knees weakened, and Bill fell on the floor of the chamber. He could only watch and listen.

"He's not here," he heard his father say. "He's staying the night at a friend's house."

"Oh, God." Sparky jumped from the bed and to the door, and Bill stood up fast. Sparky had barked and alerted the intruder that the child was still here. That set a chain of events into action that may have led directly to his father's death.

I have to save them. That's what it's all about. Save them. Save me, too.

He darted toward Sparky, picked him up, and crept under the bed. He held the old dog close and covered his eyes with one hand and his mouth with the other.

"Shhh, Sparks. There's nothing we can do. If we go out there, dad dies. If we stay here, there's a chance. That's all we got."

"I want your cell phones, jewelry, valuables and any cash you have," the intruder said. "Tell me where everything is and no one needs to get hurt."

His heart was beating through his neck and out the top of his head. Everything pounded. He buried his face into Sparky's side, and tears rolled down his cheeks. It was all too real. And the only way to win this simulation was to sit here and do nothing.

Bill heard his father comply, and the intruder took what he wanted. Then his bedroom door swung all the way open. Footsteps approached the bed, and Bill saw those shoes, the same dark shoes that were embedded in his memory from that terrible night. The shoes approached the bed, stopped, stayed for a moment, and then turned around and walked out. Seconds later, Bill heard the front door slam shut, and his parents charged into his bedroom.

"Billy?" his mom cried. "Are you okay?"

"Bill, come here." His dad reached out and pulled him into his arms. Bill hugged him back, and for a moment, he swore he could even smell his dad, the familiar Old Spice that came with him when they moved into his grandparents' house, that scent that came out of nowhere, springing tears of memory until, like the end of a season and even sadder than finding the scent on an old jacket or hat, it vanished completely.

"Dad," Bill whimpered. "Mom. You both are okay?"

"We're okay. Are you?"

"I . . . I . . ." Bill coughed. "No. I don't know."

"You saved me, son," his dad told him. "I will always be here." His dad put his hand on his chest, right over his heart. "Life is finite, but love is infinite."

Bill hugged them again and he didn't want this moment to slip away, simulation or not, but the whirling sensation began once again, and like the end of a dream, his parents disappeared, and he once again was alone. Alone in this game chamber. This Fright Fest. This Rabbit in Red challenge that was supposed to be fun.

A voice once again repeated, "Congratulations. You were successful!"

Exhaling deeply, he took off the 4D equipment. A mix of nostalgia, adrenaline, excitement, and fear rumbled through his gut. He leaned against the wall, feeling dizzy, trying to find balance, trying to grasp where he was and what had just happened. As his grip on reality strengthened, his emotions changed. He pressed away from the wall and stood straight up. His mind jumped to his friends.

"Oh, God," he said out loud. He knew what Jaime would have to experience, and it filled him with anger. *And what if she fails? What happens if you fail in this simulation?*

He thought about that for a moment. What if *he* had failed? Would he have seen his father murdered again? What horrors was JB putting his friends through?

These games were supposed to be fun challenges, and even though hours ago he heard JB state that the games would progress to real fear, this was just wrong. He needed to see his friends, but maybe it was time to confront the man behind the curtain one-on-one.

JB had taken it too far, and someone had to stand up to him. Bill bit his lip and his arms shook uncontrollably. But it didn't matter. He was going to see the man behind the curtain and tell JB exactly what he felt.

Chapter Fifteen

"Take me to see JB," Bill told the assistant Captain Spaulding.

"JB is busy overseeing the simulations."

"I don't care. I need to see him, *Chester*!" Bill was fuming. It felt as if even the short blonde hairs on his head were trying to stand straight up.

The surprised eyes behind the Captain Spaulding makeup studied Bill. "I can let him know, but that's all."

"Fine," Bill grumbled. "But do it now. Please. It's important."

Bill walked slowly toward the commons, but he kept an eye on Chester. Chester had walked the opposite way of the commons, past the game chambers, into a part of the studio Bill had yet to see. Once he had turned a corner, Bill followed him.

It wasn't much further. Beyond the game chambers appeared a large glass door. Through the glass door, Bill saw one gigantic monitor, at least 80 inches wide, more than a dozen smaller monitors, a computer station, and one large black rotating chair. It reminded him of a CNN newsroom on U.S. Presidential Election Day. A few hours ago, he might have been impressed. But right now Bill wanted to break every single screen.

Seated in the chair, turning his attention from one monitor to the next, was Jay Bell. On the large monitor, JB rotated between different screens, and all of them were of the contestants in the game chambers. JB had been watching each person battle his or her simulations.

Chester knocked on the door. "Sir, we may have a problem."

"Is it not something you can handle until the games are over?" JB snapped.

"Yes sir, I suppose, but —"

"Then handle it," JB cut him off, "and come back when I'm not focusing on the games."

"Yes, sir." As Chester turned around, Bill hid behind a crevice in the wall. He stood perfectly still, trying to merge with the wall, thankful for a skinny body as he inched as close as he could into this corner. Aided perhaps by the ridiculously large hat Chester wore as Captain Spaulding, which may have affected his peripheral vision, the assistant walked right past him.

Bill waited until Chester was out of sight and then crept back toward JB. Resisting the urge to barge in, he crouched outside the door, and watched what JB watched.

On the large monitor, JB focused on Jaime's simulation. Bill did not recognize the setting, so he figured this must be her fourth and final test. He cheered internally for her; she must have passed the first three challenges and saved all of the victims. But now eerie butterfly sensations rumbled in his belly.

This isn't right. He's spying on a memory, seeing something personal. Actually, maybe he should go, too. He stood up straight, resisting every urge to stay and watch. And then he heard Jaime's voice.

"Uncle Tim, no, please!" Jaime yelped from the monitor, and Bill couldn't have turned away if he had wanted to. A man stood in front of her, large and solid. He must have been as tall as Bill but was much thicker, like a solid tree trunk. His huge arms tied a rope on a fixture in this room's ceiling. Her uncle looked back with dark, empty eyes, but he said nothing. Bill could not imagine the fear Jaime must be experiencing.

She pleaded with her uncle, she cried, she yelled, and she even tried to physically pull him down. Of course, none of these things worked. Bill remembered from the simulations of *Scream* and *Psycho* that the secret was not to battle the "evil" directly, but to find an alternate way, a distraction of some kind or a clever manipulation of the setting.

Jaime was losing this simulation, her emotions trumping her logic and forgetting that this was a game. Anger rose through his lungs and he wanted to shout and charge at JB. But he also wanted to give Jaime a chance to win and was worried whatever he might do now could have some kind of negative consequence.

Jaime sat down on the floor below her uncle, her knees pointed up, hugging her legs and crying. Her uncle stood on a chair and tied the rope around his neck.

"C'mon, Jaime." Bill whispered. "C'mon. Get up!"

Jaime wiped tears from her eyes and looked around the room.

"That's it. C'mon."

She stood up, looked around, and focused on an object next to her uncle. More rope. Her uncle had a rather large rope and had cut enough of it to hang himself, leaving more off to the side. Jaime picked it up and moved directly in front of her uncle's vision.

"If you go, I go," she told him.

She tied a noose and threw it over another fixture on the ceiling. She grabbed a chair and stood on it. She put the noose around her neck.

But her uncle didn't seem to be stopping. He was looking at her now, more than he was before, but he was still moving, creeping off that chair as if he were moving in slow motion. Bill's heart raced for Jaime. He clenched his fists and bit his tongue so as not to scream.

"Save me," Jaime said and jumped.

Bill gasped. Jaime had kicked the chair out from beside her and now hung there choking. Bill stood up, forgetting where he was, not caring about getting caught. What if she died in the simulation? She'd lose the game for sure, but how did the game know between what was real and what was virtual? Could she die for real?

Bill looked behind him. Could he go to her individual game chamber and pull her out? But he didn't have to.

Back on the large monitor, her uncle took his noose off from around his neck, stepped off the chair, and went to Jaime's aid. He lifted her up, untied the rope from around her neck, and hugged her.

"I'm so sorry, Jaime. To you and everyone. There will always be things in this world we will never understand. I love you." He hugged her tight, and she hugged even harder back, gasping for air, choking on her tears and trying to catch her breath.

"I love you, too," she cried back. And her screen went to black. "Congratulations. You were successful!"

Bill cheered silently. He had to wipe tears from his eyes, some that were triggered by seeing Jaime's simulation, some that were triggered by anger. How could JB put anyone through that?

He kicked open the door to JB's main chamber.

"You son of a bitch!" he barked at JB. "What are you doing?"

JB turned in his black chair like a villain out of a classic film, and Bill was stunned to see that JB also had tears in his eyes. He swiftly wiped them away at the sight of Bill. JB inhaled deeply and looked at Bill with sharp, critical eyes. Frightening eyes, really.

"Sit down, boy," he said. They locked eyes, and Bill said nothing. "Sit down," he repeated with greater emphasis.

Bill held his gaze firmly, but noticed a smaller chair off to the side. He sat down, never once removing his eyes from JB. He noticed JB looked older up close. There was gray through the sides of his hair, and his forehead was too large for his face, mostly due to a receding hairline. The rest of JB's hair was black and his eyes were even darker.

"What troubles you, Bill?" he asked.

"You can't do this to people. You can't do this to us. You have to know how crazy all of this is."

"Correct me if I'm wrong, but you seemed to rather be enjoying yourself."

"I was until the last simulation. That's too much."

"I see." JB sighed and folded his arms in his lap.

"Horror is fiction. It's fantasy," Bill told him. "It's not real."

"The last simulation was not real either, son. It was only a horrific fantasy."

"How did you make those? How did you find our fears?"

"Bill, since you and all the others won the initial challenge, I've been studying you, too. You should always be careful what you write on the web. E-mails, blogs, Facebook posts, digital chats: anything sent electronically can be uncovered with the right tools and technology. And also of course, the moment you downloaded the Rabbit in Red app on your phone to answer the riddles and accepted the terms of agreement that no one bothers to read, I had total access to all the history and data you accessed on your phone. I had to learn as much about all of you as you tried to learn about horror. It's all part of the game."

Bill tried to do a quick mental inventory of everything he used his phone for. He thought about all the websites he visited, the texts he sent, the pictures and the videos.

"That's a total invasion of privacy!" he snapped. "How could you? And that last simulation? That was too much. You saw

Jaime's tears. That was not fantasy. That was real!"

"I see your tears now, too. And I know you saw mine. Calm down, my boy. Let me tell you a story." JB took a deep breath and sipped a glass of water. "Would you like something to drink? You look parched."

"No," Bill lied, fidgeting in his chair.

"Very well. Where to begin? When I was a young boy, I had fantasies of writing horror stories and making movies, much like a lot of your friends. I wrote a lot of crap, too," he laughed. "Aliens, monsters, creepy insects, anything that could go bump in the night. My first attempt was a story called *Tarantula Man*." JB rolled his eyes. "You get the idea. It was all largely unoriginal. Many of the horror films you see today are exactly the same. You have a group of teens who get chased by a madman in between their parties and sexual exploits. You have a troubled couple living together in a house terrorized by ghosts or demons. But not all demons are in the form of slashers or ghosts. Those movies can be fun, as you and I both know. When I was younger I did . . . I explored all sorts of creative avenues to understand horror."

His eyes rolled up, clearly thinking of the past. He coughed and shook his head ever so slightly, as if ejecting the thoughts from his mind.

"When I started this studio," JB continued after a moment, "I wanted to explore terror and fear from all angles and perspectives. You once wrote to Jaime, and forgive me for having read it, that the horror in fiction can prepare us for the horror in real life. I very much agree. But the real horror already exists inside of us. The horrible memories you have of watching your father murdered and struggling with your mother at home: that's real terror. Jaime's struggles to make sense of her uncle's suicide: that's terror. You see, I brought you all together in this contest for many reasons. First, I wanted the smartest young minds out there when it comes to horror. You've proven yourself quite worthy through the initial riddles and re-enacting great horror scenes. Second, I wanted original and clever young minds. More than those who can re-enact and memorize. But minds that can still be innovative and adaptive. You've proven yourself worthy there too, kid, and congratulations. That's all fun and games, yes?"

JB leaned forward in his chair, looking intensely at Bill. "But I have greater ambition when it comes to you and your friends. I also want to find those who can deal with their own terrors, who can come to peace with them, and who can maybe use those terrors to contribute to art and provide insights that may help others deal with their own personal fears. That's why this second round was more intense, and that's why you're here. Had I told you everything to expect in advance, then I wouldn't be able to see how you would naturally react to it, and that's what I was evaluating. Sometimes we can prepare to face our fears, but more often than not, our fears surprise us and come out of nowhere, a sudden storm on an otherwise sunny day."

Bill wasn't sure what to say. He was still angry, he still thought the last simulations were too much, and he wasn't sure if he could even really trust JB.

"Aren't you concerned about what could happen for those who can't deal with it?" Bill challenged. "What about those who can't make peace with them? Don't you think you can cause more harm than good by testing us on those?"

"That is a concern, yes." JB frowned. "But it was a risk I was willing to take. Any great adventure inherently possesses significant risks. Don't you feel better having hugged your parents and having seen them together, even if it was only virtual reality? Don't you think Jaime will feel better after her uncle saved her and tried to say something to her to make sense of a tragic mystery? I wanted to test you, but I also wanted to help you. Art can also be therapeutic, don't you see?"

"*You* took a risk?" Bill's jaw dropped open. "You didn't do shit! We took the risk. Art can be therapeutic? You have a messed up idea of what art is. And all this for what? An internship here? You really think people are gonna want to work with you after all this?"

"Bill!" he snapped. "Horror is not all fun and games. You overcome your fears, you understand terror, you embrace it even. This adventure, my dream, Mr. Wise, is not for just any fan of horror. In time, I hope you'll see that, only then will you be ready for what I have to offer you. The reward will match the challenges, and there is more to it than meets the eye."

"What is it?"

"Patience is also a virtue I desire in our winners, Bill." JB paused for a moment, letting the momentary irritation fade away. "Finish this weekend with me, Bill. You'll get all of the answers soon. In the meantime, do you have anything for me?"

"Um, what?" Bill wondered.

"I see. I guess you haven't figured that part out yet."

"I don't know what you're talking about." But the moment Bill said those words, he did have a clue. He pictured the axe hiding under his bed, the axe that was a symbol along with the rabbit on his gloves.

"I see that you haven't. When you figure it out what it means, tell me, and if you're correct, I'll give you another answer. Now, Bill, this game is not only about you. I have footage from all of the other contestants to watch before the results are posted. Many of our players are very talented. I suggest you don't back down for a second."

"The third and final round is tonight, right? Is that going to be as bad as this one?"

"All I can tell you is that everything happens for a reason. You're here because you have passion and because I recognize and value that passion. But it takes more than a couple of games to determine what a person is truly capable of. Until then, go and comfort your friends. I'm sure they have just as many concerns as you. We'll talk again after the games. I have more work to do, and so do you. Goodbye." JB turned around back to his monitors.

Bill thought he should go right to Jaime and comfort her. Or tell her about everything that had happened. But he was overwhelmed. He needed a moment to process these thoughts. There was so much to figure out, and one of the things he had to question was whether or not he could trust JB. Bill had always liked him. He connected with the ideas in JB's newsletters, and he was captivated by the games and other innovations in this studio. He saw a passion in JB that was admirable, a passion so few adults in his life possessed. JB walked the walk. But now, these games had taken a dark turn, and Bill wondered if they'd get even darker before the night was over.

He returned to his room. He would just take a few moments to gather his thoughts and rest. He went to the duffel bag that he had brought with him and pulled out a paper copy of all of JB's online newsletters that he had printed in case he needed to reference them.

He flipped through the pages, skimming them until one entry caught his eye.

Teenagers are the best subjects for a horror film. The problem with most horror films is that they have been used for the wrong reasons. They are on film to have sex and party and be punished for it. Of course, teens also represent a large part of the movie-going audience, and that's how films make money: make a movie about teens, put lots of sex, gore, and partying in it, and they are sure to come in masses with friends to laugh and groan at the images on screen.

But there's a better reason to focus on young adults. A part of their mind is still a child's mind, with a child's delights and a child's fears. When you're forty, you've battled your demons through alcohol or counseling or total repression. When you're sixteen, your demons are still vivid, your terrors uncontrolled, and while you may be silent about them to friends and family, all it takes is a little creativity to dig a bit deeper in the subconscious mind to find true terror. The childlike demons are present and alive and unrepressed.

When they've finally silenced those demons, they become adults, fixated on boring routines. The bills are the demons, not a haunted memory from a lonely day of one's childhood. One secret to great horror is to find those demons, bring them to the conscious mind, and then put them on screen. You see, a teenager's mind is also part adult as well as child, and then we see a true battle: Will the young person revert to childhood, hide, run, and cry when confronted with real evil? Or will the young person find strength and courage and stand tall to beat down the demons once and for all?

Could JB be trusted? Was he a genius or a madman? Or perhaps both? Bill had digested enough thought for now. It was time to find his friends. They had a lot to talk about.

Chapter Sixteen

"Bill!" Jaime cried when he returned to the commons. She hugged him tightly and rested her head on his shoulder. "I'm so glad you're here. That last game. Oh, God. It was terrible."

He let her tell him the full story without interruption. He wasn't sure yet if he should confess that he had watched, worried she might interpret it as an invasion of privacy. He listened to her tale, picturing each moment in his mind from the video feed. She didn't leave out a single detail, and she didn't exaggerate or change her story at all from what Bill had seen. Listening to her raw honesty about this moment, Bill felt closer to Jaime than he ever had before.

"Oh, I'm so sorry," Bill told her, hugging her once again. "That's absolutely terrible. Are you okay now?"

"I don't know." She rested her head on his shoulder again. "Part of me wants to find JB, march right up to him, and strangle him. How could he do something like that? I thought this was supposed to be fun."

"Yeah, me too."

"What about your last game? What happened?"

Bill told her about his simulation, also including every detail. The absolute terror of being back in his old house on that very night, worried he'd have to see his father killed again. The joy he felt when they survived and hugged him and talked to him.

"But in the end, we were both successful. I guess that's something. Maybe in some messed up way JB was trying to help us," he suggested, thinking of his conversation with the man behind the curtain. "What about the others?"

"I haven't seen Rose or Wes yet. Look around. There's only a few of us here so far. They must be struggling with the simulations. I hope they're okay."

The assistants were lining the stage with a lunch buffet, and Jaime and Bill helped themselves to a modest plate. They were both hungry but also so nervous and exhausted from the games that they weren't sure they'd keep any food down. Still, they tried: some turkey sandwiches and potato salad to start. Slowly, more contestants returned to the room, and as Bill and Jaime's stomachs started to settle, Rose and Wes returned.

"Are you guys okay?" Jaime asked them.

"Yeah," Wes said, but he was clearly shaken also. His puffy cheeks glistened from sweat or tears or both. "But that was absolutely terrible. So that's what JB meant by real terror."

"What were your simulations?" Jaime asked hesitantly.

"I was back in junior high," Wes said, sighing deeply. "In the locker room. PE class. The boys were all undressing for gym. I dreaded those moments. Always have. Why do schools have to humiliate kids? Whenever I took my shirt off, kids would point and laugh. It was worse this time though. I entered the simulation in a locker room and was surrounded by mirrors and laughing kids. And I was only wearing my underwear. How could JB do that?"

Wes looked down, holding back the pain, searching for strength. "My classmates were terrible. In the horror of the locker room, they laughed at me. 'You got more belly than you got ass,' one shouted. 'Can you even see your dick? I bet he pees like a girl.'"

He looked up at Rose and blushed, his dark skin even darker in that moment. "Sorry to be crude," he added. "But they were terrible. The kids all laughed and pointed, and then in the simulation, and here's where it gets even more messed up, they turned into small, evil clowns. I know it's going to sound weird. I've told Bill this, but for as much as I love Stephen King's *It*, I'm terrified of clowns." Wes took out his clown nose stress ball and squeezed. "I barely made it through the *It* module, too. But anyway these kids turned into little clowns, and they chased me around, taking pictures of my nearly naked, fat body on their phones."

Wes fought back the tears and squeezed the ball harder. "Somehow the pictures they took on their phones ended up posted on every locker. Every single damn locker had a picture of me in my underwear. The little clowns carried me into the girl's locker room, where they did the same thing. They took pictures, posted it on the locker room walls, and the girls laughed with the clowns. I rolled into a ball and let them laugh. It felt all so real."

"What did you do?" Bill asked.

"I tried not to cry and then thought to myself why JB would create this simulation. The first thing I thought is that he's a complete psycho. But I tried to think of something else, something that would give him the benefit of the doubt for making me experience this. The only reasonable answer I could come up with was that I had to be comfortable in my body and stop caring if people laughed. So I stood up. Me and my underwear. I let them point and laugh. And I smiled at them. I smiled and walked right past every one of them, not hiding a thing, standing as straight and tall as I could. I laughed with them. I said out loud, 'This is who I am. I'm not the bad guy. Anyone who takes pleasure in hurting someone is the bad guy.' And then they all went away."

"Wow," Jaime said. "What a terrible thing but good for you, Wes. That's bravery."

She hugged Wes then, and Rose jumped up and put her arms around him, too. Bill said empathetically, "Hey, make room for me in there. You're awesome, man. Good for you." The three huddled around Wes in a moment of pure friendship.

Maybe the situation was pretty horrifying, but this weekend was the first time he ever hugged any friend. Thinking back to just the other day — another boring day when Bill sat at in a lunch room at high school with his nose in a book — seemed like ages ago. He never wanted to let these new friends go.

"You know, it actually felt pretty good at the end," Wes said.

"What about you, Rose?" Jaime asked.

She looked away, and Bill was reminded of how Rose first looked, back on TV when a reporter interviewed her. Rose had a way of looking in the distance, thinking of something else, or perhaps not wanting to think at all.

"A couple of summers ago," Rose started very slowly, clenching her purse tight against her chest, "my family and I went camping. I had a little brother, Johnny. He was only seven years old." She paused, ran her fingers through the back of her red hair with one hand, grasping her purse with the other. "He died on the camping trip. He was chasing me in a field. We were having such a great time, laughing and running. He tripped on a rock and landed on some kind of in-ground bees' nest. I can still hear his cries as they stung him again and again."

She paused for a moment. Wes reached out and put an arm around her shoulder, and Rose smiled at him. "I ran back to help him, but they stung me too, and I cried out for my parents. By the time they got there, Johnny must have had twenty bee stings. His arms and legs swelled up like red balloons, and dad had to rush him into the city, but it was about a forty-minute drive to the nearest hospital. Johnny was allergic, and by the time my dad got him to the hospital, Johnny had passed. My dad held him in his arms at the hospital entrance, but there was nothing they could do."

Rose paused and wiped tears from her eyes. "In my simulation, I was playing with Johnny again, in that same field, and he was chasing me. I knew he could fall and land on that bees' nest at any time, so the moment I saw him, I yelled and ran toward him. I was like, 'Pretend this is freeze tag and don't move!' He slowed down and looked at me. 'But you haven't tagged me,' he said back. I was almost to him when he stepped right on the nest. But I wasn't going to let them sting him. I dove and threw my body on the ground, trying to cover the bees, trying to be their only target so Johnny wouldn't get stung. They stung me all over and Johnny cried. He said, 'No, Rose. Thank you but it's supposed to be me. I love you always, sis. And I'm always here. In your memories. And in your art.' He hugged me then and the simulation ended."

There have been too many tears today, Bill thought, seeing more roll down Rose's sweet face. "It was terrible to relive it. But you know what? It was so nice to see him and hug him again."

She opened up her purse with the *Speak only if it improves upon the silence* quote and took out a picture.

"I don't keep much in here," she said. "A couple of his pictures mostly." She showed them the photos, and it was like looking at a younger, male version of Rose. Johnny had the same short red hair, but his face was covered in twice as many freckles.

"Oh, Rose, I'm so sorry," Jaime told her.

"He's right though," Rose said. "Or whoever programmed him in the simulation is right. He's always with me. Never forgotten."

Jaime was the first to hug Rose, and the boys followed. They kept their arms around one another for a few moments. "Three of us lost someone close to us," Jaime said. "I wonder how many others here have lost someone. Do you think that has anything to do with why we were selected?"

"You guys lost someone, too?" Wes asked Bill and Jaime. "Wow. You guys make my nightmares look like daydreams. I don't even . . . I don't know what to say. Nothing I experienced even compares."

"That's not true," Bill said. "If we're friends, we need to tell you everything." Bill went first and shared the details of his father's murder and how he re-enacted it in the simulation. Then Jaime told the story of her Uncle Tim. After several moments of silence as everyone absorbed one another's nightmares, Bill continued, "But here's the thing, Wes. Don't compare your pain to someone else's. I would never say my life has been harder. That's not fair."

"He's right," Jaime said. "It's like if I break a finger, but you break a leg. I know in my head that your pain may be greater, but dammit if my finger doesn't hurt like hell."

That made Wes laugh. "You bring up a good point though, Jaime. I don't think we're here only because of our knowledge and passions. We're here because we've all had haunted pasts, in one way or another."

"And those haunted pasts can create some terrifying art," Rose said.

Bill nodded. "I need to tell you guys something. Something JB said. I confronted him —" But a commotion broke out in the commons before he could tell the story. The breaking of plates and scattered yells diverted their attention to the corner of the room. Daniel knocked the lunch plates and silverware off the table and was yelling at Dexter Lange. They stood up, and Daniel shoved him.

"You shut up." Daniel pushed him. Dexter shoved him back.

"I didn't expect to see you cry." Dexter laughed. It was odd seeing them confront one another. Daniel's bleached blonde hair juxtaposed the dark, spiky hair Dexter wore. They matched one another in muscle, but Dexter had a deeper look of crazy in his eyes.

Daniel raised his fists and bit his lip, trying to hold back. "You suck," he spat and shoved Dexter again.

"No, I think you do." Dexter smirked, barely moving an inch back as Daniel thrust at him.

Daniel looked around at everyone else in the commons. "What are you all looking at? Losers!" Then he kicked at a chair and ran from the commons back into the boys' sleeping quarters.

"What's that about?" Wes asked.

"Wow. His game must have been bad," Jaime said.

"I hope he had a lot of bees. God, I hate bees," Rose said.

The commotion at Daniel's table settled into whispers as the few left there must have been discussing what happened. Bill considered trying to move closer to hear, but before he could do that or tell his friends what he discussed with JB, the man himself walked on stage and grabbed the microphone.

"Ladies and gentlemen," JB started. He looked fresher now than when Bill had spoken to him last. JB had put on a blue blazer, as if a single piece of clothing could attract greater confidence and trust. "What a tremendous showing you all had in our second round of games. These were harder, required spontaneity and originality on your part, and as you know ended with a personal game, something different for everyone. A lot of you have been upset, but that's what real fear does. We can't play in the fiction of horror without remembering the true realities of fear. These were dark games, but I hope they also gave you some sense of relief at the end. I tested you to see if you could manage your personal terrors. But I also wanted to create something that would act as a catharsis, as only art can do."

He walked closer to the edge of the stage and looked at them with an earnest expression. "When you've had time to process it, I hope you will understand my real intentions. And if you truly want to work in this industry at my studios, I need to know everything about you, and more importantly I need to know if you have what it takes to overcome horror. The games are not over yet."

He paused and looked hard at each contestant. Bill thought JB held eye contact for a few extra seconds when he focused on Jaime and himself.

"Now it's time to unveil your current standings. Your second set of games were graded based on four elements: the practicality of your choices — whether or not your actions would have really worked, the originality of your choices — were you unique from others, the overall time it took you to complete the module, and of course whether or not in the end you were successful in overcoming your fears. Let's take a look at how all of you placed in this second round."

The screen behind JB on stage came to life once again, and Bill looked around the room. He counted only sixteen contestants. With Annie missing and Daniel having stormed off to his room, there should still be seventeen. Who else wasn't here?

The results appeared on screen, and Bill's table of friends remained quiet as first place revealed a new contestant.

"In first place, congratulations to Dexter Lange!" JB shouted.

"Well that blows," Wes said.

"In second place," JB continued. "Rose!"

"Way to go, Rose!" Wes turned into a total cheerleader. But Rose looked down, still holding the picture of her brother in her hand. This news also meant she had knocked Jaime and Bill out of the top, and Jaime could read the shy and humble expression on Rose's face. Jaime was a good sport and congratulated her, too.

"In third place, Bill!" JB stated and Bill's table erupted in applause.

"For our fourth place in this round, we say congratulations to Jaime!"

"I'm sure it's only because of time," Bill said. "You'd be even higher but you took a little long with your uncle." Catching himself, he added, "Based on what you told me, I mean."

"Yeah," she replied. "Thanks."

JB went through the additional places. So far no one else they knew had been named, not Daniel or Wes until ninth place.

"In ninth place," he continued, "Wes!"

"Yes, Wes!" Bill congratulated. "You're in the top ten now! That's huge!"

"Good job, Wes." Rose gave him a little hug, and then Jaime stood up and did the same.

"You guys gotta stop with all the group hugs." Bill laughed. "Oh-right! Let me in!" And the three wrapped their arms around Wes.

"Thanks guys," Wes said. "Better watch out now. I'm right on your tail."

"Do you guys feel weird cheering?" Jaime whispered as JB read off more names. "I feel so conflicted. I want to win this, but after the last simulations, I don't know . . . it feels . . . wrong to be excited. Do you know what I mean?"

"Yeah," Wes said. "What if it gets worse?"

"Knowing JB, it's only going to get darker." Bill frowned. "But we've gone this far. We deserve some cheers and happiness for what we've had to deal with. Don't feel weird, J. I say we use any anger at JB's simulations and put it into winning this contest. Then we can all tell him to go to hell when the weekend is over."

"I like that plan," Rose said. "I'm not quitting. I'm not giving up. But when all is done, he can kiss my ass." A little surprised at the intensity in her voice, the others laughed with Rose, ignoring the rest of the names JB had been reading until he got to Daniel.

"In seventeenth place, Daniel!"

"Holy cow," Wes said. "He went from first to almost last!" Looking around the room, they noticed that Daniel had still not returned.

"And in eighteenth place, we have Leroy."

Bill looked around for a reaction, but he didn't see Leroy either. He remembered Leroy was the guy with Daniel who laughed at pretty much anything the jerk jock said. JB added, "I'm afraid Leroy left us. As reflected in his score, he did quite poorly, and the final simulation was too much for him. He ran out of the game chamber without finishing it. We haven't found him yet, so if you see Leroy, please report it immediately to me or one of my assistants." JB looked directly at Bill. "It's too bad, but I must say Leroy was a *fool* not to finish. There's such a great reward waiting for the winner."

Jaime leaned in and whispered into Bill's ear. "Why did he say 'fool' like that? And was it just me or was he looking right at you?"

Bill shrugged, but he agreed with Jaime. Something about the way JB said it gave him goosebumps. Those remaining looked around the room. They knew enough about horror to feel that something wasn't right here, but no one knew what to do about it.

"You have the third round of games this evening after dinner. Remember the rankings I'm showing you are for each individual round, not your total ranking. The totals will be revealed at the end. You can bet that there will be many more surprises before our night is over. You won't want to miss out on that. Now, this third round of course will be the hardest yet. Maybe you should take a nap. Keep your minds focused and your bodies energized. I'll speak more of the next round after dinner."

Giving them no time for questions, JB turned quickly and left the commons.

"I simply can't imagine how much worse it can get," Jaime sighed. All of their energy was drained. The adrenaline and fun they felt earlier were gone, and they were wiped. Yesterday seemed like a year ago.

"I think we could all use some rest before we do anything else," Wes told them.

"Which kid was Leroy again?" Rose asked.

"He sat with Daniel and Dexter," Bill said. "As much as we may not want to, we should talk to them both. Figure out what happened. Then we can ask about Leroy. Who knows? Maybe when we look around we'll find more weird stuff like the axe. It has to mean something, right? Some part of a larger puzzle that's going on?"

"I agree with you," Jaime told him, "but I also agree with Wes. We're no good to anybody, not even ourselves. Set the alarm on your phone for two hours from now. If we are going to survive tonight, we have to try to rest for a bit. We barely slept last night, and who knows how long tonight will be. Let's meet back here in two hours and make a plan to talk to hashtagDbag and look around. Okay?"

"Okay," they all agreed.

Wes and Bill walked into their quarters, and Rose and Jaime into theirs. Bill still needed to tell them about his conversation with

JB. Although he wasn't exactly looking forward to it, he knew he had to talk to Daniel as well as Dexter. And they all had to go looking for Leroy now in addition to Annie. There must something else out there in the endless halls and rooms of this studio that would help make sense of what was happening.

But the mind was sharper when rested, and everything looked a little blurry after a sleepless night and intense morning. He needed to close his eyes. He needed a dreamless rest. There was enough stuff made of nightmares with his eyes open. *Give me a peaceful hour, that's all I ask,* he thought, and he closed his eyes, hoping his brain would recharge quickly. There was so much more to do.

Chapter Seventeen

Bill's hope for a dreamless rest, no matter how brief, of course did not come true. After all the images and action, his brain could not rest, even if his body was exhausted.

He was at his dad's funeral. It was a closed casket, since much of his father's face had been shot off. He remembered a stranger speaking about his father, saying wonderful things. At age eight, little Bill didn't know what the word "eulogy" meant, but if he'd been asked then he would have said, "Some guy who never knew my dad tried to say lots of nice things." It didn't make sense in his child's mind.

His mom hugged the guy who said all the nice things about his dad. He wasn't a close family member or friend, but she grabbed him and cried on his shoulder. "What do I do now?" she sobbed over and over. "What do I do? What do I do? I don't know what to do!"

Other than the terrible night his father died, this was the first time he realized his mom was not all-powerful. A child's parents were supposed to be superheroes. They could protect you from anything. But now his dad was dead, and his mom was crying and didn't know what to do. It was that moment that the young Bill knew his parents weren't superheroes. They weren't invincible. And that meant they couldn't protect him. Not really.

The scene switched and it was a little later that day. It was time to take the coffin with his daddy and put it in the ground, but Sally Wise had asked for a moment alone to say goodbye. Once the others had left the room, she grabbed on to her son and waited until everyone had left.

"I have to see him, Billy. I have to know it's really him in there. That it's not just a box we are putting in the ground. I have to see him."

She went to the coffin, still clutching onto Bill, dragging him along whether he wanted to go or not. She opened the side of the casket. There was Arnie. Sally gasped, but then leaned in closer.

"It's not as bad as I was afraid of," she murmured. "Do you

want to see your dad one more time, Billy?"

"I guess." Bill shrugged, not really knowing what he wanted.

Sally pulled him closer, and Bill looked into the coffin. His father's face and jaw were bruised, and flesh colored mortician's makeup covered the side of his head where he was shot. That was the last time he'd see his dad's face. Not a smile, not life, only bandages, darkness, and bruises: that wasn't his father. And so he refused to say good-bye.

Sally looked at her son, but she didn't comfort him.

After the burial, Sally bought a gallon of vodka and drove to her parents' house where they'd stay for a while. She locked herself in her old bedroom and drank herself to sleep.

*****

"Shh."

Bill awoke with a hand over his mouth.

"Don't say a word."

The image on top of him slowly came in to focus. Daniel wasn't wearing his usual grin, however. He possessed a look of desperation and whispered, "I didn't want you to scream and alert anyone. That's all. Please listen." He slowly moved his hand from Bill's mouth.

"I need your help," Daniel confessed.

Bill sat up, adjusting himself to this surprise, trying to think of how to respond.

"Look, I know you think I'm an asshole. I *am* an asshole. But something's not right here, and I know that you know that, too."

"Okay," Bill muttered, still groggy and confused.

"I knew Leroy. He was weird, but he wouldn't run away. All he wanted to get out of this was friends. Not the toughest kid, but I don't see him giving up. He wouldn't run away," Daniel repeated. "I think he was kidnapped."

"Kidnapped?"

"Like Annie."

"Like Annie? What do you know about that?"

"I know JB is up to more than he's telling. The two kids in last

141

place both run away? Coincidence? No, man. They were taken."

"Taken?" Bill repeated.

"I know it," Daniel stated. "I saw it. Leroy, anyway."

"How?"

"When I . . . uh, when I finished this last round, I saw Leroy. Two of the assistants—Samara and Sam—were escorting him out of his game chamber. He didn't disappear. He's been taken somewhere. And if it's true for him, you know it's true for Annie, too."

"Why are you coming to me?" Bill asked.

"Because you and I . . . well, I think you're like me."

"I'm not an asshole."

Daniel frowned. "Hey. I do what I have to do to win. You'd do the same."

"That's not true," Bill argued. "My passion isn't about my ego."

"Yeah?" Daniel challenged. "Why do you want to win this game?"

"I . . . I . . ." Bill closed his mouth. If he couldn't explain it to himself, he definitely wasn't going to try to explain it to Daniel.

"You see? You think you're a smart guy, and you have passion. I have passion, too. We're the same."

"No, we're not. I have passion, but I don't have to prove myself or get people to go along with me. I'm in this game only for myself. I love this stuff. It was an adventure."

"And to win," Daniel said. "To show Jaime and your parents and whoever that you are really smart."

"Jaime? Maybe. My parents? My mom barely talks to me and probably doesn't remember I'm even here. And my dad is dead, asshole." Bill looked away. What was Daniel's motive? He took a deep breath and wondered how much more he really wanted to share.

For once, Daniel looked normal. His slouched head and posture, sitting at the side of the bed, could almost be interpreted as empathy.

"Why don't you ask Dexter to help you?" Bill tried to hurt Daniel more, thinking of the fight those two had in the commons after the last round.

"You think I'm an idiot? There's something really wrong with that dude."

"What do you know about him?"

"I know he has no heart."

"The same could be said about you," Bill replied.

Daniel looked down at the floor. "Do you want to know what my simulation was?"

"I guess."

"It was every day of my life. It started in my home at breakfast before school. My dad teased me about my haircut, and my mom never stood up for me. My dad finds a way to tease me every day. 'Oh, you're good at basketball?' he'd say. 'Try a man's sport like football.' So I tried out for football. 'How come you let that guy tackle you? I never got tackled as much as you,' he'd say. I spent every day after school in the damn weight room because of him, trying to get bigger. I became a gym rat to prove myself to someone who would never care, no matter how well I did in anything."

Daniel took a breath and glanced up at Bill. Bill rolled his eyes but gestured for the other boy to continue.

"This last game of JB's — my dad kept yelling and yelling at me." Daniel looked at the ceiling, the floor, anywhere but at Bill. "He was the villain. I didn't know how to defeat him. Never have. In the simulation, I tried to show him what I could do—that I could bench a lot or run fast or slam a ball. I kept showing him everything I could, but he kept laughing. This went on and on until the screen went to black and said, 'Sorry. You have failed.' I was furious. Furious at this stupid game and furious at my dad and furious at myself. I stormed out of the game chamber, but as I did I saw Leroy being escorted by Samara and Sam. I didn't think anything of it until someone told me Leroy was missing."

Bill tried to process everything Daniel had told him. He didn't want to feel sorry for Daniel. And, yeah, maybe he did have an ego; if nothing else, Bill wanted to be right that Daniel was the hashtagDbag they accused him of being and that he deserved anything bad he got.

But as he listened to the story about Daniel's dad, it started to make sense. *If you're never accepted, then you can go to extremes to prove yourself.* Some people didn't care, but Daniel clearly did.

"I was so mad after I failed," Daniel continued, "that I must've had tears in my eyes when I left the game chamber. That's when Dexter saw me. He cracked a joke, totally heartless. And I even thought we were friends. I told him to go to hell. After he left, I stayed in the halls a bit longer to, you know, stop looking like shit. But Leroy never came back."

"Do you know what you needed to do to win that last simulation?" Bill asked.

"No," he confessed. "I seriously tried everything."

"There's one thing you didn't try. You needed to stop trying."

"What are you talking about? That's dumb."

"I'm sayin'. . . I think it was designed to get you to recognize that sometimes no matter how hard you try, there will be people who don't approve. You need to stop giving a shit. If you had done that in the simulation, I'm guessing you would have won."

Bill studied Daniel's face as a light bulb moment of discovery blew up in his eyes. "Damn!" Daniel said. "Damn that JB! Damn this game! I could kill him."

"So, why is it again you are coming to me with all of this?" Bill asked.

"I guess . . . I think . . . I know you're . . . smart. Even if I didn't want to admit it. You got to work with the best of the best to win." Daniel looked down at the floor. "Even if they may be better than you."

"Tell me how you won the first round. Did you cheat?"

"No!"

"Really?"

"Hey," Daniel defended, "I knew the movies in that first round like the back of my hand. I love horror, too. Those movies were my escape. From my dad. From everything. I must have watched them a thousand times."

"Oh-right. I believe you," Bill admitted. He really didn't want to admit that someone like Daniel — such an ass on the outside — could know more than him, but it was clear not everything was as it seemed. Daniel might have had a good memory, but the fact that he cared too much about what others thought of him resulted in a rather distasteful display of narcissism.

"Hey. Regardless of what you think of me, I'm trying to do something right. Will you help me find Leroy?"

"Okay. But first, let's gather my friends. They can help us."

"I've never been one to ask for help."

"I can tell," Bill snorted. "There's a first for everything. You know, not asking for help is what an asshole does, asshole.

Daniel eyed Bill curiously. "Where'd you learn that?"

"From my friends."

Daniel paused for a moment. "So I'm asking for help. Am I still an asshole?"

Bill laughed. "Yes. For now. But you're making me reconsider."

"Okay. That's something. But Bill, I have one more thing I need to tell you."

"What's that?"

"After we figure out this missing person thing, I'm still gonna win this game."

"Bring it, man. I do best with some competition."

"See? You are like me." Daniel grinned.

Bill rolled his eyes. He'd rather not be similar to an arrogant, over-confident know-it-all. *So don't be an asshole, asshole.*

*****

Bill noticed Wes's fake yawn. And that stretch? Bill had to hold back a laugh. Hadn't Wes seen enough movies to know an over-exaggerated stretch is exactly what you shouldn't do if you want people to pretend you've been asleep?

"What's going on?" Wes asked as he continued to stretch.

"Hey. Daniel came to us for help to find Leroy," Bill told him, jerking his head toward Daniel. "I agreed we should work together."

"Um, really?" Wes questioned.

"Daniel knows more about Leroy than we do." Bill raised his eyebrows and nodded, hoping Wes would see that Bill wasn't totally sold here either.

"If you say so."

They left the room to go get Rose and Jaime, but they didn't have to go far. The girls were already walking toward their room.

"Hey," Jaime greeted. "We thought we'd get you boys up. Not much time before the next round, so if we're going to find . . . um, what are you doing here?" she said when she spotted Daniel.

"He's with us. For now," Bill said. "I'll explain later. But he wants to find Leroy, and he came to us to help him."

Jaime looked Daniel up and down. "Hmm. Okay. But we aren't going to take any bullshit. You got that?"

Daniel nodded, but Jaime continued to look at him suspiciously.

Bill hoped the others wouldn't reveal too much about their search for Annie and the discovery of the axe, which still rested underneath Bill's bed. He was willing to work with Daniel, but he wanted to play it safe and not reveal every card in his hand. He also didn't want Daniel to know about JB's earlier conversation with the assistants in the *Halloween II* hall Wes and he had overheard. With Daniel's ego, Bill thought the boy could easily flip out if it was discovered Bill and company had a little extra insight on the previous round of games. He also wanted to tell the crew about his face-to-face chat with JB, but he wasn't going to do it in front of Daniel. *Never reveal your entire hand unless you're one hundred percent sure nothing can go wrong,* he thought. And he knew this night was far from over.

"Let's cover new territory," Bill suggested. "We checked the outside halls last night when Annie went missing. There's definitely more to this place beyond the game chambers. Let's go that way."

The group agreed. Bill knew they'd finally see JB's main monitoring chamber where he was able to watch all of the contestants. But he'd let that be a surprise as they didn't know he had been past the game rooms at all.

"Freddy's claws and Jason's balls!" Rose exclaimed. "What is that?" They had walked beyond all of the game rooms and were now at JB's monitoring room.

"I've never seen so many TVs!" Jamie laughed. "These must be connected to our game chambers. JB has to watch somehow, right? He must watch us here. And what was that you yelled, Rose?"

"Right," Bill agreed. They stopped and stared outside the large glass door. JB's black swivel chair was tucked perfectly under a main table which held the largest of the monitors, the one on which Bill had watched Jaime save her uncle. All the monitors were turned off, and JB was nowhere in sight.

"Wow." Daniel gave a low whistle. "All of this is such incredible technology. JB must be loaded."

"No doubt," Wes said. "The man's a billionaire." He looked at Rose. "So, Freddy's claws and Jason's balls, eh?"

"You shut up," she said with a smile. "I don't know where that came from."

They laughed for a moment, and then continued on their quest. Moving past JB's monitoring station, they entered another large, warehouse-sized room. The back wall was covered in green screens, something used to capture special effects and different settings right here in the studio. The room had dozens of different types of cameras and light fixtures.

"See if you notice anything unusual," Jaime suggested.

"It's all unusual to me," Bill said.

"It's some kind of storage area is all," Daniel said. "Doesn't look weird to me."

"Let's keep going," Jaime told them.

On the opposite side of this storage area, they pushed two large double doors open and entered a new hallway.

"Now we're getting somewhere," Wes declared. "Look at this!"

A pair of black rail cars on a track, much like a child's ride at a carnival, emerged from the other side of the heavy doors they had pushed open. The rest of the hallway was dark, but there was a control switch on the side of the wall by the cars.

"Should we go for ride?" Jaime asked.

"Absolutely! What could go wrong?" Bill replied. "You guys get in the cars. I'll hit the buttons and jump in."

Rose and Wes sat in the front car, and Jaime and Daniel took the rear car. Bill felt a wave of jealousy he didn't like, but he pressed a green button labeled start and jumped in the back car. It was a tight fit, and they had to squeeze close together. The cars started moving at a very slow place, but as they moved forward, different sections of the hallway lit up.

Wes turned around. "We're in a fun house!" His eyes showed excitement and curiosity. "I've always loved fun houses."

As the cars moved forward, animatronic clowns, like the one from *Killer Klowns* that first greeted them on the outside of the studio entrance, jumped out from the sides of the tracks.

"Never mind what I just said," Wes joked. Skeletons dangled from the ceilings, madmen hid behind caged bars, and each machine greeted them with piercing screams or lunatic laughter.

"This is great!" Rose laughed.

"Yeah," Bill said. "Let's not forget what we're looking for though."

She nodded, and all of their smiles faded. It was easy to get lost in the magnificent wonders of this studio, but they were on a mission: find clues about anything that might lead them to Leroy or Annie.

The fun house car turned slightly, and they witnessed a spectacular spinning light show that made them feel as if they were falling. The lights made the area appear as a tunnel, and the illusions moved clockwise as fast as shooting stars. Bill had to close his eyes.

"This is making me feel sick," Jaime groaned.

"Yeah, seriously, this is messed up," Daniel agreed.

"Close your eyes," Bill said.

The cars passed through the spinning tunnel and stopped.

"Is everyone okay?" Bill asked. "That was trippy."

"Yeah. Dizzy. But okay," Jaime answered and the others nodded. They stood up, trying to get a grip on reality and find their balance.

"What's this?" Daniel asked.

They were now facing several mirrors that were formed to make a narrow path.

"It looks like a maze," Rose said. "But, you guys, back there—"

"Cool!" Wes said "Let's check it out."

The mirrors were as much of a mind-bend as the spinning

tunnel. They first went to the right, but found themselves in a dead end. Then they tried the left. Another dead end.

"What the hell?" Daniel asked.

"The mirrors are creating an illusion of a path and an illusion of a dead end, I think," Wes said. "Let's go back to the right."

They followed Wes, squeezing in between mirrors, some of which employed classic fun house illusions, making them look very small and fat or very tall and skinny.

"See, it's a dead end," Daniel told Wes when they reached the end of the right path again.

"No." Wes smiled. "Look at this." It looked like he was walking directly into the mirror, but as he predicted, the mirrors only presented an illusion of a dead end. There was a very small path that went beyond, and they had to feel for the path with their hands on the mirrors. It could not be seen.

"This is amazing," Bill said. "How do they do that?"

"Vision is a funny thing," Jaime said. "We can be tricked into seeing anything."

Beyond the mirrored path, they found themselves at the end of the fun house hallway to another door. Wes tried it, but it was locked.

"I wonder where this goes," Wes said.

"Damn!" Daniel double-checked the door. "Now what?"

"What's that?" Rose asked.

Near the door was a small chest, and Wes walked over to open it. "Holy shit. It's gold!"

"Are you kidding?" Jaime asked.

"No. Look." Wes was telling the truth. Inside this small chest near the locked door was a stack of gold coins. "Do you think they're real?"

"Real or not, they've been put here for a reason. Some other kind of clue?" Bill wondered.

"Let's take some with us. Who knows what it could mean," Jaime said. "Should we head back?"

"Wait, you guys," Rose started. "There was something in the spinning tunnel. I tried to keep my eyes open the whole time. I saw some kind of trap door on the floor."

"I guess we have to go back one way or the other." Wes shrugged. "Let's walk this time and check out that door."

They slipped back through the mirrors, and the spinning light greeted them again. "I can manage this, somehow," Rose said. "Hold hands, close your eyes, and follow me. I'll get us there."

Rose guided them in a single line, each one holding on to the person in front and behind them, eyes closed, trying not to be sick.

"Here," she said. "Check it out."

They opened their eyes, the light in the tunnel still spinning.

"That's a trap door all right," Bill said. "But look, it's chained shut." A small silver chain had been tied around the handles of the door.

"So what do we do now?" Daniel asked.

"We have to break into that room."

"With what?" Daniel wondered.

"I have exactly the thing." Bill hesitated for a moment, looking in each of their eyes for understanding. "It's under my bed."

Chapter Eighteen

"What's under your bed?" Daniel asked Bill.

"There's something we should tell you," Bill said. "But let's talk and walk. How much time do we have before we're supposed to be back?"

Daniel took out his cell phone to check the time. It was running on a very low battery and, like the others, had no service inside the studio. "About an hour."

"Okay, that gives us enough time to get back to my room and then back down here and see what's behind that trap door. But we have to hurry."

They ran out of the fun house, Rose still leading the way until they could escape the spinning tunnel. Quickly moving on, they passed JB's monitoring station, still empty, and the hall of game chambers, also vacant. Bill told Daniel the story of their search for Annie.

"We met the girls in Annie's room," he said quickly. "It was pretty identical except that it had an old typewriter on the desk. From there, we explored the main hallways we saw when we first entered the studio. The *It* hall, *The Shining* hall, and the *Halloween II* hall. Outside of *The Shining* hall, we found an axe. We figured it had to be a clue to something, and it seemed all too obvious based on where we found it that it was the axe Jack chased his family with in the movie. So I held on to it and put it under my bed. We can use it to break the chains and see what's behind that trap door."

"Wait a sec." Daniel stopped. "What about the typewriter in Annie's room?"

"It was missing the letter n," Rose told him.

"Oh, and wasn't there something in the desk?" Wes asked. "It was a bunch of paper. But only the top sheet had something written on it. What was that again, Bill?"

"Fast Cars."

"The letter n?" Daniel yelped. "Fast Cars? You didn't catch that? None of you?" He looked incredulous.

"It didn't ring a bell," Bill said slowly, trying to reconsider those details.

"Haven't you read Stephen King's *Misery*?"

"I'm *trying* to read his entire library," Bill said defensively. "But no, I haven't read that."

"None of you have read that book?" Daniel asked.

"I've seen the movie," Wes said, and the others all nodded.

"Shit, you guys!" Daniel yelled. "That axe isn't about *The Shining*. It's about *Misery*."

"Um, explain," Jaime demanded.

"Okay," he started. "The book is about a writer. Paul Sheldon. He's gotten famous writing a series of novels about a character called Misery. Paul gets into a bad accident and is rescued by someone who claims to be his biggest fan—Annie Wilkes. *Annie!* She takes him in and finds Paul's latest manuscript. In the book, it's called *Fast Cars*. It's not about Misery at all and she hates it. She nurses Paul back to health and during that time, the latest Misery novel comes out. She reads it and becomes furious because Paul killed off Misery and planned on ending the series. She gives him a typewriter, which is missing the letter n, and forces him to write a new Misery book. When Paul tries to escape, she cuts off his foot with an *axe*. She even cut off his thumb with an electric knife when he complained about the missing letter on the typewriter."

"Wow!" they gasped.

"I can't believe I skipped that book!" Bill slapped his own forehead.

"You know what else?" Rose added. "When there was a buffet of food after the first round of games, the only silverware on the table was an electric knife. Another hint, I guess?"

"So the psycho in *Misery* is named Annie. And the first person missing is named Annie," Wes mused. "She had the same typewriter and manuscript from the book to give us clues to the novel. And then there's the axe. So why was the axe outside *The Shining* hall?"

"And wait a minute," Wes said. "Annie was in last place at the end of round one. Leroy was in last place at the end of round two. Is that a coincidence? If Annie's name was a clue, then what the hell does Leroy's name mean?"

"I can't think of a single Leroy in any horror story," Jaime said. "Maybe it doesn't mean anything."

"What about the gold coins?" Wes asked. "Is there a Leroy in a story connected to gold?"

"There must be, right? But I don't know off the top of my head," Bill confessed. The others shrugged as well. "Let's stick to the original plan for now. Get the axe, break open the trap door, and see what we find. That should help give us some answers."

They all nodded and continued toward Bill and Wes's room. Bill mentally berated himself the entire walk back about not catching the clues to *Misery*. He prided himself on being a King expert. He tried to tell himself it would be impossible to have read everything the man had written, not yet anyway. But if he missed something that Daniel picked up so easily, was he really ready for the final round of this game? There was so much out there, so many movies and books. How was one person supposed to know it all?

Bill also tried to remember everything JB told him in their face-to-face conversation. JB knew that Bill had the axe. What exactly had JB said about it?

When you figure out what it means, tell me, and if you're correct, I'll give you another answer.

Bill wanted to run to JB with the solution, even if it was Daniel who discovered it, but at the same time, they needed to know what the trap door was hiding. Which to do first?

He still needed to tell the others about this conversation, but he hesitated to do so in front of Daniel. Daniel had been a big help in making the *Misery* connection, but Bill wondered how much they could trust him. And if these mysteries were perhaps some other game JB was playing with them, did he really want to give Daniel any extra edge? Bill shook these thoughts away. No one else knew what JB had told him about the axe. He had time, and they could begin by finding out what was behind the trap door.

With less than an hour until the final round of games was to begin, people had already started gathering back in the commons. The group received quite a handful of stares, and a couple of Daniel's friends who had always sat with him at his table shared the same look of disbelief when they saw the five walking together. Bill examined the table of friends and Daniel's reaction, and he saw Daniel nod and wink back at his friends.

Was Daniel playing them somehow? Or was it a nod and a wink to reassure his friends that nothing was wrong?

"Hold up," Wes whispered. "Um, how exactly are we going to sneak an axe past everyone in the commons? We're already getting stared at. An axe isn't something we can slip in our pocket."

"Shoot," Bill said. "I hadn't even thought of that." He shook his head, frustrated again at another little detail he hadn't considered.

"What should we do?" Daniel asked.

"Let's talk in my room," Bill suggested. "At least we'll have a bit of privacy."

Entering the boys' room, Bill's first action was to check that the axe was in the same place. He breathed a sigh of relief seeing it still there and sat on his bed. Jaime took a seat on the end of Bill's bed. Wes and Rose sat on the other, and Daniel remained standing.

"You're right," Rose said to Wes. "We can't walk out across the commons with an axe. That will look a little odd, I'm guessing." She smiled.

"Maybe we could ask one of the assistants to carry it across for us?" Daniel suggested.

"They have to know what's going on, too. Don't you think?" Jaime asked him. "It's best we do this on our own."

"But how?" Wes wondered.

They sat thinking, the clock ticking down to the third round on this incredibly strange Halloween weekend.

"I have an idea," Jaime said. "If we want to avoid getting seen by anyone, I think there's only one possibility." They others leaned in, and Jaime softened her voice. "Whichever of us finishes first in this next round comes back here right away. That person moves the axe to the fun house. We can hide it in the spinning tunnel for now. Place it by the trap door. Anyone who finds that area is going to be too dizzy to see it. Then we'll meet up after the third round and see what's in that door."

"But what happens after the third round?" Rose asked. "Isn't that the last round?"

"I don't know what is going to happen," Jaime said. "But we don't go home until tomorrow. Everyone's return ticket home is for tomorrow, right?" They all nodded. "So we know we will be here one more night. It may be the end of the games, but we'll have time to meet and figure this out. And I think this is all part of the game, too."

"It's a twisted game." Wes sighed. "And it only gets weirder as we go."

"Yeah," Jaime agreed. "So what do you guys think?"

"I think it's our best bet. Good idea, Jaime," Bill told her. "Okay, so as soon as you finish this round of games, come right back here, get the axe, and hide it near the trap door." He was looking at all of them. "If it's not here, assume someone else finished before you and already got it."

"And don't go exploring alone," Rose added. "I have a weird feeling about all of this. No matter what, hide the axe in the tunnel, but wait as long as possible for us. Or at least one of us. Nothing less than a pair. I don't think anyone should be searching alone, you know?"

They all nodded again.

"Okay, I'm going to meet up with my friends," Daniel said. "I'll do my best to make sure they don't think anything odd is happening."

"What are you going to tell them?" Bill asked.

"I'll say that you guys had some info on Leroy, and so I went to listen out of curiosity." Daniel shrugged. "Then I'll tell them you're all weird and your ideas are weirder and make fun of you. They'll eat it up and won't think anything of it."

"HashtagDbag," Jaime whispered under her breath.

"Hey," Daniel said putting a hand on her shoulder. Bill tensed. He was getting tired of how often HashtagDbag was touching Jaime. "We all have a role to play. We all wear different faces. Life is like the movies, or the movies are like life. Whichever. The face I wear around them is not my only face."

"Why wear that face at all?" she asked him.

Daniel groaned. "It's easy to wear. And it fits." He removed his hand from her shoulder, and Bill relaxed a little. Daniel walked out of the room but turned in the doorway. "G'luck, guys. See you after the games."

"Bye," they said together.

"Man, what do you think?" Wes asked after Daniel left.

"I don't trust him," Rose said. "Something's off. And one of us better win this round before him. I don't trust that he'd wait for us."

"Agreed," Jaime nodded. "Game faces, everyone. Let's win this thing."

"Wait" Bill huffed. "I've been dying to tell you guys something!"

"Gentleman, and ooh, ladies, hello to you, too." A voice laughed from the hall. It was Captain Spaulding, aka Chester. "Fifteen minutes until you need to be back in the commons. I suggest you freshen up a bit. This next round is going to be a killer." He laughed again. "Girls, shall I escort you back to your own quarters?"

"We can get there fine on our own," Jaime said.

"Very well. Don't be late now." Chester smiled again, a creepy, yellow-stained teeth smile precisely like the Captain in *A House of 1000 Corpses*, and left.

"What is it, Bill?" Jaime asked him once Chester was gone.

"I've been wanting to tell you since it happened, but I didn't want to say it in front of Daniel," he started. "I had a one-on-one with JB. I was upset after the last round of games. I couldn't believe he'd use real memories like that. These games were supposed to be fun, right? After I finished my games, I stormed out and demanded to see him."

"What did he tell you?" They all wanted to know.

Bill started with how JB had known about their fears, how he had searched for information on their personal lives from blogs, social media, anything they wrote or was written about them online, as well as access to their phones when they downloaded the Rabbit in Red app. He told them how JB defended the fear simulations, how JB was ambiguous about the reward for winning the contest, but that it seemed much more than just an internship and cash. He told them what JB said about the axe, and his promise of another answer or something when they had figured it out. Finally, he told them that he asked JB about the third round tonight, and that JB said testing a person's ability to deal with terror took more than a couple of games.

"That's incredible," Wes said. "You should go tell him about the axe now!"

"Even though we didn't figure it out?" Bill asked. "Should we give Daniel some credit, too?"

"I don't know," Jaime said. "He wouldn't do that for us."

"And that's exactly why we have to give him credit when it's due," Rose added.

"Yeah, okay. But now or after the third round?"

"Might as well finish round three," Jaime said. "We've only got a few minutes, and we should focus on one thing at a time. Let's stick to the plan, but after we check the trap door, let's tell JB what we've discovered. What about everything else JB said? Do you guys trust him?"

"I don't know what to think," Bill admitted. "Part of me likes him. What he said makes sense, kinda. But I think even the most ambitious minds can take things too far."

"Yeah, especially if they have a ton of money to throw around like he does," Rose said. "There's a lot we don't know about JB. I just wish our damn phones worked in here. If we could at least text one another in case . . ."

"Right," Jaime said. "In case one of us goes missing next."

"Remember what Daniel said. He saw Leroy escorted away," Wes said. "JB is telling us that Leroy's missing. It's a game within a game. Nothing to worry about, right?"

"What do we do if it's not a game?" Rose asked. "What do we do if we're really in trouble?" Rose, Jaime, and Wes all looked at Bill.

"We fight," he said. "No video games, no wireless gloves, no 4D effects. We punch the sons of bitches in their faces and run like hell. Can you guys do that if you're in trouble?"

They nodded, albeit hesitantly, and Bill smiled.

"Okay," Bill said, taking a deep breath. "Let's do this together. Let's beat the hell out of these games tonight. Let's check the trap door and go to JB right after. Together. We're a team now. I don't care who wins."

They all smiled. "Okay, now remember," Jaime said to all of them, putting her arm around Bill's waist. "I know we have our doubts, but if things get scary, if they get worse than they did in the last round, we have to tell ourselves it's only a game. I don't know how JB can make anything worse or scarier in the next round than what we've already seen, but I have no doubt that he will try. Beat the challenges, and then we meet back in the commons. Okay?"

"Oh-right," Bill agreed.

"Oh-right," the others echoed. "Let's do this!"

Part II, Round III

Kill the Rabbit in

Red

"We should never try to deny the beast, the animal within us."

—Dr. George Waggner from *The Howling*.

"I've seen enough horror movies to know that any weirdo wearing a mask is never friendly."

—Elizabeth from *Friday the 13ᵗʰ Part VI: Jason Lives*.

"We came, we saw, we kicked its ass!"

—Dr. Peter Venkman from *Ghostbusters*.

"It's been a funny sort of day, hasn't it?"

—Barbara from *Shaun of the Dead*.

"Darling. Light of life. I'm not gonna hurt ya. You didn't let me finish my sentence. I'm not gonna hurt ya. I'm just gonna bash your brains in."

—Jack from *The Shining*.

"Trust is a tough thing to come by these days." —MacReady from *The Thing*.

Chapter Nineteen

"My friends," Jay Bell greeted everyone back at the commons. "I hope you've been having a defrightfully good time!"

JB chuckled into the microphone and examined the contestants remaining in the room. The remaining contestants no longer greeted him with cheers and applause.

"I understand that by now you all have experienced more than a game," he said. "You've experienced terror. Real terror from your memories of what frightens you the most. But you must understand that this is no amusement park. This is a test. You've demonstrated great knowledge in re-enactments, you've revealed your creativity in saving the victims, and," he scanned the room and focused on the two empty chairs where Leroy and Annie previously sat, "most of you have faced your fears. Some of you overcame them. Some did not. Our second round of games was intense for all of you, but you see I had to test not only your horror knowledge, but also your ability to overcome genuine horror. The reward, my friends, will be worth it.

"Now, take a deep breath with me." He inhaled slowly. "Let it all out." He exhaled loudly. "Do it again with me," he repeated. "Do you have what it takes to continue? You do not have to stay, and I cannot make any promises that this next round will be less frightening. In fact, it may be the scariest yet!"

JB cackled into the microphone again. His presence appeared bigger than ever, the size of Daniel and Dexter combined. "So, are you all with me? Stand if you wish to continue. Stand if you wish to finish this game and KILL THE RABBIT IN RED!"

Daniel jumped up, the first to rise. Bill followed, along with Jaime, Rose, and Wes. Slowly, everyone else in the room stood up, and not a single person remained seated.

"Excellent!" JB said. "Now, shall I preview the next round? I think you'll need all the help you can get."

He had managed to cheer up and re-energize the crowd. A group to the right of Bill's table clapped, and there were even a few "woos" and "yeahs" from the contestants.

"Haha, you will love the next part of our Fright Fest!" JB

continued. "But first, to be fair, you should know there are other mysteries at play here. Not everything will be solved in the game chambers. For those of you who have discovered other mysteries, come to me when you have solutions, and I will reward you appropriately."

Bill exchanged looks with Daniel, and Daniel's eyes grew wide. Bill knew, even more so now, that they would have to beat this round before Daniel. The others in the room looked around in confusion, except for Dexter. Bill caught Dexter staring at Daniel with anger and suspicion. It wouldn't be long, Bill thought, before others knew that more was going on at Rabbit in Red than the 4D Fright Fest.

"Let's focus on your next challenge," JB continued. "In this next round, you will not be a victim or a hero or a savior. You will be the villain! You will be evil itself!" He shouted and the screen behind him on stage lowered. "Let's take a look at what's in store for you next!"

The black screen came to life revealing a ghostly white mask, the iconic mask of the famous *Halloween* slasher. "In your first contest, you will become Michael Myers. An audience for any movie always enjoys a happy ending, don't you think? You rooted for Laurie Strode to escape from Michael's wrath, but you knew all along that surely she would make it, yes? In most horror films, we know many of the side characters will get axed."

He grinned and focused on Bill. "But we also know the main character in an overwhelming majority of films will survive. There has to be a sequel, right? There has to be a reason for audiences to cheer at the end and feel a sense of relief and redemption as our hero or heroine takes out the bad guy. But what if that changed? What if our hero tragically died, and horror films ended with a celebration of the villain instead? That is your challenge tonight! You will combine your knowledge of the film with your originality and creativity. The quickest to find, catch, and kill the star wins!"

A few people cheered, but Bill felt sick to his stomach. He could already picture himself in the game chamber, chasing the innocent heroine and killing mercilessly. This was no eight-bit video game. The simulation in the chambers felt like reality, and the thought of killing an innocent person, even if it was fiction, produced a morbid sense of doom in the pit of his stomach. Jaime reached out and held Bill's hand. The tension he felt told him that she also had a bad feeling about this.

"*Halloween*, especially the original, has always been one of my favorites," JB said. "It's a simple story Hollywood has tried to clone time and time again. This time though, you must kill Laurie Strode, and you must do so quickly if you want to win my contest."

The classic John Carpenter *Halloween* theme played in the background as the screen went to black. The next image to appear on the screen was also a mask, and its shape slowly formed a leather imprisonment that enclosed the mouth, leaving a few gaps for breathing, but preventing whoever would wear the mask from biting. It was the face guard worn by Hannibal Lecter.

"Oh, God," Jaime whispered to Bill. "He didn't simply kill. He ate his victims."

Bill felt his stomach turn again, and JB continued. "In the second game, you will play as the one and only Hannibal Lecter. You will start in your jail cell from *The Silence of the Lambs*, but you will find that I've left the jail cell open for you. Your goal is to kill Clarice Starling, our FBI agent and heroine of the film. In this particular game, I'm really testing your tolerance for gore. You will receive points not only for killing Clarice, but for what you do with her after." JB laughed.

The crowd groaned and JB chuckled even harder. "Care for dessert now?"

The screen blacked out, and this time there was no mask, but instead a face of a crazy-eyed man, hair a mess, eyes of the devil. It was Jack Nicholson, the actor who played the character Jack in *The Shining*.

"You should have known that this classic would appear based on the halls that led up to the commons here. One of my favorites, of course, and weren't you a little sad that Jack never gets the satisfaction of killing his son Danny?" His smile grew impossibly large. "You'll start on a stairway in the Overlook Hotel and work your way up to your wife, who is swinging a bat in your face.

You've lost it by this point, and if you don't know this part of the film, well then I don't know how you've made it this far. But there's a trick here. A catch. This will be the hardest of all. I'm not telling you why. You'll have to figure it out, but I warn you that you need to kill your victims in the quickest amount of time to earn the highest score. So try not to take too much time on those stairs."

JB laughed one last time, to some kind of inside joke that only he got. Bill and Jaime looked at one another and shrugged.

"Those are your three challenges in this round. Head back to the commons, when and if you finish. You have only one hour to complete these. If you cannot finish in one hour, you will be disqualified. We'll meet back here at that time to reveal the final scores. Good luck and get ready to KILL THE RABBIT IN RED!"

He marched off the stage. The assistants lined the front of the stage and motioned everyone to come forward.

"This is it, huh?" Jaime asked Bill. "We have to finish to win, and, even then, we have to be the quickest."

"We've made it this far." He reached out and hugged Jaime. She put her head against his chest. He bowed his head, his face gently touching her hair. He wanted the games to be over, if for nothing else to have this feeling again, to hug Jaime at the end, to strengthen their friendship, to be possibly something much more.

She pulled away slowly and looked into his eyes. "Good luck," she whispered and leaned in and kissed him gently on the lips.

Bill swallowed hard. This was what he had hoped for all weekend! He didn't want to let her go. He didn't even want to speak. *That inner dork will open his stupid mouth. You know it will happen!*

Shut up, stupid! She likes the inner dork. He blinked hard and smiled.

"You, too," he said simply. Jaime smiled back. That made him feel almost as good as the kiss.

Off they went, hand in hand, led by the assistants to the game chambers. They shouted a good luck to Rose and Wes, and Bill even locked eyes with Daniel for a brief moment and nodded.

Everything happened so quickly, and in another blink of the eye, Bill was back in the game chamber. He took a moment to look around. Was it only yesterday that he was here for the first time? It felt much longer than that. He smiled at the memory of his first game, the pure fun moment of becoming Jason to beat Freddy. His smile morphed into a nervous frown as he put on the 4D helmet, thinking of the fearful memory of saving his mom and dad.

What was his mom doing now? Was she thinking of him at all? It had been a full day here now. He had texted her when he landed at the LAX airport to tell her he had arrived safely and would be home on Sunday, but of course had been unable to make or receive contact since then. Strange how so much could happen in such a short amount of time. He put on the 4D gloves, looked at the dark symbols of the rabbit on one hand and the axe on the other, and waited for the vision of black to come alive in a new round of games.

The bloody white rabbit in the ominous red box awaited him on screen, then the *Halloween* theme played and a pumpkin appeared on screen. He felt the room move and experienced a wave of nausea, even though it was only the shift of visuals making him feel dizzy. He was transported into the pumpkin itself, and looking around, Bill saw the orange threads and seeds from inside the pumpkin. Then the pumpkin exploded, seeds and orange goo flying everywhere. JB had had fun programming these images, for sure.

The ghostly white mask of Michael Myers appeared, spun around, and inserted itself onto Bill's face. He was now looking into a mirror, and he had transformed into Myers, wearing a long, dark jumpsuit, and holding a butcher knife in his right hand. His vision was limited now thanks to the mask, and he had to fully shift right or left to see his surroundings.

JB had programmed the game to drop Bill as Myers off in the street across from where Laurie Strode was babysitting that Halloween night. She was pounding and screaming at a door, but no one would help her. Bill knew he needed to catch her quickly and so he started to run. Strangely, the movable floor had increased in resistance, and no matter how fast Bill tried to run, Michael would only walk. Like in the movie, Myers never ran. He stalked with a patient and determined walk that, regardless of practicality, somehow made for creepier and more suspenseful scenes. So Bill walked toward Laurie Strode.

She was in front of her house now, or rather the house where she had been babysitting, banging on the door and screaming for the kids to wake up and let her in. Bill continued to walk toward her, and she looked back over her shoulder, shrieking, crying, and screaming as only Jamie Lee could. The children let her in before Bill could catch her, and now he had to think. He knew she would go upstairs, lock the children in the bathroom, and hide in a closet. In the movie, Michael would find her in the closet and get poked in the eye with a clothes hanger, and she'd run to get the kids and tell them to go to the neighbor's and have the police called. Then she'd collapse foolishly on the stairs as Michael would get up and go after her once again, but by then Dr. Loomis, Michael's psychiatrist, would appear and shoot him.

Bill did not have much time at all, and he suspected he needed to accomplish his task before Loomis arrived. Bill walked to the side of the house and broke a window, not caring about the noise. Laurie was panicking and not thinking clearly. She'd go to that closet, and Bill would have to guard his eyes and get her there.

He walked up the stairs and to the back room. He examined the closet where he knew Laurie was hiding. He felt an odd adrenaline rush to experience horror from the perspective of the villain, even though he was horrified by the fact that he had to kill Laurie, the girl he rooted for no matter how many times he watched the movie.

He gripped his knife firmly and instead of punching the closet door as Michael did, giving Laurie time to prepare, grab a hanger and turn it into a weapon, he kicked down the closet door as hard and fast as he could. He shattered it almost at once but gave it a second kick to fully expose his victim. There she sat, hunched against the corner, screaming and reaching for the clothes hanger. Bill grabbed her by the hair and pulled her up. She flung her arms and tore at his mask. The mask shifted making it harder for Bill to see, and Laurie somehow dropped free. Bill lifted his arms to adjust the 4D helmet, trying to see exactly through the eyes of the mask. By the time he could see again, Laurie had her weapon and she thrust the twisted hanger straight into his eye. In that exact moment, Bill lost vision in one eye completely. He tried to adjust the mask, but it was useless. JB must have programmed it this way, and now Bill's vision was even more limited through one hole in Michael's mask.

Laurie was getting away and Bill worried he was using too much time. He ran on the floor of the game room, even if it did little good, and chased her down before she could get to the kids. He knew if she got to the children, they'd scream and run down the street, which was what alerted Dr. Loomis to come and save Laurie and shoot Michael. Bill picked up a chair and threw it across the room at Laurie's back. He hit her squarely in the upper shoulders and she fell down crying. He walked toward her and grabbed her once again. She clawed at his face, which shifted the mask even more, making Bill's field of vision virtually nothing. He had no time to waste. He grabbed her throat with his left hand and shoved her straight against the wall. Saliva poured out of her mouth, snot ran from her nose, and tears dropped from her eyes.

"I'm sorry. I have to do this," Bill said and Laurie's jaw opened all the more. Michael, of course, never spoke in the movies, but Bill felt guilty for what he was about to do, even though he knew this was only a virtual reality.

With his right hand, he thrust the knife into Laurie Strode's heart. He pulled it out and blood dripped from his knife and oozed out of her chest and mouth. To be sure, he slammed the knife one more time into her heart, and her body went limp against the wall. Bill Wise had changed the ending of *Halloween* and killed off Laurie Strode. The innocent would not be saved. The villain had won.

The screen turned to black, and Bill was again congratulated by the computer. He hoped he would have a single moment to recover before the screen changed. He was sweaty and sick to his stomach, and trying hard not to think of what he had just done. It was one thing to shoot and slash at characters in a video game. It was something else entirely to feel it, to hear the screams, to be looked in the eye in such an unsettling way. It felt all too real.

But Bill was given no time out. The screen shifted and Bill saw the Hannibal Lecter mask appear and spin on the screen before finding its way onto Bill's head. Bill had more vision now, sight returning to both eyes, but he struggled to breathe. He couldn't open his mouth all the way, and the mask prevented him from taking a delicious bite out of one of his victims. JB had told them before the games that they'd be in the jail cell from *The Silence of the Lambs*, although this time the jail cell would be open.

Bill looked around at his setting. A simple cot and toilet, lots of books checked out from the library, and those ominous prison bars in front of him. It didn't look open at all, but Bill tried to move the bars to the side and discovered they were in fact unlocked. He looked down the prison hall. There was Clarice now, coming to interview him. In the film, Clarice interviewed the imprisoned Hannibal Lecter to find information about Buffalo Bill, a serial killer who skinned his victims. Bill watched as Clarice walked toward his cell, expecting nothing more than another interview. He wondered why JB made this one so easy, and then he realized that this game wasn't about capturing Clarice. It was about what he did with her after. His stomach turned.

Bill tried to hide off to the side of the cell, waiting for Clarice to appear exactly in front of the cell's door. When she appeared, Bill quickly slid the cell door open, grabbed Clarice, and pulled her in. She started to scream, but Bill clasped her mouth, silencing her with all of his strength. He looked around the cell for a weapon, but of course there was nothing so convenient readily available. He took a deep breath, but Clarice, a trained FBI agent, elbowed him in the stomach and punched him in the groin. His grip loosened and she started to pull away, but Bill slammed her against the wall. She punched him in the stomach and the face and turned to escape. Bill grabbed her again and with all of his might he threw her into the back of the cell. Charging at her, he tackled her to the floor. He dragged her over near the toilet, took her head, and plunged her face into the little toilet water available.

He felt disgusted at himself and yet exhilarated. *It's only a game*, he told himself, remembering Jaime's advice, and applied more force on Clarice's head into the toilet. Her body wriggled, kicked, and twisted, but Bill remained strong. Minutes passed and finally Clarice's body went limp. Bill prayed for the screen to go black and to hear a message of congratulations, but no such luck. He knew JB had something much more twisted in mind. He looked around the room, but there was no weapon, no object sharp enough to do what he thought he must do.

In the corner of the screen, a box with a question mark appeared out of nowhere, like a Mario coin box. "Damn," Bill said aloud, knowing JB was simply giving him a gift. Bill hit the box, and a saw appeared on screen. Grabbing it with his wireless glove, he held the saw.

"This is what I have to do, right?" he grumbled to himself. He knew what he had to do and he knew he was wasting time. "This is so nasty."

But he did what he needed to do. *It's only a game. It's only a game. It's only one hell of a sick, twisted game.* He took the saw with one hand and grabbed Clarice's head with the other. He pressed the saw into her head, slicing back and forth. Blood poured out, and Bill groaned.

It's only a game. Only a game. He closed his eyes so he didn't have to see and dug the saw deep into Clarice's skull. "Only a game," he mumbled, starting to sound a little crazy now. The blade was extraordinarily sharp and cut through rather easily, like a knife sinking into a ripe orange.

At least JB made that easy for us.

Bill saw her brain. It looked like a loaf of hamburger, a bloody brown and red. "Damn you, JB. C'mon!" he shouted. He knew that JB was watching them.

Hannibal the Cannibal would enjoy a tasty feast, and if that was what it took to finish the games, then that was what Bill needed to do. Next, he cut open the mouth guard around his mask with the saw. Then he scooped out a chunk of Clarice's brain, slowly brought it toward his mouth, opened wide, inched the bit of brain closer and closer.

Bill's gag reflex kicked in, and he belched a bit of vomit. Fighting the urge to puke, he swallowed hard and closed his eyes. *How many times do I have to tell myself this isn't real?* But it felt real. He swore he could smell it somehow, a stench like a rotten egg mixed with a bloody wound. He opened his mouth. He put the chunk of brain inside his mouth. It *couldn't* be there, but he swore he could feel its thick, slimy texture. He opened his eyes and swallowed.

And then the screen went black. "Congratulations," the voice said. "Wasn't that fun? Now only one more game."

Bill's stomach still churned when the face of Jack from *The Shining* appeared with wild, uncombed dark hair and possessed eyes. Like the masks from the previous games, the head spun, whirled, and attached itself to Bill. He looked around at his surroundings and tried to settle the sickness in his stomach. He found himself at the bottom of a staircase in the Overlook Hotel, staring up at Wendy, his wife. Wendy had a baseball bat and mumbled in fear at Jack to stay away. Moving quickly, because Bill desperately wanted these games to end, he charged up the stairs at Wendy but found himself blocked. It was like some kind of force field. Bill could run and the floor moved, but the images around him were frozen. She was right there in front of him, but Bill couldn't get to her. He was stuck.

Is there a glitch in the game?

Then he remembered that JB said there would be something tricky here, a catch that they'd have to figure out. Bill looked around the room. Nothing grabbed his attention. Nothing seemed out of place. He walked back down the stairs. *What do I have to do?*

He charged back up the stairs at Wendy, still there, but every time he approached her, he was blocked by some kind of invisible barricade. Wendy didn't run away, and at closer inspection, Bill saw that she was also literally frozen in this simulation. She wasn't moving, talking, or breathing, but waiting for Bill, waiting for him to figure out whatever the trick was to move forward.

Bill ran down the stairs and back up twice more, which only required a brief back and forth motion on the movable floor, but nothing changed. He tried to leave the room and go another way, but the simulation also blocked Bill in this particular room. There was nowhere to go.

"Think," Bill demanded. "Think. What is the trick?"

Bill considered this scene from the movie. It was an epic scene

— Jack had finally lost it, and looked demonic and tortured, nearly foaming at the mouth as he moved toward his wife, a wife he deeply loved, but was now determined to kill. Bill remembered thinking that it was this scene in Kubrick's film that really captured the loss of humanity in Jack and turned him into pure evil.

"That's it!" he yelled. He talked out loud, wanting JB to hear that he'd figured it out. "Don't take too long on those *stairs*, you said!"

Kubrick was famous for the overwhelming number of retakes he forced actors to do in each scene. According to Hollywood legend, this particular scene was shot 127 times. Kubrick wanted the scene to be perfect, and it took 127 retakes to get it exactly the way he wanted it. It was an absolutely ridiculous and OCD kind of thing to make one's actors do. That thought made Bill smile. It was also exactly the kind of thing JB would make people do.

He had now run up the stairs four times. He needed to run up them 123 more, and then he'd be able to pursue Jack's wife and son. He took a deep breath and started running back and forth. It was taking longer than he wanted, and he knew time significantly mattered in this round. He sure hoped he was right or he'd have wasted a heck of a lot of time.

He counted each run of the stairs out loud and finished 126 times. "Okay, here goes nothing. Or should I say, *here's Johnny!*" He ran up the stairs one more time.

Like an Easter egg in a game, he found the trick and broke the frozen spell. He wasted no more time. In the film, Wendy would escape and hide in the bathroom, where Jack would break down the door with an axe. In that famous scene, Danny escaped outside and ran into the hedge maze of the hotel. As cool as the hedge maze was, Bill hoped he didn't have to pursue that route, as it would take even more time.

He tackled Wendy immediately at the top of the stairs, took the bat, and in a moment of pure brutality that would haunt Bill's future nightmares, he swung the bat at Wendy's head as hard as he could. He smashed her skull completely in, and her face now more closely resembled the face of Jason Voorhees than it did Wendy

Torrance.

Bill had one more task: to find and kill Jack's son, Danny. Bill tried to push away all rational and conscious thought and simply immerse himself into what, he repeatedly told himself, was only a game. He knew Danny would be hiding in the master bedroom, and that was where Bill went. He charged through the doors, and there was little Danny. The boy let out a scream, ran toward Bill, and slid right between his legs. Bill, stunned at Danny's quick reaction, turned around to run after the kid, but Danny was incredibly fast. The boy was down the stairs and through the lobby doors. Exhausted, Bill ran as fast as he could after him. They would have their final confrontation in the hedge maze after all.

Outside, snow covered the hotel grounds. Danny had a head start, but left convenient footprints for Bill to follow. Bill remembered from the film that Danny would eventually back track through his footprints to throw off his father.

Bill moved even quicker. How much more time did he have to complete these challenges before the hour was up? JB had only given this round a time limit, which Bill supposed was to eliminate people who couldn't figure out the trick of 127.

He ran into the maze and took no time to gawk at the impressive size of the hedge-lined labyrinth. He had lost visual of the boy but continued to follow the footprints. Danny was at the point where he was about to backtrack, but Bill must have been faster than Jack: he had caught up with the boy.

"Danny!" Bill yelled.

"You're not my father," Danny cried.

"I'm not your father," he agreed. "And you're not real." He charged at the boy, tackling him on the snow. He put both hands around the boy's head and snapped the boy's neck, hard and fast.

Danny lay limp in the snow, and Bill stood over him.

Bill looked up in the game chamber and spoke directly at the camera. "Jesus, JB. This is too much. Way too much."

"Congratulations," JB's voice announced darkly, and the screen turned to black.

Bill tore off the gloves and helmet, sweat dripping down his back, his hair drenched. He wiped his face, pretty sure that tears had merged with sweat.

"It was only a stupid game," he said aloud, thinking of everything he had done.

He fell to his knees and vomited on the floor, heaving and heaving until nothing else would come up.

He wiped at his mouth and looked up. "I hope you enjoy cleaning that up."

He was exhausted, soaked in sweat, dizzy and empty from the vomiting. But he stood up nonetheless.

He cracked his neck from side to side, walked forward, and exited the game chamber.

There was still more that had to be done, and now was no time for a break. It was time to get the axe and see what was beyond the trap door in the fun house. He simply hoped he had enough strength left to swing it.

Chapter Twenty

The axe was gone. Bill stood on one knee, bent over his bed, confused and shaken. The axe was no longer here. The most obvious thought was that someone must have beaten his time in the third round of games. He thought he had done very well, especially considering he discovered the trick to unlocking *The Shining* stage quite quickly. Who beat his time? And did that mean he lost the game?

He stormed back to the commons. Only minutes had passed since he exited his game chamber and discovered the axe was missing. No one else was here yet. Curiosity overwhelmed him, and without thinking he drifted past the game chambers. He paused for a moment at JB's monitoring station. JB was inside, watching the players on several different screens.

Should he tell JB that he had made the connection to the axe and Annie and get an answer? But now the axe was missing, and Bill had a pretty good idea who must have it. Now wasn't the time to confront JB. Now was the time to see where the axe was and, perhaps more importantly, where the hell Daniel was. Bill moved onto all fours and quickly crawled past JB and his monitoring station.

Rushing through the movie studios the group had previously explored, he returned to the fun house. Why wasn't there a way to shut off all the crazy lights and effects? He already felt sick. He closed his eyes and tried to feel his way through so he wouldn't get dizzy, only opening them briefly to check for the location of the trap door. He held his breath as he opened his eyes.

The trap door was open.

He felt his heart skip a beat and his pulse quicken. Not only was the axe missing from under his bed, but the chain around the trap door had been broken. He looked around the tunnel, trying to focus, looking for someone, a shadow, a clue, something, anything. But there was nothing to be found. For a moment, he considered exploring inside to see what was beyond, but he heard the voices of his friends in his head.

Don't go alone.

He had already broken that promise, but he couldn't just sit and wait, especially with the axe missing.

Back through the fun house and past JB's monitoring room once again, Bill returned to the game chambers. He couldn't see or hear anything from the outside. He contemplated going back toward JB to try and see who was still playing, but he desperately wanted to find Daniel.

He ran back to the guys' sleeping quarters and busted into Daniel's room. No one was there. He checked every single room, but there was no one to be found.

It had to be Daniel, right? But his mind jumped to a dozen possibilities. Daniel could have told anyone where the axe was. He could have told his entire crew about the trap door. Or maybe Rose, Wes, and Jaime already finished their games. They only decided not to go alone. If any duo had finished before Bill, surely they would have taken the axe.

He ran into the girls' sleeping quarters and knocked on Rose and Jamie's door. No one answered. He opened the door to confirm no one was there, and all he saw was an empty bedroom.

"Damn!"

He ran back to the commons again, but no one was there. He turned around. It was time to confront JB.

"Wes!" Bill yelled, running smack into him on his way to JB's monitoring station. "Did you just finish?"

"Yeah," Wes mumbled. His dark skin looked much lighter than normal and sweat covered his body.

"You okay?"

"I don't think so, no. I feel sick."

"But you beat it!"

"Yeah. Thank God we didn't have to climb real stairs. There's no way I would have made it a hundred and twenty-seven times up and down. But the short back and forths on the floor weren't too bad."

"Have you seen anyone else?"

"You're the first. Did you move the axe already?"

"No. The damn thing's missing. It's not under my bed. I checked the trap door and the chain has been broken and the door is open. Someone beat us to it."

"Daniel?" Wes asked. "Or the girls? Do you know?"

"I don't know. I don't know what else to do but go to JB. Let's go."

"Bill! Wes!" Jaime shouted from one of the game chambers. "What are you guys doing just standing out here?"

"I've been running all over," Bill said. Both boys walked up to her. "I wasn't sure who finished. Wes just finished, too, but the axe is missing, and the trap door has been broken."

"Of course it is," she sighed. "Nothing is easy here. Did you go inside?"

"No, I came back for you guys first."

"We need to get to JB then," Jaime said.

"Can we pause for a minute?" Wes mumbled. "That round was too much. The brain, Clarice's brain. I about threw up in my helmet."

"Don't feel bad," Bill told him. "I got sick at the end, too. More than I think I've ever been sick in my entire life."

"I would love to rest, too," Jaime said. "But we need to finish this."

"Oh-right." Wes tried to smile, stealing Bill's words. "What about Rose though? Should we wait for her?"

"I don't want to leave Rose in the dark, but I think she'd understand," Bill answered. "One of us could stay and wait for her."

"No, Rose is smart. We said don't go alone. She'll wait for someone, and if no one shows up, she'll understand that we were in a hurry for answers. Especially since someone clearly has a head start on us."

"Okay," Wes said reluctantly. "Yeah. Let's go then."

"Let's check the trap door first," Jaime suggested. "We may not even need JB. We should see what's in there first. It could be Annie or Leroy."

"Agreed," Bill confirmed. "If it's a dead end, then we come back to JB."

The three walked as quickly as possible. Not quick enough for Bill's taste, but faster than a normal pace. They crept past JB who was still watching the games. This time Bill tried to see who was still playing, in particular if he could see Daniel or Rose. But he saw neither. JB was watching one of the other contestants stumble around in the Overlook Hotel, still not having figured out the secret. Once the group moved beyond and made their way to the trap door, they leaned in and tried to listen.

"Hear anything?" Jaime asked.

"No." He looked back at Jaime. "Ladies first?"

"Such a gentleman." She smirked. "You should go first, being our wise leader and all."

Bill managed a small smile, leaned in closer, and discovered a small ladder. He swung himself around and climbed down. Bill reached the bottom and scanned the room. It was dark, so he took out his cell phone to use as a flashlight. He briefly noticed that he still had no signal, but now the battery was in the red, too. *Of course it is.* He saw only an empty room, about the size of a high school bathroom, that must have been used for storage, he guessed.

"C'mon down. No one's here."

Wes and Jaime took out their phones, too. They were surrounded by walls made of stone, and, at closer inspection, they found a small cot in the corner of the room.

"Over there," Jaime whispered, gesturing toward their left. Using their phones to guide them, they examined the tiny bed, and then their jaws dropped at what they saw next: the axe that had been underneath Bill's bed was now on top of this cot.

"Did Daniel leave it?" Wes asked.

"I guess so," Bill replied. He picked up the axe and examined the bed more closely.

There was another chain. Another broken chain. A chain nailed to the back of a wall behind the bed. A chain that could have held someone.

"I'm beginning to wonder what was locked in this room," Jaime said. "And now that the room is unlocked, I'm wondering what may have gotten out."

"You're creeping me out," Wes told her.

"This whole thing is creepin' me out," she said.

"There's nothing here now. Daniel — or someone anyway —

found the axe, broke open the lock, and came in here. But you don't have chains on a wall for no reason. And you don't lock a door for no reason."

"What do we do now?" Wes asked.

"We have to go to JB. We've got to get some answers. These games aren't over yet," Bill said. "And something else is going on here. Something big."

Chapter Twenty-One

The three rushed back toward JB's monitoring station, Bill with the axe in hand, Wes and Jaime by his side.

But JB was gone. The monitors were turned off, and the room was empty.

"Now what?" Jaime asked.

"Maybe he's getting ready to address everyone again back in the commons," Bill responded. "Let's put the axe in your room for now, Jaime. I don't know if it's a good idea for us to just be carrying it around in front of everyone, and we don't know if we actually need it or not."

They ran to her room. "How about in here?" She opened the closet door. "Wait, this wasn't here before."

"The vacuum?" Wes asked.

"Yeah, I swear this was empty. There wasn't a thing in here before."

"It's only a vacuum," Wes said. "Maybe there's housekeeping or something that we haven't seen."

"I guess." She put the axe behind the vacuum and shut the door tight. "Okay, if this thing goes missing again, I'm gonna go crazy."

"Right?" Bill said. "Let's check the commons. See who else is back."

When they returned to the commons, the other contestants had just started appearing. One after the other, the room filled up once again with tired, pale faces.

"I bet the time limit is up," Jaime told them. "Look, no one seems happy. I wonder if they all ran out of time."

They spotted Dexter, standing where Daniel had sat earlier, and he wore a perplexed, frustrated look on his face. JB's assistants were setting food and refreshments out on the front tables as everyone took their seats.

"Where's Rose?" Jaime asked.

Bill counted the number of people in the room. Only two were missing, Rose and Daniel.

"Where could they be?" Wes asked. "Look, there's Captain Spaulding!"

From behind, Chester, the assistant dressed as Spaulding, approached the stage. The room quieted, and Bill studied the other contestants. Most looked exhausted, barely able to keep their eyes open. Except for Dexter. There was something about the look in his eyes that made Bill shudder.

"Good evening," Chester began. "I'm glad to see some of you can still eat after the last game. You've all given our cleaning staff some extra work tonight." He chuckled. "What a Halloween—one you will never forget, I am sure. But I'm guessing you want to know the results, who won, and all the details about the grand prize! I wish I could tell you. I really wanted to be able to tell you. But I'm afraid that . . . another person has gone missing."

All sounds of conversation and eating stopped at once. Everyone straightened up a little more in their chairs and gave Chester their undivided attention.

"I have specific orders," he continued, "to send you to bed and to tell you to get packed and get ready to leave in the morning. But I wouldn't be able to sleep tonight if I did that. Leroy and Annie are still missing. And now Rose."

Wes stood up, his mouth open and his fists clenched. Chester looked at him for a moment, then seemed to come to a decision.

"Guys," Chester said urgently, "you need to pack your bags tonight and get the hell out of here. I cannot guarantee your safety. JB is . . . well, he's not himself. Look . . . we can't wait until morning. Get your stuff, head out front to the main entrance. I'm arranging transportation to get you all out of here." Everyone was glued to their seats except for Wes, who remained standing and breathing heavily. "Get up! Go. Now!"

Like a swarm of bees, everyone started moving at once. Everyone except Bill and Jaime, who stood up with Wes.

"Bill —" Jaime started.

"I know. We have to get to JB. Do you think he's lost it? Do you think he'll hurt Rose?" Bill asked. "God, who knows what could be going on in this place!"

"We have to find her!" Wes shouted.

"What about Daniel? And where is Dexter going? Look!" Jaime pointed to Dexter, who was moving toward the game chambers, not their sleeping quarters.

"I have a feeling they know something we don't, and I don't much care for that." Bill started walking in the same direction as Dexter.

What is going on? What happened to Rose? Where were the other missing players? Why wasn't Daniel back? What about Dexter? What had been locked in the trap door room? Dozens of questions bounced through Bill's mind as they followed Dexter.

"Wait!" Bill stopped, and Jaime and Wes ran into him. "Just in case. Let's not be empty-handed this time." Wes looked beyond Bill, clearly worried about Rose and not wanting to waste a single second. But he nodded, turned, and led the way to Jaime's room. *Yes, just in case we need it, we better have it,* Bill thought. *And I have a terrible feeling that we're gonna need it.*

*****

They retrieved the axe from Jaime's closet, and then the threesome went straight back to the game chamber and past JB's monitoring room. All of the screens had been turned off, but Bill saw something that made him pause.

"What's that?"

Jaime opened the door, and the three went inside. Sitting on the desk by JB's enormous black leather chair was some kind of dessert in a glass bowl.

"This is totally random," Jaime said.

"What is it?" Bill asked. "It looks like it hasn't been eaten, either. Just a big bowl of what, pudding?"

Wes dipped his finger in it and sniffed. "Chocolate mousse. My mom makes this stuff."

"Weird," Bill said. "And what are these?"

"They look like magnetic keys. Shit. Take them. And c'mon. We're wasting time. We have to find Rose." Wes grabbed a key and led the way back out.

"Now where do we go?" Bill asked.

"There's something beyond the fun house," Wes said. "Remember? Where we found the gold? And now we just happen to conveniently find a key, right? Maybe this key will open a new door."

When they passed through the fun house, Jaime tried her key on the door where they had found the gold coins earlier. The key opened the door, and they entered a long hallway, with doors spread out every twenty feet or so, like the hallway of a large hotel.

"These must be the studio rooms," Wes said. "Different settings and stuff for filming."

"Where do we start?" Jaime took a deep breath. "Studio One?"

"What do you think is behind that door?" Wes asked.

"There's only one way to find out." Bill took his key card, unlocked the door, and pushed it open.

They were greeted by an incredibly round woman, wearing a long sleeved green shirt wrapped in a darker green vest with a gold necklace and cross charm around her neck. Most frightening though, she was holding a gigantic sledgehammer against her right shoulder.

"We don't want none here," she chirped. "Go away."

"We're looking for our friends," Jaime said. "Annie, Leroy, and Rose."

The woman smiled, showing a mouthful of teeth, somewhere between frightening and welcoming. "Oh," she replied. "Oh. Thank you. I'm Annie. Come in now." The three carefully entered the room. "What can I do you for?"

"Not you," Jaime continued. "We have reason to believe a young girl named Annie is here."

The woman frowned. "So I'm not your friend?"

"I didn't mean that," Jaime stammered.

"It figures. I don't have any friends. Well, except for dear old Paul. I should get back to him. You three run on now."

How could one person's voice sound so pleasant and so menacing at the same time? This had to be Annie, the main character in Stephen King's *Misery*. She had rescued and then imprisoned her favorite author, Paul Sheldon, and forced him to write a story for her. In the book, she used an axe to cut off his foot to keep him from running away. This woman was holding a sledgehammer now instead of an axe, her weapon of choice in the movie. *No more simulations*, Bill thought. *JB's making the movies real.* This was flesh and blood, standing and breathing right in front of them. *What are we supposed to do now?*

"Ma'am," Bill started. "We have to search your home."

"On one condition." The woman smirked. "That stays here. I don't allow strangers to bring dangerous things into my home."

Bill looked down at the axe. He lifted it up slowly, and she grabbed it easily with her free hand. Then she cocked her head to the side, smiled, and threw the axe into the back of the room. She faced them, snarled, and readjusted her grip on the sledgehammer.

"Now you just have to get by me!" With that, she swung the sledgehammer like a baseball bat at their heads. The three screamed, ducked, and ran into a table off to the side with a bunch of animal figurines. *What the hell?* Bill rolled and hit his head. He could feel the air from the sledgehammer and saw a penguin figurine drop to the floor.

"You almost broke my penguin," Annie said. "My little ceramic penguin always faces due south." She marched toward them, her heavy feet slamming on the floor and making the room shake.

"Is this for real?" Jaime asked. As if to answer her question, Annie raised her sledgehammer, looked at them, and said, "Hi pumpkins. Such kidders." And she swung the hammer again.

"Move!" Bill yelled. "To the back!" The three jumped to their feet and sprinted to the back of the room, as far from the reach of the sledgehammer as they could get.

Even though they hadn't read the book, they were familiar enough with the film that they knew that in the end Annie kept Paul locked in a basement. *That's what we have to find,* Bill thought, looking around frantically.

"There! Over there!" Bill shouted and pointed at a door that he hoped led downstairs.

"Not so fast!" the woman yelled, bringing the sledgehammer down toward Bill's head. He rolled to his right and frantically looked around the room for some kind of weapon. His thoughts bounced from *this can't be real* to *it's another game* to *JB's gone completely crazy and has someone literally trying to kill us.*

No time to figure it out. He saw the axe in the back of the room, but there was no time to go after that. He reached out for a vase on a small end table that stood near him. The woman turned and faced him, growling.

"You can't take my friend," she snarled and swung the hammer again. Bill moved right as the hammer collided with the small table, crushing it like a boulder hitting a stick. With the vase in his right hand, Bill swung it with every ounce of energy he had left. It connected with her head, shattering into hundreds of tiny pieces.

"Oow!" Annie cried and dropped the sledgehammer on the floor. She looked at Bill and then back to Jaime and Wes, who had gathered their own weapons. Jaime held a glass milk bottle, and Wes had found some other kind of bottle. They both held their makeshift weapons high above their heads, and when Annie turned toward them, they brought them down with great force. Jaime's milk bottle cracked and shattered on her skull, and Annie stumbled to the side. Wes came from the opposite direction and slammed his bottle across the other side of her face.

Annie held her face and fell on the floor. They stared at the fallen woman. What had just happened? Whenever they thought each part of the Fright Fest was the worst thing ever, somehow things always intensified. Now JB had real people trying to kill them.

"The door," Bill snapped. There was no time to figure it out. They had to find Rose and the others. "Let's go!"

They opened the door and saw a set of stairs that led downward. "The basement!" Wes shouted. "That's where we'll find her!"

One after the other, they went down the stairs, and sure enough, there was Annie. She sat alone on a bed—none of the others were with her. Her hair was uncombed, and she wore the same clothes as the first round of games.

"Annie!" Jaime ran up to her and threw her arms around her. "Everyone has been looking for you. JB made us believe that you had run away. Are you okay? C'mon, let's get you back."

She tried to pull her up, and then they noticed the chains.

Annie was chained to the bed. She lifted her head weakly. Her shirt was soaked in drool, and she looked like she hadn't slept or eaten all weekend.

"Oh my God!" Jaime said. "Are you okay?"

Annie stared at them without moving. Her mouth opened slowly, and she whispered something inaudible.

"Speak up, Annie, please!" Wes begged.

Annie tried to swallow and then she spoke again. "If you don't hurry . . ."

"If we don't hurry, what?" Bill asked, his body now shaking.

"If you don't hurry . . ." Annie's head dropped. She didn't have the strength to finish the sentence.

"We need to break those chains and get her out of here," Bill said. "I'll get the axe." He turned around and saw a video camera in the corner of the room. Bill paused and looked back at Wes and Jaime. "Look!" He pointed at the camera. "JB is watching." Bill walked closer to the camera. "I told you once before that you had gone too far!" Fury, frustration and confusion threatened to overwhelm him. "This is messed up! You are messed up!"

He turned away from the camera and ran up the stairs. He needed to get the axe and get everyone out of here.

He paused again at the top of the stairs. Big Annie was gone. Was she hiding somewhere now? He inhaled deeply and walked forward. Annie had tossed the axe behind her when they met her at the front door. Bill tried to listen. Annie was a big woman. Surely, he'd hear her footsteps or her breathing, right? But he didn't hear anything. He darted across the room to where Annie had tossed the axe.

But it was gone, too.

A scream echoed up from the basement.

"Jaime!" Bill ran back to the stairs. It was Jaime's voice, he had no doubt. His anger doubled. *Jesus, if something happens to her, I'll . . . I'll . . .*

"Jaime! Are you okay?"

He raced down the stairs, and in his hurry, he stumbled, missed a step, and rolled all the way down. He opened his eyes but the room was pitch black.

"Bill? You okay?" It was Wes. Wes was touching him and grabbed at his arm.

"Ow!" Bill moaned. His shoulder hurt, but he stood up and

everything else felt okay. "Where's Jaime?"

"I'm here," she said.

Thank God. Bill couldn't see her, but he reached out for her, ignoring the pain in his shoulder. "What happened?" He grabbed her hand and pulled her close.

"The lights went out and something—or someone—pushed against us. I don't know what's happening. I can't see a damn thing!"

The lights came back on. Bill gasped and Jaime squeezed his hand. Annie was gone. The chains were on the bed, but she was gone. And there was bloody writing on the wall.

"If you don't hurry, she'll die," Wes read the message out loud. "That's what Annie was trying to tell us?" Wes turned to the camera in the corner of the room. "Who will die? Rose? Is this a warning about Rose? What is wrong with you?"

Wes looked around the room. In the corner on a small writing desk rested the typewriter they all had found back in Annie's room. The typewriter with the missing letter. Wes ran to the typewriter, picked it up, and hurled it with all of his might at the camera.

Then he faced Bill and Jaime. "We go to the next room. Now."

The look in his eyes terrified Bill. But Bill nodded.

"Wait, guys," Jaime said. "On the bed by the chains. It's another key."

Wes grabbed it, put it in his pocket, and ran up the stairs. Bill and Jaime followed.

Jaime pulled back and nodded. She turned to the guys and said, "Okay. To Studio Two. Let's go!"

"She's gone?" Wes asked at the top of the stairs. "Where is this Annie?"

"I don't know. She was gone when I came back up. So was the axe." Bill put a hand on Wes's shoulder. "Wait a sec, man. We gotta think. We could have been killed. And what happened downstairs with our Annie?"

"It happened so fast," Jaime said. "Lights went off. Someone pushed us. I'm guessing there's more than one way in and out of all these rooms, and someone came and took our Annie when the lights went out."

186

"Maybe we need to get out of here and call the cops," Bill said. "This isn't a game anymore. Maybe it's a game in JB's head, but this is sick."

Jaime looked at Wes. "What do you think?"

"A woman attacks us with a sledgehammer, and you think I want to stay here?" Wes said incredulously. "Hell. No. But I'm not leaving until we find Rose. You guys will help me, won't you?"

"This is all so crazy," Jaime said. She rubbed her eyes wearily. "But yes, of course. Finding Rose should be our first priority."

"But this isn't a game anymore," Bill argued. "We've seen enough horror movies to know what happens when people go deeper into a haunted house. They don't all come back out."

"Should we split up?" Wes asked. "I'm not leaving without Rose, Bill. But you could go try to get the police."

"Shit, no. We don't split up either. Are you crazy?" Bill paused and tried to quickly consider everything that had happened. He wasn't about to leave his friends alone, but he didn't think it was the best idea to keep going. "Okay, what choice do we have? We go forward for now. We find Rose."

"Where are the double d-bags?" Jaime asked. "Daniel and Dexter must be in one of these rooms, too, don't you think? Shit, should we be worried that they're in trouble, too?"

"You know, I really don't care," Wes said. "They can fight for themselves. But what about Rose?"

They heard a scream from down the hall. Bill saw the worry on Wes's face.

"That was Rose, wasn't it?" Wes asked. "Which room did it come from?"

Bill looked down the long hall. There had to be at least a dozen rooms. Behind one of these doors, they'd surely find Rose. And Leroy, too. But what else would they find? And what else would find them?

"I don't know, man." He rubbed a hand over his face. He probably sounded hysterical. "But I guess one door at a time. Studio Two?"

Wes looked focused and angry. Bill didn't see a kid who had been bullied. Bill saw a man who would do anything to fight for his friends.

"Oh-right. Let's do this together." Wes led the way to Studio Two, inserted the new magnetic key, looked to his left and right to make sure Bill and Jaime were ready, and opened the door.

This time they were greeted by the sound of gunshots.

Chapter Twenty-Two

Bill dodged to the side of the door, and Jaime and Wes hit the floor.

"Where did those come from?" Wes asked.

"I don't know. Is everyone okay?" Bill poked his head around the corner.

"I think so," Jaime said. "But obviously this means someone's got a gun. And what the hell are we gonna do about that?"

"That also means that someone could have a gun on Rose," Wes argued. "C'mon! No matter what, we have to keep going."

They crept through the door very slowly and looked around. They were in a room with huge ceilings, lush couches, and a fireplace. It was a dark room, but a mansion-sized one, full of antiques.

They had only taken a few steps into the room when the door behind them slammed shut. They jumped, turned, and tried to open the door, but it was locked.

"Dammit!" Bill cried. "I'm going to kill JB."

"Not if he kills us first," Wes said.

"Hold on," Bill said. Hadn't he learned anything in those simulations? He had to stop panicking. He had to think. "If Annie was connected to *Misery*, then could this room be connected to someone else? To Rose or Leroy?"

"Look around," Jaime said. "Does this look familiar?"

"Yeah," Wes said nodding his head. "Think about it! We had all sorts of little clues that led to *Misery*. We're in some kind of weird mansion. We heard gunshots. We found gold coins outside of the fun house. Fool!"

"Fool?" Bill said. "What do you mean?"

"And look at that stairway over there, Bill. I have a feeling we are gonna have to go under the stairs."

The light bulb in his mind blew up. *"The People Under the Stairs!"* he exclaimed. "One of Craven's films from the early '90s. The one about a kid working with an older guy to defraud a family and rob their house. They had piles of gold—the gold coins! The real twist was that the couple kept people under the stairs. And there's a character Leroy who calls the boy in the movie a fool."

"Yeah, I know the film," Jaime said, rolling her eyes. "When JB told us Leroy was missing, he looked right at you and said 'fool.'"

"But guys, the people under the stairs were more than just people," Wes said. "They were children who spoke out of turn or saw things they shouldn't have. The parents would blind them or cut out their tongues to match the so-called mistake. They were all deformed."

"That means Leroy is trapped here somewhere," Jaime said. "We need to help him. Maybe we have to get to him before we can get to Rose," she said to Wes.

Before they could discuss further, a man appeared dressed in all leather. He looked like he was straight out of the first season of *American Horror Story*, but the threesome knew this was the insane husband from *The People Under the Stairs*, who dressed in a leather outfit to chase and hunt down those who escaped from the basement and hid in the walls. He held a pistol in his right hand and pointed it directly at Bill's face.

"You know what we do to those who break into our house?" the man asked. "We KILL!" At the sound of that last word, a Doberman Pinscher appeared, growling from behind the man in leather. "KILL!" he shouted again, and the dog charged at them.

"RUN!" Jaime yelled, and they sped to the right of the room where they saw a staircase. They ran up the stairs, hearing the barks and growls from the dog right on their heels.

Halfway up the stairs, they heard the man in leather yell, "SURPRISE!" The stairs flattened, connected to some kind of remote control that shifted them into a slide. Jaime slipped into Wes, and Bill tried to hang on to the railing.

"You guys!" Bill yelled. "The dog!"

Wes and Jaime slid into the dog, and the Doberman locked its mouth around Wes's ankle. The man in leather pointed his gun at Bill and shot. Bill screamed, hearing a bullet fly right past his ear. He put a hand up to his face. The man must have missed. Bill let himself slide down into Jaime and Wes. He made contact and surprised the dog, who let go of Wes and now growled at Bill instead. The man pointed his gun again at Bill, but Bill jumped up over the railing and onto the floor of the living room next to it. He grabbed an old telephone and threw it at the man in leather. The man ducked, but the phone hit the button at the bottom of the stairs, shifting the slide back into steps.

"Quick! Up!" Bill yelled.

Wes and Jaime sprinted up the stairs as the Doberman turned and chased after Bill. Bill ducked behind a couch as the dog jumped over to attack him. Bill jumped on to the opposite side of the couch and ran to the stairs, where the man in leather stood with his gun still aimed at Bill. Not thinking, Bill charged the man and knocked him out of the way and then ran up the stairs toward Wes and Jaime.

They ran as quickly as they could to the top. Once there, they flung open the first door they found. They stumbled in and saw a small child's bed with a doll on top.

"In the movie," Bill heaved, out of breath, "this is their little girl's room. There's a way out from here. Look!"

There was an oversized vent, an entrance into the walls, where those who escaped under the stairs traveled through the house. Bill pulled it open, and the three climbed in. They crawled as quickly as they could, and the man in leather stuck his face in the vent.

"KILL!" he shouted. He stuck the gun into the vent and fired. They felt that whiz, through their hair, by their ears. They screamed in unison, tears burning in their eyes. A deafening vibration echoed in Bill's ears.

"Is everyone okay?" Bill shouted. He rubbed at his ears. He had felt this kind of ringing at loud concerts, but never quite like this.

"Yeah," both Wes and Jaime snapped back and continued crawling. They felt a vibration, and through the ringing Bill heard the sound of paws. The dog had entered the vents with them.

"We have to keep moving!" Bill told them.

"KILL!" the man in leather screeched again.

Crawling even faster, Bill saw what was coming ahead of them and warned, "There's a slide, guys. We're going down." He let himself slide down the vent, face first, and Wes and Jaime followed. They reached what appeared to be an actual furnace, and they kicked the main vent open and crawled out, dusty and dirty.

"Quick! Hold this shut!" Bill yelled.

The three pushed on the vent opening to keep the dog and anyone or anything else that followed from getting out.

"Over there," Jaime pointed. There was a long, thick piece of wood. "Can we put that up against the vent to keep it from opening?"

"Try it," Bill said. "Wes and I will hold this shut."

Jaime ran to get the large piece of wood and they braced it against the floor and stuck it into the vent. They slowly let go of the vent and waited to hear the dog's growls or the man in leather's commands. Instead, all they heard was silence.

"Did the dog stop before the slide?" Jaime asked.

"I don't know," Wes moaned. "Is everyone okay?"

"Yeah," Bill said, checking himself from head to toe. "I don't know how we survived. How many times did he shoot at us? Is your ankle okay?" he asked Wes.

"The dog tore at my pants, but never actually got skin," Wes said. "Thank God."

"Wow. Good." Bill looked around. "Okay, now what?"

"It looks like there's some kind of door over there." Jaime pointed. They walked to a metal-looking door with no handle. It was already cracked open or they probably wouldn't have noticed it at all. They pushed and sure enough, it opened into another small room. They could hear the screams, moans, and groans echoing from around them. Bill felt goosebumps form on his skin. Were these noises just special sound effects? Or could there be real people somewhere here under the stairs? They went inside the door and found a small room where a man sat on a bed waiting for them.

"It's Leroy!" Wes exclaimed. Leroy looked up at them, but his eyes were cloudy, as if he had just woken up. "You okay, man?"

And like Annie, he was chained to the bed.

"Oh, man," Bill said. "What happened to you? Tell us!"

"Look, Bill," Jaime pointed up at the corner of the room, where another video camera was placed.

"I don't care if we are being watched. I don't care what JB

sees." But he paused for a second to hold up his middle finger at the camera. "Let him see that." He turned back to Leroy. "I want to know what's happening. Tell us!"

Leroy licked his lips and blinked his eyes several times. "One of the assistants, I think, grabbed me at the end of my game. I don't know what's going on! I . . . how long have I been here?"

"What do you remember?" Wes asked.

Leroy shook his head. "I . . . I heard gunshots. Just minutes ago. That's when I woke up. I've been out of it since . . . it was Spaulding, I think. He grabbed me at the end of my game!"

Bill, Jaime, and Wes exchanged nervous glances. Bill wondered if they were thinking what he was thinking. He just wanted this to be some insane trick. But it wasn't a trick, was it?

"Do you remember anything else?" Jaime asked. "Has anyone else been down here?"

Leroy shook his head and tears rolled down his cheeks. "You know what I think?" He sniffled. "I think JB put us through those games to find the best of the best. The losers — like me — we're just bait. It's you all he wants. The ones who performed the best. He's a hunter. And he wants to chase the most challenging prey he can find."

"Do you think that was JB upstairs shooting at us?" Jaime asked Bill.

"I don't know. Maybe." Could Leroy be right? Were they being hunted? He looked back up at the camera. Then he picked up a small chair near Leroy's bed, brought it up over his head, and smashed the camera to pieces. That made him feel a bit better.

The others stared at Bill for a moment. He looked them each in the eye. He didn't know what to say or do. But they hadn't found Rose. They'd have to keep going. But would they also have to face JB?

Something caught Bill's attention. "Guys, what's that?" He pointed to the small table from which he'd taken a chair to destroy JB's camera.

Jaime walked over to it. It was an envelope with the Rabbit in Red logo printed on top. She looked up at Bill, then reached into the envelope and took out a sheet of paper. She swallowed hard.

"What is it?" Wes asked.

"It's a message. And I'm guessing it's from JB." She looked up at them and bit her lip. Then she read the message out loud. *"Two down and one to go. Which is the right room, do you know? We've cleaned the floor and had our dessert. Hope you find her before she gets hurt. This key will open all the doors. If you're still unsure, make this pendant yours."*

Jaime reached into the envelope again and pulled out a pendant. She held it up for the others to see.

"It's just like the riddles from the very first challenge that got us here," Jaime said. "Do you know what this means?"

They all shook their heads.

"Have Daniel and Dexter been here?" Bill asked Leroy.

"No. I don't think so anyway. I've been asleep. I must have been drugged." Leroy sighed deeply.

"That message is about Rose," Wes said. "Hope you find her before she gets hurt? Guys, we have to get out of here and find her!"

"What about Leroy?" Bill asked. He looked at the boy on the bed and wished he had the axe or something to break those chains.

"You've gotta find your friend. I understand," Leroy said, but sadness consumed his face. "Like I said, I think I'm just bait. But um, come back for me? Like as soon as you can?"

"Of course," Jaime said and put a hand on Leroy's shoulder. "We don't want to leave you. But if you're right . . . if we don't make it out of here, then I don't think anyone's making it out of here."

Leroy nodded.

"Where do we go from here?" Bill asked.

"Unfortunately, I think we may have to go back up." Wes looked back at the slide from which they had fallen.

"Great. More dog and more shooting." Bill sighed. "Okay. Up the rabbit's hole instead of down."

"We'll just check," Jaime coaxed. "If the guy or the dog is there, we'll come back here."

"Oh-right." Bill turned to Leroy. "You sure you're okay here, Leroy?"

"Is there another choice? I think you need to hurry."

If you don't hurry, she'll die.

Jaime pulled the chunk of wood holding the vent shut. There was no sight or sound of a dog or a man in leather. She started to climb up, and Wes and Bill followed. The climb up was much harder than the slide down, but they eventually made it to the top. They ended up in the small upstairs bedroom. There was no sight or sound of the dog or the man, so they walked downstairs, through the massive living room, and to the front door of Studio Two. This time it was unlocked.

"There are over a dozen rooms left," Wes said as they stepped out into the hall. "Which one do we try?"

"What about JB's message?" Bill asked. "Read it again, Jaime, will you?"

"Two down and one to go," Jaime read. "Which is the right room, do you know? We've cleaned the floor and had our dessert. Hope you find her before she gets hurt. This key will open all the doors. If you're still unsure, make this pendant yours."

"Any ideas?" Bill asked.

"Think about it!" Jaime jumped. "Remember the vacuum we found in my closet that I swore wasn't there? You thought it might have simply been a housekeeping thing, but I don't think so. 'We've cleaned the floor.' That must be a reference to the vacuum."

"And the dessert!" Wes said. "In JB's monitoring station, we saw the dessert."

"The chocolate mousse," Bill said. "And now we have a pendant. I think I know what scene we're looking for."

"Oh, yes! That's perfect!" Jaime said.

"A closet with a vacuum, chocolate mousse, a pendant . . ." Wes thought for a moment. "Got it! What are we waiting for?"

At that moment, Daniel and Dexter exited from one of the studio rooms down the hall.

"Are you kidding me?" Bill yelled. "What are you guys doing here?"

Daniel turned and gave him the middle finger. Dexter snarled back and then took out a key card and went into another studio room across the hall.

"What the hell are they doing here?" Wes asked.

"Forget them," Jaime said. "Who knows? The only thing we need to worry about is finding Rose." She paused for a moment, and Bill knew she was thinking of something else. "Guys, what if . . . what if they're after Rose? I can see JB doing something like this. He sets up one group to save her. He sets up another group to . . . to . . .I mean, all of us have saved people now, and all of us have killed."

"Then we need to make sure we find Rose first," Wes said. "And you may be right. They don't seem to know where they're going. At least we know what room we're looking for. Let's go!"

Chapter Twenty-Three

They started opening doors, looking for the room they needed to find. They recognized the creepy home from *The Conjuring* in room three and the mall from *Dawn of the Dead* in room four. The vampire den from *The Lost Boys* welcomed them in room five, but that wasn't the room they were looking for either.

Then Daniel and Dexter came out of Studio Six. Bill was just about to open the door to that room when Daniel grabbed Bill and Dexter wrapped his arms around Wes.

"Hey!" Jaime screamed. "What the hell are you guys doing?"

Bill and Wes kicked, but their rivals were stronger. Dexter and Daniel shoved them hard against the wall and then faced Jaime.

"Make it easy on us, will ya, princess?" Dexter asked.

"Go to hell," Jaime replied.

"As you wish," Dexter said. He lunged for Jaime who dodged to the left, but ran smack into Daniel.

"We trusted you," she growled as Daniel hugged her tight, but it was far from a hug of friendship.

"That was your mistake." He laughed.

Wes stood up and cracked his knuckles. He exhaled hard through his nostrils and shouted, "You asshole!"

Daniel tossed Jaime to the side like a bag of dirty clothes and faced Wes head on. Wes charged like a football player and tackled him. Dexter sprinted forward, though, faster than any athlete Bill had ever seen. Bill ran to help, but Dexter punched Bill in the stomach and threw him against the wall.

Jaime grabbed Dexter from behind, but he flipped her easily over his shoulder, and she fell to the ground with sickening thud. Wes stood up and Daniel moaned on the floor like a baby in pain.

"Ahhhh!" Wes yelled and charged at Dexter with every ounce of energy he had, but Dexter turned to the side and let the large boy fly by. Bill stood up and ran to Jaime, who held a hand against her ribs.

"Are you okay?" he asked her. If he had hurt her —

"I don't know. I think so. I guess that's what it feels like to have the wind knocked out of you."

Bill looked up, but as soon as he did, Dexter kicked him in the stomach. "There's no room for weakness in this story. Get out of my way."

"Hey!" Daniel called as Dexter walked passed him, too.

"Sorry, buddy. I only needed you to get this far. You're on your own." Bill watched as Dexter entered Studio Seven. He wanted to cuss and scream at him, but at the moment it hurt to even breathe.

Wes limped back, holding his left shoulder.

"Jaime? Bill? Are you okay?"

"I'm okay," Jaime said. "I don't think anything is broken. It hurts, but it was more shock than anything. Bill?"

"I've never been hit like that," he said, standing up, his hand pressed against his stomach. "Dexter is a monster."

"A real psycho," Jaime said.

Bill looked at Daniel with the fierceness of an animal in the wild. Daniel stood up slowly. "That fat ass friend of yours about killed me."

"What's wrong with you?" Bill snapped.

"A game can only have one winner," Daniel said back.

"What are you talking about?" Bill asked. Daniel looked at him and smiled. *What does he know that I don't?* "What's going on? What are you even doing back here?"

The three marched forward, and Daniel took a step back. He grinned but kept silent.

"You may be stronger and more athletic than us," Wes said. "But together, the three of us can take you. And we will hurt you if we have to. This is not a game anymore."

The three crept closer, and Daniel took another step back. Bill caught himself smiling a bit as Daniel's face twitched. "What do you want me to do?"

"Tell us what you know. What's going on?" Bill asked.

"Go to hell," Daniel said.

The three stood like a small army, breathing powerfully, and stared him down. Daniel stood his ground for several moments, sizing them up.

After a moment, Bill spoke. "If you're not gonna help us, then get out of the way."

Finally Daniel stepped back. "Fine. Good luck with Dexter. He's the real crazy one."

Daniel turned around. For a brief moment, Bill wondered where the jerk would go, since they seemed to all be trapped in here. But he quickly dismissed the thought. They had to get to Rose, and someone even worse than Daniel may already have found her.

Jaime opened the door to Studio Seven, and Wes bolted in first. They saw a bleak, depressing apartment style room, beige curtains draped around windows, and an empty hallway that led to a closet.

"There," Wes pointed at the hall closet. "We go in there."

Carefully walking toward the closet, they opened the door; there must be a secret passage that led to an adjacent room. They listened carefully, and Bill knew they had chosen correctly when they heard the chant of, "Hail, Satan."

The secret door led to a different room, and they were welcomed by the cries of a baby. *Rosemary's Baby*. In the movie, Bill remembered some of the symbolic items: the pendant the neighbors gave Rosemary as a supposed good luck charm, but of course it had some kind of Satanic properties. He remembered the sparse room Rosemary had, where her husband found a small closet with nothing but a vacuum and a few minor items. And, of course, there was the chocolate mousse, a dessert the neighbors had brought over on the night Rosemary had hoped to conceive with her husband, a dessert that tasted horrible, tainted by the spell of Satan worshippers. The same dessert they saw sitting in JB's empty monitoring station. JB had played another name trick on them, hiding Rose in the setting of *Rosemary's Baby*.

They entered the adjacent room within Studio Seven where they heard chanting. In this version of the setting, there was no baby, but rather a giant black crib, where Rose Dawn sat, looking frightened as about a dozen people dressed as witches surrounded her.

Dexter was also in the room, standing next to the crib. Bill's gaze moved from Dexter to one of the witches who stepped away from the giant crib to face him, Wes, and Jaime.

"You cannot have her." The witch sneered and lifted her hands as if to push them away. She wore a black dress and a large purple hat that under other circumstances would have been comical.

"Get out of my way," Wes said as he charged through the group of witches. Bill thought he would run straight to Rose, but his jaw dropped as he saw Wes head straight to Dexter instead.

"You!" Wes yelled. "You get away from her!"

The room, no bigger than Bill's living room, felt crowded with so many people squeezed in, and Dexter didn't even move as Wes approached. Instead, just before he could get to Dexter, one of the witches stepped toward Wes, grabbed him quickly, and held him tight. Wes groaned, but the woman had his arms bent back at a painful angle, and she snarled at Jaime and Bill.

Bill looked at this ridiculously large, black crib and then back at all of these people who appeared to be guarding her. But Rose was not Rosemary's baby. She was a friend, and they were taking her out of this place.

Bill turned to the witch that had hold of Wes. "Let go of him!"

Jaime turned back into the closet and ran out of the room. Bill thought he knew what she was after, and he took a deep breath. He wanted to help Wes and get Rose, but he worried about what Jaime was going to find. He turned around quickly.

"Jaime! Wait!"

Back in the other room, he saw her collide into Daniel.

"*Rosemary's Baby*," Daniel said. "How did I miss that?" He grabbed Jaime's arm.

"Ouch," Jaime cried. "Let go of me." She swung her elbow and knocked him back.

"Where are you going?"

"Go screw yourself, you coward!"

"Whatever." He turned and knocked into Bill, who stood in the doorway between these rooms. Bill wanted to knock Daniel in the jaw, but he needed to see what Jaime was after. He pushed Daniel to the side.

His suspicions were justified when she picked up a large carving knife, the knife Rosemary held in her hand when she walked through the closet in the original movie. It was the one thing missing from the scene. What was she going to do with it? Bill opened his mouth to ask her these questions, but she ran right by him with the same force as Daniel.

This is too real, he thought. *I'm not gonna let Jaime do what I think she's gonna do.*

"Let Rose and Wes go!" Jaime shouted at the witches. She held the knife up by her head, and Bill saw the most frightening look he had ever seen on her face. Her eyes narrowed, and she bared her teeth and snarled. She was ready to attack.

"Give *me* the knife," Daniel demanded and held out his hand.

"Back off!" she snapped, and Daniel hopped back at her viciousness.

A few witches in the room then came after Jaime. The others held on to Wes, locking his arms tightly behind his back. One of the witches then growled and ran toward Jaime.

Do something, you idiot, Bill thought. But between the anger on Jaime's face and the calm on Dexter's, he froze.

"I won't hesitate to use this," Jaime claimed, but the witch didn't back down. She lunged and knocked the knife out of Jaime's hand.

The witch screamed, a yell louder than anything he had ever heard. Bill shuddered, but the scream broke his paralysis, and he dove for the knife as it flew across the floor. He plunged headfirst as if sliding into base and grabbed the knife. As he stood up, some of the witches tossed Wes through a door behind the giant crib. *So many rooms.* Then another witch lowered one side of the giant crib and grabbed Rose. This witch shoved Rose through this other doorway right after Wes.

Dexter turned around, and Bill saw that the psycho's hands were tied behind his back with rope. *Is that why he's so calm? Why isn't he fighting back? Is he in on it?* Another witch pushed Dexter into the room. Daniel walked up and stood by Bill's side.

"Hey!" Jaime yelled and ran toward the new doorway after Rose and Wes. Bill went after her, the knife gripped firmly in his right hand — *if anyone is going to use this, it should be me* — and Daniel followed. Upon seeing this third connected room within Studio Seven, Bill's knees buckled and he nearly collapsed. He dropped the knife on the floor and stepped forward without thinking.

"What the hell?" His heart jumped into his throat and he rubbed his now watery eyes. It was his childhood bedroom. The room that he slept in up until the night his father was murdered. It replicated the exact visuals from the earlier fear simulation and all of his childhood memories.

"You guys," he said to his friends. "This room. It's . . . it's the room I grew up in, the room I was in when my father was murdered."

"What the hell is all of this? Someone explain something!" Jaime demanded. The witches just grinned, and Bill stumbled forward. He put a hand on the twin bed. Bill almost sat down on it to see if it felt like his old bed when he heard Jaime ask, "Rose, are you okay?"

It snapped him from the distraction. JB was using every trick in the book against them. He made the movies real, so why not make their childhood fears real, too? That's what this was, right? He didn't need an attack dog or a gun, not here. He just needed to get inside their heads. Bill looked at Rose. She looked back at Jaime with tears in her eyes. Instead of answering, her body twitched violently, and she screamed as she tried to get free. Bill saw Wes try to wiggle free, too. He tried to thrust forward when Rose screamed, but the witch that held him only tightened her grip. Dexter, with his hands behind his back, had yet to move. And Daniel just stood there watching it all.

A door from the rear of this third room opened, and a half-dozen more people entered, this time dressed as clowns with bright red hair and sharp teeth. Wes moaned at the sight.

"We have something for all of you," one of the clowns said and tossed a rope through a fixture in the ceiling. "Jaime, you could end this all. Save your friends. All you have to do is put this rope around your neck. Your life for theirs?"

Jaime paled and her jaw dropped. Bill gasped at the thought and stepped forward. "Leave her alone!" He stood tall, taller than ever, and he stared down at the clown with the noose.

Rose yelled again, this time not a barbaric cry of fear but a command. "ENOUGH!"

"We haven't forgotten about you, sweetie," a clown laughed,

and all around them they heard a swarming and buzzing of bees. Rose's face twitched and she looked around nervously.

"I hope none of you are allergic," the clown chuckled. "Be careful not to move too fast. It will only draw their attention to you. Any sudden movements and you'll be sure to get stung. Repeatedly." The clown exaggerated his smile, revealing sickly yellow teeth.

"Well, hello, Daniel," a voice called from the back. It was a tall man wearing a hooded sweatshirt. The hood covered his head, and they couldn't make out his face in the dark room, but at the sound of the man's voice, Daniel lost all composure.

"Dad? What . . . what are you doing here?" he asked.

"I'm disappointed in you, boy. You're losing this game. Always a disappointment."

"You . . . you can't be real," he said. "How?" Daniel's body shuddered, and the muscles in his face twitched.

"Oh, I'm real. You stupid, stupid boy. Words haven't changed you, so I think you need something more." The man took off his belt, snapped it in his hands, and held it up shoulder level. "Come here, boy. I have a lesson for you."

"No!" Daniel lowered his head and stared at the floor. He walked back slowly and jumped when he bumped into one of the witches. He looked up incredulously, and Bill thought Daniel was about to sprint out of the room.

It was getting hard to breathe. Too many people and too many nightmares coming together. Bill felt a tightening in his chest as he absorbed it all. The nightmares from a child's old bedroom, a noose hanging from the ceiling, sinister clowns, cackling witches, the buzzing of bees, and now an evil, abusive father had joined this dreadful gathering.

"Oh, there's still one more surprise." Daniel's father grinned. "You haven't introduced me to your new friend. Dexter, is it?"

"He's no friend of mine," Daniel whimpered. He couldn't even make eye contact with his father.

"I have no friends," Dexter said. He had been trying to loosen the rope that held his arms. Bill noticed that he was moving his hands more than before. Where was Dexter's paralyzing fear, anyway?

"This is a gift for you," the father addressed Dexter.

The father looked up, and everyone's gaze followed. Something fell on Dexter's face from above.

Spiders.

Dexter tensed, but stayed motionless as the spider lowered toward his face. The muscle in his jaw jumped, but he held still when the spider landed on his skin. The spider paused on his lips, then walked back up and rested near his eyeball.

The dim lights in the room flickered and a cacophony of noise erupted. The clowns laughed. The bees swarmed and buzzed. Daniel's father snapped his belt. A breeze pushed the noose back and forth on the ceiling.

"I've had enough!" Wes yelled, and, with all of his weight, he finally shoved the witch off of him. He marched right toward the clowns. "You don't scare me." He took out the red nose stress ball from his pocket, looked at it briefly, and threw it at one of the clowns. It smacked one right on the cheek. Its smile turned into a growl, and it hissed at Wes.

Bill ran to Wes's side while Jaime lunged for the knife he had dropped. She held the knife in one hand, and then darted toward the rope the clowns had thrown around a fixture on the ceiling. With her free hand, she yanked hard at the rope and pulled it down. Then she looked at Bill. He nodded, and she tossed him one end of the rope. Together, they ran in a circle and wrapped the rope around Daniel's father.

"Daniel, help us!" Jaime cried, but Daniel stepped backward. He looked up, but only quickly and nervously.

"I . . . I can't. I don't understand."

Bill wanted to tell him to grow a pair. Had he learned nothing from all of the games? Jaime shook her head at Daniel and faced the witch that held on to Rose. "Let her go."

Rose roared and wriggled until one arm flew from the witch's grip. Then she stomped on the woman's foot and sprang forward. Turning, she smacked the woman right in the face with an open palm.

Rose ran toward Bill, Jaime, and Wes, and all four stood their ground. As they stood in unison, Dexter yelled from the side. It was thunderous and surprising, and Bill nearly dropped the rope that was around the hooded figure of Daniel's father.

Dexter, who had freed his hands, slapped the spider from his face, and charged at Jaime. "You! Get out of my way, you bitch!" He knocked into her with great force. She fell backward and dropped both the knife and the other end of the rope that held Daniel's father. Dexter bent over her for a moment. "You have no idea what you're doing, do you?" Then he picked up the knife, turned, and plunged it into the heart of Daniel's father.

Dexter screamed again, pulled the knife out, and stabbed again. And again.

Had this been JB's plan all along? To terrify them so completely that they turned on each other and became the killers they'd always watched? To take the third simulation one step further?

The man screamed, and after the fourth time Dexter stabbed him, the man started to laugh. The laugh turned into a cackle. The other witches and clowns joined in, and some of them started clapping, until the noise in the room was a chorus of laughter and applause. Gradually, the lights in the room brightened and everyone quieted.

Dexter looked at the knife, and as it came into focus, they all saw the same thing. There was no blood on the knife. They looked at the man he had stabbed. There was no blood on him. No mark or slash on his shirt.

The man removed the hood from his head. He stood in the light, and all of them gasped.

It was JB.

He held up what must have been a voice simulator, just like the killer used in the *Scream* movies, and tossed it to the floor.

Bill looked at him and took a step forward.

"You've made it this far. I'm rather impressed." JB flashed his teeth, and Bill felt a terrible chill. He looked back at Jaime, who had stood up and rejoined the foursome after Dexter knocked her down. He stepped to the side so that he was in front of her. Whatever happened next, JB would have to go through him first.

"I just have one question for you. Are you ready to die?"

Bill lost all feeling in his body. *How can this be possible?* He looked at his friends. Wes stared daggers at JB. Rose's nostrils flared. Jaime looked as if she could kill. *You know, I think we have just enough crazy to fight JB and win.*

Bill stepped forward. He felt Wes, Rose, and Jaime move with him. They were one.

"You don't scare us," Bill said. "And we will do whatever it takes to protect our friends. You're not hurting anyone else tonight."

He breathed hard. All four maintained eye contact with JB. JB didn't even blink. He studied each of them. Then he took a step back.

"Congratulations, boys and girls," he announced. "You have what it takes to overcome horror."

"What?" Jaime snapped.

The witch, the one that originally had held onto Rose, walked over to JB and faced them. She wiped the makeup off her face and put on a long, dark wig. She had been the assistant dressed as Samara. The other witches and clowns all took off their masks and wiped their makeup from their faces, too. Sam and Pumpkinhead were there, among others the group had never met.

"Your final challenge was to face and overcome real horror," JB explained. "I promise you were all perfectly safe, but you had to be tested. This was the real Rabbit in Red challenge."

Daniel looked at the man he had thought was his father. "You're not real?"

Dexter had been standing still this entire time, his eyes and mouth wide. But he still held onto the knife, and now he shook, his eyes possessed, his mouth appearing as if it could foam at any second. He threw the knife to the floor, clenched his fist, and slugged the assistant Samara. He turned, ready to swing at anyone and anything, but then JB dashed forward and grabbed him. Dexter tried to wiggle free, but JB easily overpowered him.

Little Rose, with the bright red hair to match her name, locked eyes with JB and took a step toward him. She completely ignored Dexter.

"You have a lot of fucking explaining to do," she said.

JB smiled. "Yes, my dear. Now, would you all follow me?"

Chapter Twenty-Four

They followed JB back to the commons. Adrenaline still pulsed through his veins, but Bill was speechless. What the hell had just happened?

They walked through the fun house, past the game chambers, back to where they first met JB. All of the contestants were there, including Annie and Leroy. JB walked over to the stage, and as they entered the room, the other contestants stood up and gave a standing ovation.

Bill stepped up close to JB, ignoring Dexter who was still being held in JB's firm grip. "What is going on?" he asked for what seemed like the thousandth time this weekend.

"Have a seat, my friends," JB invited with a grand gesture. "I owe you all a *huge* explanation."

Bill held JB's gaze a moment longer, then turned toward his friends. They took their seats at their usual table, Jaime's hand in Bill's, Rose's hand in Wes's, and Daniel by himself. JB passed off Dexter to his assistants, who all held him tightly.

"There is much to say," JB began. "Please be patient and open-minded."

Bill snorted, and Jaime rolled her eyes. None of them were feeling very patient or open-minded.

"I know you've been through a lot," JB said. "First, I'd like to introduce more of my assistants. You've met my Annie. Please give her a round of applause." Everyone cheered except for the ones who had to face her in the *Misery* room. "Annie is a stunt actress. She plays a lot of tough roles, and I assure you, she can take a punch or a fall very well." The screen behind JB lit up, showing the footage of Bill, Jaime, and Wes defending themselves against Annie, footage the other contestants must have been watching when it all happened.

Bill's jaw clenched. Reliving the panic was bad enough, but the fear on Jaime's face made him furious. JB's explanation had better be damn good if it was going to make up for that.

"Studio One was equipped entirely with breakable props," JB continued. "They looked and felt real, and they broke upon impact.

That was part of your test. To defeat Annie. Her sledgehammer looked heavy and real, but had you never ducked, she still would have missed you by a hair or two, I'm sure."

JB looked over at Leroy and Annie and motioned for them to stand. "Annie and Leroy aspire to be horror actors. Their mission was to make you believe that you were all in real danger. I think they passed their test."

He laughed again, and Bill looked over at Jaime. She looked as perplexed as he felt.

"Now, welcome another one of my assistants!" The man in leather came out on stage with the Doberman by his side. "Another stunt actor and a trained movie dog! You noticed of course that the dog never bit skin. It was trained to bite only clothing. And the gun you were shot with: pure blanks! Wasn't that fun? In the final room, you found more of my assistants, all actors I've worked with. They know how to take a punch, and they've been well trained in martial arts so they could easily apprehend any of you. And Dexter," he turned toward the young man standing bound near the stage, "of course you noticed the knife you used was also a stage prop. No one was ever going to get hurt."

"What about the trap door in the fun house?" Bill asked loudly. "How did Daniel know what to do? How did Dexter know where to go?"

Dexter looked at Bill with the darkest eyes. Bill saw evil in his eyes, but also a deep intelligence. The scariest of combinations.

"Ahh, good questions." JB smiled. "Well, Daniel came to me when he discovered who was in that trap door. He also was the first to get the Annie and *Misery* connection, too. So I let him begin the *bonus* round early."

Bill glanced at Jaime and shook his head. Daniel had done an awful lot behind their backs.

"Frankly," JB said, looking around at the whole group, "any of you could have played this bonus round. When Chester, who you know as Captain Spaulding, talked to you at the end of round three, he tried to scare you. That was his job. Our winners are the ones who chose to go after the missing contestants instead of packing their bags."

Bill looked around at the others. Some lowered their heads for a moment. Others simply shook their heads, as if berating themselves for not understanding.

"But we'll get to all of that. You can imagine all of these games, this entire weekend, took an awful lot of planning. I had to confide in and trust my closest assistants to help me." JB swept his hand out to indicate the original four assistants. "You saw four of them in person all weekend, but I had dozens of behind-the-scenes staff to help make everything happen.

"Earlier on," JB said, his expression becoming sad and regretful, "one of my staff argued that this weekend was too much. Too unethical. Too violent. Too *real*. He threatened to contact parents and the police. I fired him, but good old Chester took it upon himself to prevent that disaster. You see, the man is actually Chester's brother. Chester locked his brother in a trap door in the fun house until the games were over. The trap door was a storage unit for fun house props. I didn't know that Chester had placed a cot in there and locked his brother up before our games. I do hope they will work it out."

JB paced across the stage, his eyes roving over the group until he found Bill and Jaime. "Chester's brother may have had us shut down had he not been locked up. I believe he even sent a couple of you an e-mail before I caught him? He tried first to contact Jaime and Bill by accessing my computer. Chester caught him and prevented him from contacting anyone else. When you both showed up on Friday, he threatened to call the police that very evening. Chester decided it was best to lock him up for the weekend so no one would interrupt our games."

Jaime and Bill looked at one another. It had been so long ago since they had received that warning e-mail that they had almost forgotten about it. Bill wondered if he would have gone through with this if the email had told him what he would have to face. There was no way he could have really understood it if someone had tried to tell him in advance.

He looked at Jaime again. *Yeah, okay, maybe I'm crazy, but I'd still have come.* He squeezed her hand under the table.

"All in all, I think what Chester did was admirable," JB said, "but perhaps unethical. Some will *certainly* say the same about me. But it was best to have no other distractions this weekend. I even had blockers installed to cut off your cell phone signals. As much as I love technology, it's best to live fully in the moment and not need one's phone all the time."

"Yes, there is no doubt the world will criticize what we have done here," JB said, one hand on his hip, staring into the distance as though seeing some beautiful but misunderstood dream. Then he looked at them again, as though returning to reality. "But in the end, none of you got hurt. At least not by me. And I have always had my reasons for what we did. They may not all make sense now, but they will over time. And of course there is a reward for you, too, should you choose to accept it."

"What is the reward?" Wes asked. The four friends exchanged a look that clearly said, *it had better be damn good!*

"Competition brings out the best in us, don't you agree?" JB asked. "I used rankings and promises to ignite your competitive spirits. But in the end, the winners are those who gave it their all. It's not about points or places. Our biggest winners are those who experienced the most and overcame their darkest terrors. I'm attempting something special with Rabbit in Red. I promised the winner an internship when the contest was launched, but I have even more to offer all of you. I want Rabbit in Red to be more than a studio. I want it to be an experience, an education. Not an amusement park for the public, but rather a college of sorts for dark souls like us."

Bill snorted. As everything started to settle and slowly make sense, he realized he still admired JB in a way. But he certainly didn't want to be thought of as like him, any more than he wanted to be like Daniel.

"However," JB continued. Was he ever going to stop talking? The adrenaline was fading and Bill was starting to feel exhausted. "Those who fully completed the Rabbit in Red challenge will be our first-year leaders, should they choose to attend our Rabbit in Red experience. Here, we will study, read, write, create, and explore everything horror. During your college years, you will be offered internships to work in the industry however you wish:

writing, directing, acting, editing, or anything at all! From there, I will offer you all a lucrative and full-time position to spend your life working on and creating horror for future generations. Let me be succinct here. You're all going to get the job of your dreams and become filthy rich doing it!"

JB paused as if waiting for applause. When none came, he went on. "And all of you here get a cash advance. How would each of you like to leave with ten thousand dollars in your pockets? Before you leave tomorrow, a check will be waiting for each of you. You'll have some paperwork to sign first, but then it's all yours."

He grinned, and Bill knew what that meant. The cash wasn't just a reward. It was a bribe and they'd no doubt be signing some kind of contract. *But damn, I could do a lot with ten grand!* "For the rest of you who may not have finished all of the games, you are invited back, too. You have a little more to learn, but I would love to keep working with you. You see, I always wanted to work with passionate youth, to train them myself. I wanted those uncorrupted by money or status or ego or Hollywood. Our traditional educational systems are killing creativity thanks to standardization, but here we will focus on what is more important, all those things you were tested on in the games: creativity, adaptability, originality, and innovation."

"Right," Jaime muttered. "And how to not get hit by a sledgehammer, or devoured by an attack dog,"

"Or shot by someone's crazy dad," Wes added. "Very practical."

"Don't forget eating brains," Bill said, leaning his head in.

"What about rescuing a devil baby? But I'd be a devil baby any day for ten thousand bucks!" Rose put a hand over her mouth to stifle a laugh. "I'm going to put experience as devil baby at the top of my college applications."

"We definitely learned a lot of great skills." Jaime giggled. Bill felt a case of the giggles coming, too. He was exhausted and excited all at once. They had nearly died, but then no, not really, only it sure has hell still felt like it, and it was all making him a bit loopy. Jaime leaned her head on Bill's shoulder.

"And you have all proven to be the best of the best," JB was saying. He frowned down at them and they stifled more laughter. "I wanted those who knew their horror history, as you proved with the riddles and the first round of games. I wanted those who could face their own terrors and be original and creative in saving the innocent, as you proved in the second round. I also needed those who could see through the eyes of the villains themselves, as you proved in the third round. If you are to create a villain, you need to be able to act like one. But I also desire those who possess empathy. I needed to see that you would feel upset and sick at some of the things I asked you to do. Only those who can really feel for others can create characters with heart," JB paused and looked at Dexter and Daniel, "and that's what we will do here.

"I also wanted those with experience, bravery, and wit to overcome not merely virtual terror, but genuine face-to-face terror as you proved at the very end. The four who I am inviting back as our leaders — Rose, Wes, Jaime, and Bill — you put each other before your own fears. Isn't that incredible? You overcame all of your fears. You never once hurt anyone or attacked your peers. You are the leaders we need, and that's why you experienced the tests you did."

Bill whispered to Jaime, "Maybe he needs a team of psychiatrists, not student leaders." She started to giggle again.

"What about me?" Daniel asked.

Facing Daniel directly, JB continued. "As we all know though, competition can bring out the worst as well as the best. You did win several of the contests. But you also manipulated multiple people here. You worked with our foursome there, and behind their backs also worked with Dexter. Then you hurt someone. We watched you grab and toss Jaime. She wasn't the villain. For that, for hurting one of our own, there must be consequences. It will be up to the four of them whether to allow you to return and participate at Rabbit in Red. You have much to learn and much fear to overcome."

"That's not fair!" Daniel shouted. "I came to you directly about the dude who was locked up!"

"And I thanked you for that. But success comes from working with others, and it is up to them to decide." JB looked at the four he had chosen as leaders. "You don't have to make any decision today. That's something you can discuss and figure out later."

"Forget that!" Daniel shouted. "I never want to work with you any of you again. I'll show you how much I can accomplish without you!" He turned and stormed off to the guys' sleeping quarters.

JB sighed, then turned and focused on Dexter next. Dexter's focus was on the floor. Bill wondered if he had heard a single thing JB had said.

"As for you, Dexter, you and I will have a conversation in private."

Dexter finally looked up at that. His eyes were empty and his face apathetic. He never responded verbally to JB, but his eyes said everything. They were dark and full of anger.

JB turned his attention back to the other contestants. "My friends, our character is determined by what we do for others, not what we do for ourselves. I know you don't understand everything that's happened here yet. It's a lot to digest. But my intentions were always pure. To help you overcome fears. To give you strength and confidence. To give you the opportunity to be a part of the biggest horror empire in history. That's your reward. That is what I have done for you. I hope you will see it as I do, and I hope you will join me. Not just for a weekend. For an entire school year of horror training and experiences. To create the absolute best art, better than anything ever done before."

The crowd was silent, except for the ruffling of clothes as each of the remaining contestants turned to look at one another. Some shrugged. Some nodded in a way that suggested *that money sounds great.*

Breaking the awkward silence, Jaime asked, "Will you have other challenges like this in the future?"

"That depends on you." JB shrugged. "You'll be on my team now, if you choose to join me. You have followed the Rabbit in Red and you have completed my initial challenges. If you decide that tests like this Fright Fest would be appropriate for recruiting new talent, then you will help design the next one. What will Rabbit in Red do next? I don't do the same thing twice, and with our combined imaginations, we can make everything even better. It's rather exciting to think about, yes? And you'll be able to give full input about what is right, wrong, and ethical." He winked at Jaime.

"I have one more surprise for you before the night is over. But you can relax. There's nothing you need to do but sit back and enjoy. Will you do that for me? Now, I wish I could help all of you more. I can't bring back your loved ones. So many of you lost someone you loved, as I learned when prepping your fear simulations. And, as I'm sure you figured out, I intentionally chose many of you with dark pasts. I've got quite the dark past of my own, perhaps even scarier than what any of you have ever experienced. But that's a story for another day. Perhaps those of you who return next year will hear those stories. I do think you are all stronger for having confronted your fears."

An assistant waved at him from offstage, and JB nodded. "But there is one thing we could do, using our creative resources. You've seen what we can do with simulations and designs, but there's so much more we can do when we put our creativity together." He paused and looked down at Bill. "Mr. Wise, this one's for you."

New images appeared on the screen. It was a news story about an event that had happened earlier today. A young woman reported on the story live outside a home in a small town in Illinois.

"In breaking news today, Jason Lamb has been arrested. The forty-one year old man has been connected with a series of home invasions over the past ten years. Our community and a string of other nearby communities have reported break-ins, robberies, and home invasions sporadically over the last decade, but police had never been able to find the criminal. Until today. Police received a full file of information and evidence that connected Lamb to the crimes, and here's an even stranger twist: the evidence comes from an anonymous source. Although we don't know who turned in all the evidence, police say they have received packets full of pictures and documentation connecting Lamb to the home invasions. The evidence even connects Jason Lamb to the unsolved murder of Arnold Wise, a husband and father who was killed during a home invasion nearly a decade ago. His son, Bill Wise, watched Jason Lamb murder his father. On behalf of our community and the world, we hope this gives all of the victims' families some peace. In the meantime, we are trying to contact the Wise family for a statement. More details on this breaking story as it develops."

"Bill," JB started. "Many of our contestants lost someone, but you were the only one who had a family member that was murdered. I put all of the resources of Rabbit in Red's creative team behind the investigation. Earlier, I presented our assistants with a confidential file that outlines the evidence. If you'd like to learn more about this criminal, you can talk to any one of us. I didn't want fame or credit here, which is why I submitted the evidence anonymously. You can decide if and how you want to respond to any reporters."

JB paused. "Jason Lamb. You know, I've always said you should never trust someone with the name of a serial killer. No offense to anyone with such name, but in my experience, I've found that those named after our most popular slashers almost always turn out to be assholes. And in this case, a real psycho, too. I hope, Bill, that this will give you peace, and your mother also. Rabbit in Red is a part of your family now, should you choose to accept that, and we will be here to help you and your mom however we can. There is virtually nothing we cannot accomplish when brilliantly mad people combine creative resources."

Bill didn't know what to say. There were so many emotions, he couldn't sort them all out. Jaime gently squeezed his hand. Justice would be served to a terrible person. And maybe this would help his mom, too. He could only hope.

"Sir, uh . . . wow. I really don't even know . . . I mean, thank you. Of course. Thank you." He closed his eyes for a moment. There was already so much to digest. Could this provide some kind of peace for his mother? Could this be the thing that would eliminate his nightmares?

"You are very welcome. We can talk more later if you wish. Now, ladies and gentlemen, I know you have had an eventful and exhausting Halloween weekend. It's after midnight. Halloween has passed, and winter is coming. I urge you all to get some rest. You fly home tomorrow, and I'm sure you have many stories to tell. The world has been watching. You haven't forgotten about our website, have you?"

The *FrightFest4D* website appeared on the screen behind him, with JB's image streaming in the center. Bill and Wes exchanged alarmed looks. Some of their experiences had been really personal.

JB must have seen their concern, because he rushed on. "Now, I promise none of your fear simulations were made public, or for that matter any that would attract any legal attention." He laughed. "I only gave the media a sample of our fun this weekend, but you will have plenty of people asking you questions nonetheless. You'll also each be leaving with a booklet of complete information about our upcoming horror experience, internships, possible future careers, as well as a preview of next year's theme, which those of you who return will design yourselves."

"I hope to see all of you back." He paused, gazing over them with an expression Bill assumed was supposed to convey fondness. It succeeded fairly well. "There's so much more fun to be had! I'll be in touch with all of you after you return home. You have a lot to consider, and now that you have the answers, I feel it's always best to take some time to think and reflect on your own. We will talk soon, but I hope you will be *one of us*."

JB winked, and once again left quickly without giving anyone else an opportunity for further questions. Then the assistants escorted Dexter off stage and followed JB.

"Wow," Jaime said. "This is a lot to comprehend."

"Are you okay?" Wes asked Bill.

"I think so." Bill exhaled. "That's just crazy. That JB would do that. Could do that."

"Yeah," Rose agreed. "It's amazing. It's a happy ending after all, to a weekend of terror." She smiled but shrugged at the same time.

"One of us!" Jaime yelled.

"What?" they all asked.

"Bill, do you remember the last riddle we never had time to finish?" She pressed her fingers to her temples and squeezed her eyes closed. "'Follow the Rabbit. Follow the Rabbit in Red to the turkey. Don't reject the Rabbit. Welcome it. And sing this with the quirky.' It's a reference to the song 'One of Us,' the one they sing in *Freaks*. From the beginning, JB has wanted us to be here."

"One of us," Bill repeated. "Yeah. Maybe JB wants us to accept him, too."

"So do we accept him after all this?" Wes asked. "And what do you all think about this horror college?"

"I'd give him a chance if you were here with me," Rose told him.

"You have no idea how upset I was at him and worried about you." Wes paused for a moment and looked closely at her. "But I'd risk anything to be by your side."

"And it sure beats high school, right?" Bill asked, and they all laughed. "Seriously though, what he did for my family? Finding the killer? And we *are* all okay. It's worth giving him a second chance, right?"

"I know one thing," Jaime said. "It would be nice to go to school with you. To see my best friends every day."

"That would be the best." Bill leaned in and hugged her. This was the moment he had been waiting for. Not winning a competition, but having his best friend right next to him. Bill wanted more than friendship. He knew that now, and, based on Jaime's smile and touch, he was pretty sure she felt the same way.

Is now the time to ask? Do I just say it?

He let go and leaned back, almost ready to say whatever he needed to be officially more than friends with Jaime. But then out of the corner of his eye, he saw Wes lean in and kiss Rose. Rose beamed and kissed him back. Jaime grabbed Bill's hand and giggled softly. Wes put his arm around Rose's shoulders, and they turned toward Bill and Jaime.

Damn, that's how you do it, Bill thought. *I can't follow that. Not right now. There's always tomorrow, right?* He held Jaime's hand tightly, and hoped he'd have the courage to tell her how he felt before they left Rabbit in Red and returned home.

"What do you say, guys?" Rose asked. She smiled bigger than she had all weekend. "The four of our messed up minds coming back to study and work on horror with the most messed up

218

billionaire on the planet? We'd sure have some stories to tell. And to create. What would be better than that?"

Bill took out his cell phone and looked at the group picture they had taken, back when the weekend was pure fun without the fear. The four looked blissful, and he thought that perhaps they could be happy like that again. He also thought of his mom. When he got home, he wouldn't sit by any longer. He'd get help, no matter what it took.

The people who exist in our realities are far more important than the people who exist in our stories, he thought.

Jaime opened the folder JB's assistants had given them. Scanning it quickly, she said, "Look at this, guys. The theme of our next challenge. *Burn the Rabbit.* What do you think that means?"

"It's going to be even hotter next year," Wes said with a wide grin.

"Ooh, I like fire," Rose giggled.

Bill looked at each of them and smiled. "What the hell, guys. Let's do it. I haven't felt this alive *ever*. JB is crazy, but yeah. We survived, right? Let's do whatever it takes to get back here."

"What's the worst that can happen?" Wes asked.

"What's the best that can happen?" Bill added. He looked at Jaime again. *Tomorrow. I'll tell her tomorrow.* He held on to her hand and smiled at his friends.

He felt the lines blur again somewhere between the wakefulness of reality and the fantasy of a dream world. As long as his world included real friends, he didn't care. *Let me always feel this alive,* he thought. If Jaime and his other friends would come back, then so would he, no matter how many more nightmares there might be to experience.

He now had everything it took to overcome those nightmares.

Right?

Acknowledgments

Dear friends,

We are kind of friends now, yes? You've spent several hours dancing through my horror fantasies, so it only seems right that you are more than a reader. Please don't be the Annie to my Paul, of course, but I want to thank you. This first *Rabbit in Red* book started as something that was pure and simple fun. How cool would this kind of adventure be? The story grew from the initial Fright Fest concept to embrace characters with dark pasts, fear simulations, and a mad genius behind the curtain.

At the time of this note, book two is on its way to print (it will be available by the time you read this, so I hope you get it!), and I'm nearly done with the first draft of book three, the final book in the *Rabbit in Red* trilogy. I have to tell you a couple things. It gets really crazy. Book two is to book one, I suppose, like *Game of Thrones* is to *Goosebumps*. You'll learn what drove JB to become the man he is. Bill, Jaime, Rose, and Wes will face new challenges, and it goes far beyond any kind of game or simulation. And not all will survive.

For this edition, thank you first to Horror Block for making a dream of mine come true. You noticed that Bill subscribes to Horror Block, right? I wrote that line in the summer of 2014, so it was always a dream of mine to be included. What an honor! Thank you! And thank you to Nicole at Horror Block for putting up with my endless questions and for just liking my story enough to be worthy of inclusion!

If you liked the book, leave a review on Amazon or Goodreads and tell a friend about it.

There are some other acknowledgments, too, I want to say.

To Brian McWilliams and Brandy Kennington, not only my first readers but the first to read this book and the first to read *Burn the Rabbit*. I listen to them first.

To Bryan Fitzgerald at Fitz of Horror! At the time of this writing, Fitz has over 76,000 fans and is an incredibly supportive dude who also has a ton of talent—he's doing the audio for *Rabbit in Red*! So for the friends and family in your life—tell them about the audio book. By the time you get this Horror Block edition, the audio should be available!

To Camron Johnson Illustrations for the incredible cover art!

To my lovely editor, Kathy Teel, who has put up with my relentless questions and who has critiqued and edited this manuscript with great care, professionalism, and humor. I've learned such a great deal from you, and I don't know if words can say how much I appreciate all you have done.

To Elise Dinquel Zwicky for giving the Horror Block exclusive edition a fantastic proofread! Not too many people volunteer to simply read 70,000 plus words looking for typos. That's one incredible person in my book!

To Jen Leigh, one of the first professionals to give me feedback and hope.

To an energetic band, Terribly Happy, who produced a song for the book called "Enter the Rabbit." Thank you Kyle Hamon, James Wylie, and Logan Kiesewetter. It rocks.

An extra big thank you to Logan who also produced a live action trailer for the book. You can see that trailer and hear Terribly Happy's original song for the book, "Enter the Rabbit," at www.joechianakas.com.

To my "Rabbiteers," various groups who provided such great behind the scenes support by generating buzz and discussing the book: Lauren Bernard, Tyler Brown, Kayla Fast, Shanzida Khandaker, Jacklyn Kraklow, Julia Markun, Ruben Ramirez, Adair Rodriguez, Sammy Spear, Matin Tajiev, Brooke Waldon, Alexis Whitman, Stephanie Whitman, Roger Crow, Amanda Sluga, Amanda Fox, Samara Lynn, Bailey Schmidt, Kristin LaFollette, Stephanie Jones, Tyler Deatherage, Ryan Thomas, Matisynn Ciardini, and Kalee Christian and all of you who have shared and loved this story!

My current *Burn the Rabbit* PR Team is working hard, too. Thanks to Christian Harr, Sammy Spear, Brianna Schierer, Amanda Sluga, La Verne Roz Armijo, Aaron Hamilton, Kayla Fast, Eric Heyob, Alexis Benson, Stephanie Jones, Ruben

Ramirez, Salina Porter, Amanda Fox, Tal Porter, Rachel Heckman, Justyce Blakenship, Asanta Cunningham, Britney Wagley, Zach Paine, Nashawn Webb, and Micheale Potter. What an incredible group! I'm a lucky guy to have so much support.

Also thanks to Apartment Two, a team producing brand new media, including pictures and video, to promote *Burn the Rabbit*. Find them on Facebook and Instagram.

To all the people involved in the dozens of stories and movies referenced in the book: I love your stories and I only wish to spread my love of them with the world so even more people will explore your fantastic creations.

To team member Jennifer Gadd for her critique and her help, and to Catrina Taylor, former owner of Distinguished Press, who called my creation "beautiful."

There are dozens more of you out there: the friends who are always by my side, the students who told me they were excited to read this, the parents of my students, my colleagues who cheered me on every step of the way, and so many other friends. As I write this, I realize how lucky I am to know so many great people.

When you first make that connection with someone who tells you that they're going to introduce your story to the world—that's a priceless feeling for which I will be eternally grateful. No matter your art, your work, or your business, I wish you all success.

Thanks for following the rabbit.
Joe Chianakas

Burn the Rabbit

Bill Wise can't wait to return to Rabbit in Red Studios—this time as a student in JB's brand-new Horror College. He's looking forward to learning the craft, renewing last year's friendships, and above all, to seeing Jaime, and finally asking her to be his girlfriend.

But before he even gets to see her, one of their own is violently attacked. JB goes on the hunt, and the students learn about his troubled past, which changes their views of him forever. As their project, they create Rabbit in Red's most terrifying and disturbing challenge yet, Hellfire, and use it to recruit a new class of horror students.

Then the bodies start piling up, and the mysteries become more and more dangerous. Is this another one of JB's dark games-within-a-game, or will Rabbit in Red—and everyone in it—burn in the end?

NOW AVAILABLE!

Request it at your favorite bookstore, or get it online!

Listen to "Enter the Rabbit", the hit, original song inspired by *Rabbit in Red* at **terriblyhappy.bandcamp.com**.

Thanks to Terribly Happy for the incredible song! Be sure to get their first full album, "Modern Life," available now.

Terribly Happy

Kyle Hamon - guitar/vocals

James Wylie - bass/vocals

Logan Kiesewetter - drums

terriblyhappy.bandcamp.com

Thank you to the creative team at **Apartment Two**, who produces media content for *Rabbit in Red*. For great photography and video, like Apartment Two on Facebook at

www.facebook.com/Apartment2co and follow on Instagram at

@apartment2co.

"Be creative. Be yourself. And inspire others to do the same."

The Apartment Two Team: Nashawn Webb, Imanuel Acera, Nicole Carson, Remi Sweeney, Drake Sweeney, Hieu Phan, Skylar Robards, Mallory Ingles, Wes Watson, and Thomas Blood.

Fitz of Horror is at <u>www.facebook.com/horrorfitz</u>!

A huge thanks to Fitz not only for the support but for the AWESOME work producing the audio book for *Rabbit in Red*. Get the audio book online today!